Tallie Rose

Hecate's Hollow

Tallie Rose

www.tallierose.com
Twitter: _tallierose
Instagram: _tallierose

Hecate's Hollow

Chapter One

Lemon did not remember when her father struck her mother. She only remembered the car's headlights that night, reflected off the oak in their front yard. Some might call it foolish to hit a witch. She never heard her father say anything else at all.

Hecate's Hollow, as the name suggested, was one of those rare places that didn't just tolerate witches—it welcomed them. Besides, the land was cheap, along with the real estate. So it was easy enough for them to settle into one of the old Victorians, a house that Lemon and Ruby now owned, after their mothers deemed it too much work and moved into one of the workman cottages lining Main Street.

The Hollow loved celebrations, Founders' day parades, festivals, pancake breakfasts, anything to bring in a tourist or two that would wander the streets and buy trinkets and bags of herbs. Their mothers' eyes always grew wide, watching the crowd, but fears of her father had long since vanished for Lemon. She loved her tiny mountain town, the way the wind whipped through the trees, singing songs just for her, the way the peaks sparkled in winter and changed color in autumn.

She knew every path, every rabbit hole, every stream. She'd spent her youth, barefoot and worry free, wandering the hills, scaling mountains far too large for her, bolstered only by the magic running through her veins.

Now, she pulled her pillow over her head, as Ruby's alarm clock rang through the thin walls of their house. How it could wake her up, but not Ruby, whose head was only inches away from the damned thing, she would never understand.

Her sister was supposed to open the apothecary in an hour. It was Lemon's day off and she longed to walk among the ferns and mountain laurel until she reached the riverside. She had planned her whole day around collecting the tiny blue flowers that grew along its shore, a flower she had no name for, and had never seen anywhere else.

Sighing, she pulled the pillow from her head, squinting in the bright morning sun, and pounded on the wall. Nothing. She stood, pulling on her robe and opened the door, giving Ruby's cat, Athena, a scratch. She didn't bother to knock, just threw open the door, taking in the rich smell of rosemary that hung from the ceiling because they had run out of room in the kitchen.

"Get up, you lazy loaf!" She shook Ruby, and her blue eyes fluttered open. "You have to open the shop."

"Harpy." Ruby groaned.

"I told you not to stay up all night reading cards and drinking. You always do this."

"I divined that the mothers would open the shop this morning." Ruby sat up, swinging her long legs off the bed, and grinning as Lemon rolled her eyes. "I'm kidding. They messaged me. They said they didn't want you to go into the hills alone."

Their mothers always worried, and Lemon couldn't fathom why. She sang songs with the birds and talked with the deer. Out of the four of them, she was the best with the animals, the keenest at spotting the herbs and flowers they would need, the magic they held inside. But, perhaps, she wasn't the most surefooted, and even the wildest witchcraft would not help if she actually tumbled off a cliff. "Fine."

And to be fair, she appreciated her sister's company, the companionable silence that could stretch between them, the braying laughter, and all the memories that belonged only to them. There had never been a doubt since the day Ruby's mother, Esther, named them sisters that they were, and they had never taken kindly to the other children suggesting otherwise.

"Well then, get dressed. I'm leaving soon and I'm not waiting."

"Bossy." Ruby stretched her arms and headed for her closet. "Do you have fifteen minutes to spare, your majesty?"

"I suppose." Lemon flopped onto her sister's bed. "But you're buying breakfast on the way."

Lemon pressed her hand to the bark of a hickory tree, feeling the power beneath the surface. Old and knowing, the tree's roots stretched wide, searching out the secrets of the forest, the troubles of its neighbors. A bird squawked in the tree, and as Lemon pulled her hand away, it flew down, resting on her shoulder.

A shiver ran through her. Trouble. But the birds were so different from humans, their thoughts were nothing she could understand. "I felt something. Worry through the woods. Or something like it."

"For the birds or more?" Ruby's fingers strayed into her pocket and Lemon knew she was toying with the verbena and anise satchel she always brought with her into the mountains.

"I can't tell." She shook out her shoulders. "Probably nothing to worry about. The birds aren't the most reliable."

"Maybe we'll find a raccoon." Ruby teased.

They continued on the trail, smiling sweetly when hikers passed. It was still warm, the middle of September, right before the leaves changed and the weather grew cold. Their mountains were full of people, searching for waterfalls or just a moment away from their busy lives. Tourism would pick up until the town was loaded for the Festival of Blessings, when people came from not-so-far away to get blessed by the Hollow's witches. She'd never see a spark of magic from some of the women who dusted off crystal balls or shuffled tarot cards freshly delivered from Amazon, but Lemon would never tell.

They were farmer's wives or single mothers. They needed the money to fill their cellars for the winter, when the tourists stopped coming. The roads in were too narrow, and the Hollow did not hold enough amusement, so they went to Gatlinburg or Asheville, renting cabins from corporations and buying fudge before they went to see whatever neon-lighted monstrosity had a dinner show that night.

As the hill grew steeper, Ruby took the lead. She reached out, wrapping her long fingers around a branch, and shuddered. Lemon held her tongue until they got to flatter land, but she could feel it too, the change in the air, the tension. It set the hairs on her arm on end.

"It's more than trouble," Ruby said, staring off the mountain at Hecate's Hollow below. The roofs of the houses looked so small they were barely more than specks. "There's something new."

Lemon didn't like to think of something troubling and unknown so close to her home. She wrapped her arms around her chest. "What do you mean by *new*?"

Ruby shook her head, her fingers steadily moving in her pocket. "I'm... not sure. I didn't get a good reading." Sometimes the flowers, the trees, the animals that skittered through the woods hid their secrets. Lemon's mother, Amaryllis, was better at reading their signs than either of them, but she rarely ventured into the woods anymore. She preferred staying home, knitting or reading, curled on the couch with Esther. They'd fought for their love, their time together, and now, almost twenty years later, they were rarely apart.

"Should we be concerned?" She looked around, but there was nothing amiss, just trees heavy with new buds. "Let's go to the spring." Sometimes the crystal clear water spoke more than anything else in the forest. Though she hadn't planned to go there, and she'd left most of her herbs and roots behind, she could find flowers here somewhere, and a rock would make-do as a mortar in a pinch.

"I don't know." Ruby's eyes darted toward the path that led them home and then toward the cliff side. "We need those ingredients for the shop. Maybe we should stick to the task. The forest always has problems. For all we know it's an invasive plant, carried in on a hiker's shoes."

If Ruby saw the irony in her words, she didn't give it away. Though they were invasive themselves, hailing from the coast, they were the keeper of these woods. If something invasive was growing Lemon would pull it from the roots.

"Well, why don't you get the herbs and I'll go for the spring?" They'd separated before. They were no more likely to get lost in these woods than they were walking down Main Street. The trees and shrubs would whisper directions, the squirrels would lead her way. And Lemon couldn't leave without finding out what had happened in her forest.

"I don't know." Ruby pulled on the strap of her bag. "We can do both together."

"We'll miss lunch." Millie's Diner had fried chicken on Thursdays, and Lemon had been thinking about it since she had woken up. It was greasy and full of calories, and she planned on several servings.

"You and the chicken." Ruby pulled a granola bar from her jacket pocket and threw it at Lemon. "If you miss it, I'll fry some chicken tonight." She continued to grumble as she started to walk again. "There's trouble in the woods. Let's split up." Her imitation of Lemon was eerily spot on.

Lemon followed her sister. It had rained recently, and the descent was slippery. She shoved the granola in her pocket, watching for roots that might trip her.

The path towards the spring was barely a path. The locals had not shared their secret with the tourists, so the trodden earth was covered with moss and lichen. Branches hung low, casting strange shadows that flickered in the breeze and morning sun.

She looked for squirrels, bees, or beavers that might let her glimpse into their mind and spill their stories, but they scurried from her and she did not give chase. Still, every tree she touched sent its warning, though they did not scream of urgency or fear. Something new. Something dangerous. She could feel it in the sap, in the fallen fruits and deep roots.

Something had come to the Hollow.

She ran through the creatures she knew of in her mind, the failures and curses of witches that had become a blight upon the land a century ago. But they were all so rare now. Most heavy curses that could transform a person, mar their spirit, required not just a witch but a Hathorne as well. They were the dirtiest of hypocrites, in Lemon's opinion.

Magic flowed in their veins. It was the only thing that allowed them to stop witches, yet they sought them out, twisting their words and fabricating foul deeds in order to prosecute them. Of course, it mattered little to the government. They had never been in pursuit of justice, only control, and there were few members of Congress interested in standing up for the witches.

Still, to curse someone, especially a witch, as those crawling creatures usually began, was technically a crime. The Hathornes wielded their special brand of anti-magic to strip power from the witch and allow the curse to be put hold. Even on a human, curses held better with witch magic, allowing it to turn bone and skin, transforming a human into something else.

The Hathornes rarely advertised this facet of their power, preferring to look like law-abiding citizens. Her father had been one, though he had hidden it well. And his power had been small, much smaller than her mother's, so he seldom used it, preferring fists and cruel words.

"You have your thinking face. I don't think it's that serious, Lem," Ruby said, pausing by a boulder to tie her shoe. "You just need to get out more. You're spending too much time in the woods. When's the last time you got laid?"

Lemon flipped her off. She knew exactly when and that it had been far too long, but the list of Hecate's Hollow lesbians was short, and the tourists that came through were often coupled. Leaving Lemon in a rather long dry spell. "More recently than you, asshole."

Ruby let out a bark of laughter so loud she startled the crows, who took off into the skies. They continued teasing each other until they could hear the sounds of the spring. Leaves, brown and red at the edges, floated along its surface.

Ruby discarded her bag and bent to pluck them from the water, while Lemon found a stick to trace shapes in the sand. She peeled the clothes from her sweaty body, and Ruby did the same, both of them giggling like schoolgirls. Though others knew of the spring, the power it held was a secret between them.

They had discovered it as teenagers, when they'd hidden in the woods drinking wine coolers and Kahlua they'd stolen from their mothers. They'd also discovered that just past the trees was a long fall down to the creek. Luckily, at least Lemon saw it that way, it had only resulted in a broken arm for Ruby. And one screaming mom.

Anson Mills, the town doctor, was used to setting breaks. He said without broken bones he'd have no business at all. Children constantly played in the hills, just as their parents and grandparents had done before them. And of course the tourists, always believing they were better outdoorsmen than they were.

"Ready when you are," Ruby said. They linked their hands, fingers slipping together with familiarity, and sunk into the cool water. Often Lemon wished it was a hot spring, but the water was clear and cool and they both sighed at the power. For thousands of years, the spring had stood, collecting the secrets of the mountain from the underground streams that fed it. Thousands of years it had sat silent without witches to whisper its secrets to, and now it spilled them to the sisters.

Lemon sprinkled dried petals, witch hazel, and wormwood into the water, and it frothed and gurgled. A high, keening note emanated from the stones that held the pool, and they both closed their eyes, faces turned upwards. There were advantages and beauty to being a witch, and sharing secrets with the spring was one of them. It did not always talk, but when it did, it seemed like the most glorious thing in the universe.

Visions blurred through Lemon's mind, animals whelping, couples fighting, the secrets of the townsfolk whispered in the woods. Those secrets were safe, rarely even discussed between Ruby and Lemon, taught from the cradle that witches should not abuse their power. Then something else. Dark smoke and blood—splatters of it. A woman screaming. A deer, strong and majestic, fallen and writhing. And then the visions were gone, and Ruby's hand, still held in Lemon's, trembled. Clouds, gray and puffy, had formed in the sky above them.

"Oh," she breathed. "Maybe we don't get those flowers today. That was..."

Lemon nodded, rising from the spring as rain drizzled on them. It had done nothing but rain for weeks now, and she had hoped to be out of the woods before it started again. At least it wasn't pouring. She squeezed out her hair and offered a hand to Ruby. "That was fucked. I've never seen anything like it before."

They needed to tell someone, the mayor perhaps, or town council. Their mothers definitely. Something lurked in the woods, something that downed deer, left them bloodless. Her mind raced. If something cursed lived here, they couldn't hold the festival. They needed to find it, see what they could do. Often the answer was death, even if it wasn't the creature's fault. Curses were tricky to cast, even worse to undo. The magic often took the victim's mind, and once lost, they could not be brought back. And undoing a curse required the blood of the Hathorne who had cast the spell, but unless you could prove their involvement, the government would not force them to cooperate.

On other days, they spent hours at the spring. They would lie on the hot, gray stones until they were dry, passing joints between them, and laughing as though the whole world belonged to them. She was sure Ruby had one tucked somewhere in her bag, she always did. But not today, not in the rain, not with her heart pounding.

They pulled on their clothes, then Lemon heard the snap of a branch. She glanced towards Ruby. The forest went still, but her sister hadn't noticed. She was too busy digging in her bag, searching for something.

Against her better judgment, Lemon turned towards the noise. The rain continued, fat drops that fell on her face and splashed off the forest floor. She moved quickly, darting over rocks and branches, without saying anything to Ruby.

Something crashed in the forest and she could feel the slick, oily magic from whatever it was. She should turn, run away, but curiosity drove her onward. She had never seen someone cursed before. Thoughts of Hathornes, of the booming voice of her father, cursing witches even as he married one, came to her.

The rain grew heavier, dripping into her eyes. She heard the creek and then Lemon was falling, her feet above her head, crashing over roots and through brambles. She tried to reach out, grab something as she tumbled down the embankment. Above her, Ruby was screaming. Lemon's fingernails cracked and shattered against rock but she found no grip.

Something flashed before her eyes. Strong arms wrapped around her, stopping her fall, sweeping her up. Her head hurt, her arms, her back. Everything hurt. She thought it was Ruby, and she moaned her thanks, reaching up to rub at the lump on her skull that was forming.

"You're most welcome," said an unfamiliar voice.

Lemon's eyes popped open and looked into those of a pale brown, like hardened amber. Coppery-brown hair hung in heavy sheets around the woman's face. She was beautiful, in the way of a well-forged knife, honed and dangerous. Then she smiled, sharp incisors and lips too red. Her skin too pale.

Her senses came back to her. Of course, Ruby wasn't holding her. She couldn't lift Lemon. This woman shouldn't be able to lift her either. She struggled to get away, and the woman put her down, right into the winding waters of the creek. Ruby was still at the top, muttering words Lemon couldn't hear.

Vampire was the first word that came to mind, but this woman was in the sun. She wasn't burning, nor was she sparkling, which were the only two options Lemon knew of.

"You." She took a step back, nearly slipping again on the algae-covered rocks. This was the dangerous new thing. This was what had taken down the buck.

The woman put up her pale, slender hands in supplication. "I've been looking for you."

"Absolutely, fucking not." Ruby rushed down the embankment, nearly tripping herself, and blowing powdered herbs as she came.

The woman's eyes widened, and she clutched her neck, gasping for breath. She collapsed to her knees, fear lining her face. Ruby's hand closed around Lemon's and tugged. As they struggled up the slope, Lemon glanced back at the woman. She writhed on the ground, still clutching her throat. Lemon had never seen Ruby do magic like that. She'd never done it herself, but she knew it. And the words touched something in her brain—memories of Esther on the night they had fled.

They were out of the woods before the rain started to pour, and when they got back to their home on Maple Street, Lemon did what she never did and locked the door while Ruby ran for the cupboards.

Chapter Two

Neither Esther nor Amaryllis spoke when Ruby and Lemon finished their tale. Amaryllis twisted her hands in her lap, as though she longed for her knitting.

"I have only seen one cursed before," Esther finally said, standing to stoke the fire. "It is illegal and immoral."

This was nothing Lemon didn't already know. What she wanted to know was...everything. She had so many questions she thought she might burst, but she knew their mothers would have no answers. But why had the woman helped her, not let her break her neck as she tumbled? Most cursed things were twisted, horns and hooves, but that woman was beautiful. But the blood.

Ruby might have questions as well, but she stared ahead into the flames, settling into herself as she was wont to do when she was frightened. Lemon would draw her out later, when the sky grew dark and their house was warm and full of the scent of cedar.

"She can't be a vampire, right?" Lemon asked, looking towards her mother.

Esther smiled. "I think not. I have never heard of one. It is a myth the same as werewolves, or zombies, or whatever else men dream up to frighten each other."

"But she *looked* like a vampire and I'm pretty sure she drank deer blood." There were blood spells, of course, dangerous and hard to catch, slipping through fingers like grains of sand. Lemon had never tried one. She preferred more natural magic, the sap of a tree, the strength of the wind. Flowers and herbs and divination.

"Just because a thing looks like something doesn't mean it is." Esther turned towards her. She had the same blue eyes as Ruby, but her red hair was graying at her temples. "I will let Mayor Ellis know. She can decide where we go from there. Esther and I will put wards around your house. The creature may know you're a witch—"

"Well, I don't think she was looking for me because of my incredible good looks." Though one could hope.

Amaryllis cut her a look. "I'm glad to see she has not frightened the sass from you. But you must be careful until we have caught her. We will need a counter spell, or the authorities." Distaste laced the final word. The police had done nothing when they reported her father. He was a Hathorne, one of them. What did they care about the word of a witch?

But this was not the city, nor a town with patrols and men emboldened by their badge. The jail was more of a drunk tank and they knew every police officer, they'd all been born in the Hollow and in the Hollow they would die. They'd given up state funding years ago when they'd voted to refuse Hathornes admittance to the force. The town respected the witches and did not trust the Hathornes, so, if her hand was forced, Amaryllis would contact them. She always called it professional courtesy and might as well have held her nose, but she did it. They were still cops, but it was better than elsewhere.

Esther finished fiddling with the fire and dusted off her hands on her skirt. "Well, enough talk of that. We will not handle this problem before the sun falls, and I'd like to start on these spells. Come, come." She clapped her hands. "Where is your sage?"

Their mothers rustled around the house, refusing to let either Lemon or Ruby help, forgetting in their fear that they were no longer children but capable witches. So they sat in the kitchen, a container of Rocky Road between them, rehashing what they'd already told their mother.

"She wasn't... I could smell the curse, like rotting mushrooms, but I didn't get that slimy coat of fear on my tongue."

"Well, I did!" Ruby assured her through a mouth of ice cream. "And what the hell were you thinking, just taking off like that?"

"I didn't want you to get hurt." The excuse was feeble, but she didn't have a better one. "You know me, not heavy on the thoughts. We need to go up to the attic, lug out some of those books. There has to be a way to reverse whatever was done to her."

Ruby's eyes narrowed. "Lemon...." She sat down her spoon and crossed her arms. There was something so solid about Ruby, as sure as the old oak in the backyard, as constant as the ticking of the grandfather clock in the hallway. She would always be there for Lemon, no matter how ill-formed she thought her plans were.

"I'm half Hathorne. There's hope. If anyone can undo a curse, it would be me."

"And tall, pale, and gorgeous isn't having effects on your brain? Only the goodness of your heart, I suppose?" Sometimes Lemon thought Ruby was a bit of a cynic. Often Ruby called her aggressively mercurial. She hoped they balanced each other out.

Lemon filled her mouth with ice cream, pondering the question. If the creature had claws or fangs—well, she did have fangs—if she had horns or fur, would she be as keen to help her? She liked to think she would, always eager to offset the Hathorne blood that ran through her, to prove she was a witch, helpful and kind. She brought salves to Dr. Mills office for his patients, brewed potions for the townsfolk whenever they asked. She did what she could to help.

Still, those eyes. She had not seen terror or cruelty in them, but pain. Deep and well etched, like a river through rock. Perhaps it could not be undone. Sometimes it couldn't—often. "It's our job to help, Ruby Carmine."

"Tell the mothers that, then."

"Tell us what, dear?" Esther peered in, her arms full of sprigs of lavender. "We're almost done."

Lemon eyed Ruby. If she told them, then Lemon was going to tell about the stash of weed she kept under her bed. She ground her jaw until it hurt, trying to convey all the ways she was going to make her regret opening her mouth. Not telling mom was their number one rule. Not until there was blood.

"Nothing. Just teasing."

It was clear from Esther's face she didn't believe a word either of them said, but they were grown women, and she'd learned long ago they didn't betray each other's secrets. Before the Hollow and its townspeople, it had only been Ruby. The other children would tease Lemon, knock her down, scream and spit, and call her witch. She had cried herself to sleep, wishing the witches were still in hiding.

And then, Ruby had shown up. Strong and fierce Ruby, who had hit the children back and pulled her from the ground. She'd brought out the wildness in Lemon, while Lemon had soothed Ruby's anger. And one day Lemon had confessed how she hid in her tree house while her mom screamed. She never saw the fights, but she saw the bruises, the way her mother would flinch.

Ruby must have told her mother because not long after that Amaryllis had shown up, asking if they'd like a playdate. Like Ruby and Lemon, their mothers had become inseparable, though something more than friendship had grown between them.

Lemon never asked many questions about that time, because she didn't care. For the first time, her mother had started to smile. She'd started to do magic again. And then they had fled and Lemon's life had begun. No one pushed her down. They asked for charms and spells. Waitresses smiled and ruffled her hair. She was accepted.

That night, after their mothers had left, Lemon double checked the locks on her window. She brought in cloves of garlic, which made Ruby laugh, and she pulled the sheets up to her chin before she went to sleep. Despite her bravado, she did not like to think of that cursed woman watching her, looking for her. Even beautiful eyes had no business peeping in through her window.

Unfortunately, things rarely went as she hoped. She woke to Athena's tail brushing against her nose. "Ugh. What have I told you about your ass and my face?" She moved the cat to the other pillow.

Athena meowed. Lemon shushed her. Athena stood, meowing again, and jumped from the bed to the bench in front of the bay window.

Something scurried beyond the screen. And Lemon could feel it again, the oily taste on her tongue. *Fear.* She was a witch, a powerful witch, but she was also in her cupcake pajamas, without spell or herb or potion. She grabbed the baseball bat she kept under her bed. Magic was great, but a bat to the head also found results.

"Go away." She hissed at the window, as Athena settled onto the bench, purring. This was stupid. There was nothing out there, only her imagination running wild. How did she even know that woman was cursed? Perhaps she was something else, a lost traveler, an infertile woman seeking potions.

Except she had held Lemon in her arms like a child. She thought of Bram Stoker, Anne Rice, Charlaine Harris. What would they say? "Stephenie Meyer, bless my soul." She slithered out of bed. She needed to be like Elena or Bella or Sookie. Buffy really. She'd had that whole Spike thing. Fuck, she watched too much TV.

Really, she should get Ruby. Unless it was a raccoon. Or the tree outside of her window scratching the glass, its supple branches moving like fingers. She tightened her grip on the bat and took a step closer.

She couldn't see anything outside the window, except the leaves of the tree, swaying in the midnight wind. Just a tree. She owed ol' Stephanie a fruit basket. But she wanted to be sure, to press her nose against the cool glass and peer into her yard.

Athena brushed against her face, pressing her nose into Lemon's cheek. She wasn't Lemon's familiar, she'd never gotten her own, but still the cat gave her strength. This was silly. She pushed back her curtains and peered out the glass.

Her eyes adjusted slowly, the only illumination from the porch light Ruby had forgotten to turn off after she sat outside smoking. She let out a long breath. Nothing. The wind changed course, brushing the leaves in the other direction and she saw it—movement. A lone figure standing on the grass.

She waited for the oily feeling of fear to rush through her, but it didn't come. Instead, it was the acidic tang of curiosity. What did the woman want? What had happened to her? She knew curses did not always take the mind right away, or take it in even worse ways, making them believe they were still their old selves while anyone around them could see they were not. But if the woman had wanted to hurt her, it would have been easier on the creek bed.

She could have left her falling, her head banging against rocks, her skin scraping against roots. Let her land face down in the water. But she had grabbed her. She had cradled her gently. Lemon looked at the cat and yellow eyes looked back.

"Am I a fool?"

Certainly she was, but Athena only meowed, so Lemon pulled on her slippers and wrapped her robe around her. She glanced into the mirror. Her short blonde hair was sticking up, mussed by pillows. She tried and failed to flatten it.

Usually the stairs creaked, but she whispered curses at them, frightening them into submission and they held her secrets as she descended. Only the front door stood between Lemon and the cursed woman. Oh, this was stupid.

Fear and anxiety finally caught up to her curiosity. She should wake Ruby. But Ruby's wildness was always put aside in favor of keeping Lemon safe, especially when the danger was real. As children they had run through fields and leapt from roofs, kept safe only by the magic in their blood, but they'd also hid from bears that wandered into their yards and kept their protections in their pockets.

Still, her hand slid against the cool metal of the doorknob. She pushed it open and the cool fall air washed over her. She could see the woman more clearly, standing under the tree, still as a statue.

Waiting.

Lemon was afraid, but not the fear that came from her preternatural senses. Regular human fear. Hot adrenaline.

Stepping onto the porch felt like stepping onto the plank, the moment before a leap. She waited at the steps, unsure of what she should do, ready to retreat back into the safety of her mothers' wards.

The woman took a step forward. "Lemon Leblanc." Her words moved across the space between them, twining through the grass and thinning the air.

Lemon's fear melted away. She took a step and then another, until she was also standing under the branches of the sweeping oak, bathed in moonlight. She glanced towards the moon, sending a silent prayer to the goddess of the night to keep her safe. "You were looking for me."

"Yes." The woman's skin was pale and silver. Seeing her under the moonlight seemed wrong to Lemon, as though she had been copper before, bursting with light like Helios himself. Cursed indeed. "I'm Claudia." She offered no last name.

"You're cursed." Lemon longed to reach out, run her fingers over Claudia's skin, feel the dark magic of sorceresses and Hathornes running beneath the surface. She had never felt it before, would not dare to do the dark magic, fueled by blood and spite and hate.

"A cruel joke by a cruel man." Claudia looked towards the house. "He knew they were my favorite stories. Another thing he could take from me, like the sun."

"But you were out during the day."

"Under clouds and shadows. I do not burst into flames. But it has gotten worse the longer I'm cursed. I am not a true vampire. But I burn like I laid on a beach in August. Food tastes like ash, and I crave blood. I cannot enter homes without invitation and my heart does not beat. I don't know if I can survive even if I find a cure."

"But why me?" She was no famous witch, none of them were. People in nearby towns knew the witches in Hecate's Hollow practiced, but they also knew they hid, though they may not know from what. Their names did not spread further than the foothills. It would not have traveled to whatever city held women this beautiful, whatever city held Hathornes so bold they would curse a woman and leave her still speaking. Curses were against the oaths they took. Though she knew they were still done, they did not leave the victims to tell the tale.

Unless he was not one of the order. Unless it was just his blood, not his heart, that led him to his anti-magic. She had heard of them, rogue Hathornes bound by nothing, but did not know any. But how would she? She knew little of the world beyond the mountains.

Claudia moved with grace, pushing herself onto one of the lowest hanging branches of the oak. "I ran when it happened. I couldn't get in my house and I was afraid of what he might do to me. It would be easy enough to turn me into his friends, not mention his part in it, and have me killed. They don't care about ending the curses and who will stop them? So I fled, and I came to the mountains. I've heard the tales, the tiny outposts that revere witches. Every witch in Chicago talks about it. When they get frustrated, they say they will disappear into the Smokies. Your name was mentioned, they said you were kind, that you help people. I hoped you might help me."

Lemon took her in, the sharpness of her features, the clarity in her eyes, her perfectly cut hair, unlike the haircuts Lemon gave herself, sometimes aided by Ruby and always aided by a bottle of wine. Claudia didn't look like someone who needed help, she looked like someone who would deny Lemon a loan. But she'd come to ask for help.

Lemon ran her hand through her hair and pulled her silk robe tighter around herself. "I don't know what I can do. I've never broken a curse. I make salves and potions for stomach aches. I talk to the birds and read cards."

"But perhaps, you could try."

Lemon would not know where to begin. And this woman was cursed. She knew the tales; the warnings told to witches from the time they were babies. Undoing a curse was nearly impossible. Nevertheless, this one did not seem so bad. Claudia was not a raging beast. This seemed more like a practical joke. "Would it really be so bad to live like this?"

Anger flashed in Claudia's eyes. "To drink blood? To live in darkness and shadows? How will I earn money? Where will I live? I know I'm asking a lot, Lemon. I will beg it if I must, but curses can be reversed. I have money, I can pay you. You can have my vampire blood."

"Whoa." Lemon put her hands up. "I do not do blood magic, nor do I know of any spells that require *vampire* blood."

"Maybe you can come up with some." For the first time Claudia smiled. It lit her face and made Lemon's breath catch. "Look, if the answer is truly no, I will leave but... will you think about it?"

"Of course I'll think about it." What choice did she have? Even if her heart didn't urge her to help, she wanted to see the end of this mystery, to unravel its strings and get at the heart of it. Lemon was no fool. She knew there were many things not being said, and she wanted to hear them.

She wanted other things as well. Things best suited to twilight and stars. Smooth skin and rough breaths. But those things were not what compelled her, because she did not believe she would ever achieve them. She would help if Claudia were a hag, because her heart had not been changed, and her mind was clear, and no living thing should be forced to live that way.

Claudia leapt from the tree on nimble legs, landing steady. "I'll meet you tomorrow, as the sun goes down. I saw a bakery."

Though she knew she shouldn't, Lemon smiled. What would the people of the Hollow think of her and Claudia? "Okay, but I need to tell my moms and my sister before I go out in public. News travels faster than a cat lapping chain lightning around here. We can meet in the evening."

Claudia nodded. "I'll see you at sunset." And she swooped in, kissing Lemon on the cheek and was gone into the night.

Chapter Three

To avoid her sister, Lemon pretended to be sleeping until she heard the front door shut. Then she waited another minute. Ruby had been known to outsmart her a time or two.

She couldn't stop glancing out the window as she pulled on her clothes and brushed her hair. There was nothing out of place, no way Ruby could know, but her chest was still full of guilt. She didn't keep secrets from her sister, but she knew she wouldn't approve. She'd seen the way Ruby had looked when she had mentioned Claudia before.

She shoved her wallet in her back pocket and pulled on her jean jacket. As soon as she was off her property someone was yelling at her. Her neighbor, Betta McCray was plump and pretty, with red hair piled high on her head and an attitude that could swing quickly from almost annoyingly pleasant to hostile.

"Shug, what are you doing walking by yourself? The way you are with your sister, I thought the two of you were joined at the hip. You opening the shop by yourself?"

Lemon shook her head. "Nah. My mama's got it." She couldn't help it. One second around an accent and she picked it up, like ants on sugar.

"Well, you be careful. My dog was barking up a storm last night. I'm sure it was just a deer or something, but it's always worth checking over your shoulder. Say, you planning on mixing up a batch of healing potion anytime soon? Only thing that works for my knee, you're going to put Doc Mills out of business."

"Come in this afternoon. I'll make some when I get in." She smiled and started back up the path towards Main Street, replaying

27

for at least the tenth time, her conversation the night before. And the more she thought on it the closer Lemon got to bursting.

She'd never been one to keep things to herself. She loved to over share, and this was the biggest story she'd ever had. A vampire had come looking for her in the night. She was ready to call the Times, HBO, at least the local newspaper, The Hecate Herald.

Except she had to tell Ruby before she did that. Some might call it codependence, but they called it sisterhood. Still, she knew Ruby was going to be spitting mad, and she wasn't sure she was ready to hear it.

She slowed her pace as she made it to the Main Street. The Hollow was beautiful in the fall. The leaves were giving up their summer colors, changing to red and orange and yellow. Pansies and chrysanthemums dripped from window boxes and the grass outside homes was slowing its growth, promising cooler weather. Lemon wanted to kick off her shoes and feel the blades between her toes.

She trailed her fingers over the barks of trees, feeling the rings beneath, the wisdom and power in their age. Even the buildings seemed to sing to her, of all the stories they had seen. It was the kind of day that begged her to stay outside.

Where was Claudia now? In some motel? Did the rules of entry apply to that? She knew she'd seen shows cover it, but she couldn't remember. And besides, Joss Whedon wasn't exactly the foremost vampire expert.

"Hey Lemonade. You're late," Amaryllis said as she entered the store, the thick metallic smell of magic washing over her.

"Sorry, I was..." She tried to come up with an excuse. "Can I tell you something?"

Her mother put down the petals she was threading together and walked around the counter, wiping her hands on her apron embroidered with Red and White Apothecary. "Of course, darling."

Lemon ran a hand through her hair, chewing on her lip. Where to start? "I saw the woman again... the..." the word vampire stuck in her throat. "I don't think she's dangerous... yet." Lemon knew enough about curses to know they grew in scope. "She said she enjoyed the tales of the undead before, that it was a cruel joke."

Amaryllis cleared her throat, her mouth moving into a thin line. "The cruelty of the Hathornes knows no bounds. What does she want from you?"

"What does anyone want from a witch? Help. She wants me to undo the curse before someone catches her. We can't tell the town yet. No matter how much they embrace us, they won't embrace someone who drinks blood."

Amaryllis scrubbed her face with her hand. "I have never undone a curse; few witches have. But if you want to take it on..." She sighed. "I'll help you. But Lemon...."

"What?" Her stomach seemed caught in her throat and magic, usually so reassuring, seemed to vibrate around her. To undo a curse, she would have to feel the sting of anti-magic, draw the will of the Hathorne from Claudia. She would need his blood. It was not a task for every witch.

"Keep your brain involved but not your heart. This is likely to fail. The reason the cursed are not left to wander is not just cruelty. They are dangerous. Once the magic sets in, it can be impossible to unravel. I know of very few successes."

"I can't just leave her like she is." She stared at her hands. They had done so many simple magics. She spoke to birds and traded secrets with the deer. But somewhere in there was the blood of a Hathorne, though she had never found it, never felt it bubble to the surface. She knew there were few like her. Maybe it would help. "I haven't told Ruby."

"She won't take it well."

Her mother was right. Ruby would understand the desire to help, but she'd see the danger first. She'd be plagued with images of Lemon's neck being treated like an all-you-can-eat buffet. "How long do you think I have before it's too late?"

"Two months? Maybe three. A vampire..." Amaryllis chuckled coldly. "Fangs instead of the usual claws. But that's how people get hurt. They appear the same at first, until the moon is whole again. And each time their bones bend more, their mind becomes clouded, until who they were is gone, until they are nothing but a beast."

Lemon straightened a jar of crystals on a shelf. "But why?" She'd never understood it. "The Hathornes are supposed to stop witches from doing unjust magic, but curses are the most unjust of anything. It doesn't make sense."

"Hathornes are hypocrites, you know that. They claim to stand for justice, but there is no trial, no council, before they dispense their so-called justice. And if they capture a witch, are juries sympathetic? Are we judged by our peers?" She paused and Lemon knew she was thinking of her father. But he was fuzzy in her memory, his face a blank slate. She could only remember the tenor of his voice, always yelling. "Curses are illegal. If they are caught, they are punished, but they rarely are. Who can name them when their victim no longer has vocal cords? I've seen women turned to snakes, to beasts of the ocean."

Though she did not voice the thought, Lemon wondered if perhaps being a vampire was not so bad. She might keep her mind? In most vampire lore, they kept a sense of themselves. But she doubted whoever had cursed her would be so kind. The bloodlust would take over, and Claudia would be gone. She barely knew her, but she thought of her sister, of mother. Wouldn't she want someone to help them? And she knew she wouldn't be able to sleep at night if she did nothing. "Where do I begin?"

"If she can find the Hathorne who cursed her, his blood will aid any antidote, and well...he seems to have turned her into the perfect vessel for it." Lemon nodded, and her mother grabbed her arm. "You are not foolish for this. I admire your big heart. You have always wanted to help. I have tried to help the cursed before. I remember one woman, her bones slowly curved, hair sprouted from her skin,and in the end she was gone and the man got away. As I said, try to guard your heart."

Lemon nodded again, but it seemed an impossible task. How did she stop herself from caring? "Can I see the real spell books?" The ones her mothers kept in the attic, the kind they would never sell. Ones full of dark magic, hard magic. Not the magic to heal small cuts or soothe an aching throat. Those books held love spells, spells to steal a voice, to transform and conjure.

"Are you sure you want to do this?" But Amaryllis's fingers pulled at the chain around her neck. There was always a moment for witches, where they decided who they would be, a moment when someone came who needed something more than what could be found in an apothecary. Someone who needed real magic, potent magic, the kind of magic that took more than stirring and crushing herbs. Some witches turned from it, because there was no going back once that magic ran in your veins. More would come once they heard you could help. And the magic would long to be free.

She'd heard of witches losing themselves to it, addicted to the rush of powerful magic. And undoing a curse? She'd need to call on the goddesses of old to harness the power of the moon and stars, to feel the ache of old trees and the spark of new life. It was not something everyone could do, and she was not sure she was one of those strong, magnificent women who pulled off charms and brewed real potions. But her mother handed her the necklace she always wore, the one with the key on the end.

And she suspected somewhere in those books was the answer to what had happened to her father. Why he had not chased them? Why she had not heard from him?

"There are many things I have kept from you, Lemon. Not out of cruelty, not because I didn't trust you, but because I kept them in my heart, and I was not ready to let them go. Magic is a gift, but it can be a burden. I will speak to Esther. We could try to do this for you."

Lemon knew her mothers danced under the moon. They buried things she did not ask about, to soothe the ancient magic in them. The magic they had set free twenty years ago, releasing it from its cage for the rest of their lives. Sometimes they left for weeks, and neither of their daughters asked why. Witches held secrets, deeds they did not speak of. Sacrifices like stones around their necks. "I think I can do this, mom. I think I have to try."

"As do I. And I will not fight you on it. Do what you need to do. I always told you that in the end all we have is each other, and I meant it. Go read the books. Esther will not stop you, either."

As Lemon left the apothecary, a chill moved through her. Some witches never had this day; the need for that ancient magic never came to them. She never knew which she hoped to be. Her life since leaving Charleston had been simple. The wind seemed to whisper to her, more urgently than ever before. She did not turn her face towards the breeze. The birds swooped low, but she did not call out to them.

Her feet continued their steady march towards her mothers' house even as her mind was elsewhere. She'd heard of curses lifted, usually on some news report with a smiling reporter and a crying family. But she'd also seen the failures, the shrugged shoulders and sad eyes of Hathornes standing by while police explained what a terrible, terrible crime it was, but how they had no leads, did not know who to charge.

And then it was only death, though families would cry and plead. There was no return for a cursed mind. The beasts roaring in cages, swiping their great claws. And then the public outrage. Why were the Hathornes not watched better? Then the counter argument, a witch must have helped. Perhaps witches were the problem. And then it would die down until the cycle repeated.

She reached her mothers' house and grabbed the stow-a-key rock, flipped it over, and let herself inside. The house was cluttered in the best way, plants and pictures, thick rugs and overstuffed pillows on velvet couches. She listened carefully for Esther's footsteps or the sound of the television, but nothing came. She must be out.

The garage was even more crowded than the living room, with boxes boasting of holiday decorations and old memories. Several of them held her name and Ruby's. She reached up, pulling down the stairs to the attic and a musty smell wafted down with it. As she ascended the stairs, she could feel the air thicken with wards, but they let her pass.

There, standing before her, were the antique trunks she had never been allowed to look inside. Lemon longed for Ruby. She had always thought if she ever made it inside these trunks her sister would be with her. She needed to tell her what she planned to do, but Ruby would not be as understanding as Esther. Family first, she would remind her. How many witches had died at the claws and teeth of the cursed? Her sister would not want to see her among them. And she could not blame her.

She knelt in front of the boxes reverently and pulled the chain from around her own neck. It was warm in her hand. She slipped it into the lock and it clicked open.

The tomes were old, and, at least in this trunk, had laid untouched for some time. A fine layer of dust coated them and then Lemon's fingers when she ran them along the covers. Thick leather and stitched spines. Under them were notebooks with cardboard covers and handwritten spells. She turned the pages carefully.

There was so much in them, spells to fight the plague, to keep away an enemy, and to kill one as well. Diagrams of patterns to be carved into cedar or drawn in the sand. Potions for love and hate with ingredients she had never used. Things she had never considered, to turn the waves, to call a storm.

Spells for the unfaithful, to steal magic, to kill a witch. And others as well, smaller spells, the ones she knew, to cure colic or hurry along a seedling. Reverence flooded her system, thankful for every bit of magic passed down from her ancestors that now flowed through her veins. All the men and women who had written these spells.

She pulled the ones on curses, putting them in a pile. She would need a trunk of her own, a lock, a key. How had her mothers gotten away without being cursed? She knew it was in these books somewhere, whatever spell had been done to Giuseppe Diggory, but they had never spoken of it, and eventually too much time had passed to ask.

The shadows grew long without Lemon realizing. She was already prone to finding herself lost in books and these captured her mind. With a start, she realized she had plans. She would need to go to the bakery soon. But what would she tell Claudia? That she had no way to get half the ingredients listed, that she had never used magic like this before? That she didn't understand why Claudia had come to her, out of all the witches who roamed the mountains?

And she hadn't told Ruby yet. She should. Her phone was heavy in her pocket but she didn't pull it out. She'd rather tell her in person.

She returned the books to the trunks and locked them away once again. She knew some of the ingredients, but they were like the blue flowers near the river, unnamed except by witches. Some of them were hard to find, on the tops of peaks, behind waterfalls. Some ingredients were not only hard to get but illegal, and morally dubious, like elephant tusks or the tears of a newborn.

And each spell had been devised by the witch who had broken the curse. She doubted they were interchangeable. Pulling the magic from a slithering serpent with two heads could not be the same as pulling it from a beautiful woman who drank blood.

On the way out of the house, Lemon checked her reflection and fixed her hair. Dust covered her shirt, and she did her best to get it off. She rummaged through the coat closet, finding several of her own in there, and settling on the leather.

It shouldn't feel like a date, it definitely wasn't, but there was a certain excitement to it. And all of those feelings mingled with trepidation. This was a big choice, and she wasn't sure why she was agreeing with it. But she'd always longed to test her magic, to see how steely she was at her core. She could prove herself.

The trepidation grew with each step into town. She would be in more danger. The Hathornes rarely prosecuted lesser witches, women who had never found the limits of what they could do. It was the strongest among them who found themselves on trial, if you could call it that, when there was no jury. Was she ready for that? Was she a fool?

Chapter Four

The Widow's Peak bakery was one of the most controversial establishments in Hecate's Hollow. Opened by Lavinia Green after the death of her third husband—another hiking accident—and funded by life insurance money, some people called it callous, especially considering the name. But Lavinia could bake better than anyone else and her coffee was the best in town, so eventually people moved on from their complaints.

For the first year it had only been open in the day, like most bakeries, but staying late one night to prep, Lavinia had noticed the stream of drunks walking by. Her bakery was midway between the only bar and the only hotel. So she'd extended the hours, shutting down midday and opening again at nine.

Lavinia smiled at Lemon as she walked in, her dark skin gleaming in the lamplight, where it wasn't covered in flour. She had been one of the first witches to welcome them to the Hollow all those years ago. She'd been young, younger than Lemon was now, but she'd kept an eye on her and her sister as their mothers unpacked. And she'd never asked about their fathers, though Ruby's wasn't a mystery. He'd been a friend of her mother's, and even after a drunken night and a big surprise neither of them had wanted more. He showed up a few times a year, more of an uncle than a father, but it never bothered Ruby. She'd seen what fathers could do.

Claudia was sitting at a wooden table, with a checkered tablecloth and an untouched croissant in front of her. She had leaned back, her long legs stretched out under the table, her hair fanned over the back of the chair.

Lemon hesitated. This could not end well. Claudia was gorgeous, and Lemon had always been a sucker for a pretty girl. If she hadn't found a solution in a month would she really be able to step away? There were ways to end it with kindness, potions that brought death gently, given in dire circumstances, and that was how most of the cursed found their end.

Claudia would be another tragic tale; so many older witches had them. Trying to help, not sleeping for weeks, feeling hopeless and helpless as they made potion and draught and tincture until their fingers bled and nothing changed. Until death was the only kindness they could offer. But most of them said the same thing— at least they did not go alone, at least someone was with them.

Against her better judgment, her feet moved forward, and she sat across from Claudia who smiled when she looked up. Except for the faint silver sheen of her skin and her elongated canines, nothing about her said vampire. Though what did she expect her to look like, a cape and red eyes?

Lemon smiled back, opening the limited menu Lavinia put out at night. She kept her voice low. "So I've been thinking, and technically, you *are* a vampire."

Claudia growled. "No, I'm not. *Technically.*"

"Teeth, blood lust, night time. You'd know the stories better than me. Do you feel a need to choose between two handsome men, approximately 200 years older than you?"

"I'm going to bite you." Claudia growled again, but she finished with a wink and Lemon's toes curled. She could feel herself blush and hid behind the menu as the not-exactly-vampire continued to talk. "I know I'm asking for a lot, but I thought it might be easier than other curses. You don't need to change my form. I'll keep looking like this if I have to. I just want to eat food and go out in the sun."

Lemon peeked over the laminated pages, another thought occurring to her. "Can you die?" What would she do if she couldn't? Stake her through the heart? Gross.

"I haven't tested it, but I cut my palm and it stitched back up. And no, I'm not allergic to silver or garlic. I do drink blood."

Also gross. "Human?" Lemon ran her thumb along her neck, and Claudia followed it with her eyes, answering that question.

They both stopped talking when Lavinia showed up at their table, putting a blueberry muffin she hadn't ordered in front of Lemon. "Here, honey, you're looking thin."

Lemon wasn't sure she was looking too thin by anyone's standards, but she took the muffin, picking off a piece as Lavinia retreated. She had a hundred questions for Claudia, who still hadn't touched her own food, but she started with the one that had been bothering her since their first encounter. "How'd you find me in the woods?"

To Lemon's surprise and excitement, Claudia blushed. "I, uh, can smell you."

So vampires could track by scent—except Claudia wasn't a vampire. She had been a witch and now she was a victim. Lemon kept thinking of her as something mysterious, some pre-civil war relic with a mysterious past, but she was just a woman, and by the looks of her, barely older than Lemon. Not a dark soul, not a bride of the darkness.

Still, she had *smelled* her. Lemon glanced around the bakery. People were looking at them from behind mugs and quiches. As the moon rose, Claudia's skin shined brighter and soon the townsfolk would be in a tizzy trying to figure out exactly what she was. Or just gossiping that Lemon was on a date with some strange, out of town woman. "We should get out of here, and then you should tell me what I smell like."

Claudia nodded, throwing a sheet of her chestnut hair over her shoulder and standing. Lemon got a full view of her outfit for the first time. Maybe she did look like a vampire, or at least she had more lesbian street cred than Lemon did, with leather pants and Doc Martens.

Not that there was much in the way of queer street cred in Hecate's Hollow, despite the higher than average collection of lost souls that had made their way to the town. They'd take in anyone who wandered in unless they caused trouble. There just weren't many streets and the only thing resembling a gay club was Drag Queen Storytime at the library, and that was just one guy—Gunter Greyson—and he already worked there.

"You be safe out there, Lemon-Lime!" Lavinia called after her. "Don't go worrying your mamas."

Lemon could have sunk into the sidewalk. There was nowhere without eyes in the little town. Mrs. Aberdash was already waving by the time they hit the end of the block, her little dogs yapping at the end of their leads.

Claudia bent down, extending her hand, and the dogs reared up, snapping in earnest now. She righted herself, apologizing while Mrs. Aberdash did the same, chiding the little dogs, but her eyes narrowed, and her lips moved into a thin line as she hurried away.

"Animals don't like me very much anymore. I keep forgetting." Claudia looked at her boot-clad feet. Lemon didn't know her well, but she could see the mess of emotions swirling over her face. Not a vampire at all.

Her sister was going to kill her for this. She'd been putting off texting her all day and strategically avoiding her, a fact Ruby was sure to have noticed. But she had to do something. "Do you want to come to my house?"

"If you think that's best."

Lemon led the way beneath the swelling moon. The night was thick with the scents of fall, apples, bonfires and crisp mountain air.

She plucked some leaves as they passed to put in jars later. Bats flew chittering overhead and Lemon looked up, but they did not stop. Their frantic fear of Claudia was heavy in the air. She should be afraid. She knew she should. But she had to try.

"I miss it," Claudia said, eyeing Lemon's pocket where she'd stowed her pluckings. "I can't feel anything anymore. I'm cut off from the magic. It's a different kind of death."

Lemon couldn't imagine what it would feel like to not be able to feel the roots beneath her feet, to know the birds by their wingbeats, or touch a plant and know what it might do, to urge it to bloom or wilt. She'd never been without it.

"I'm sorry," Lemon told her. Claudia nodded, and they fell into silence as they turned from the square, up the narrow street that led to her house, so close to town. "Do you know why he did it? It's very unusual."

But, before Claudia could answer, they were greeted with the off-key chorus of "The Best" coming from the open windows of Lemon's Victorian. She laughed, throwing the door open, to find Ruby doing her best—yet still terrible—Tina Turner impersonation while spinning Athena around the room.

She froze as the door opened and the cat jumped from her arms, scampering up the stairs so fast her legs moved several times before she did. Ruby's eyes went wide, and she closed her mouth, dropping her arms to her side.

Lemon put on her best smile, wide and welcoming, and hoped that her sister wouldn't leap across the threshold and throttle her. Well, she was doing this. No going back. "This is Ruby! Ruby, you remember Claudia. Come on in, Claudia." She looped her arm through the almost-vampire's and led her into the house.

Ruby's face went pale, and then red, nearly the color of her hair. "Lemon. A word." Her gaze darted from Lemon to Claudia to the doorway, clearly trying to decide what to do with her now that she was in the house. "You stay here. Don't move."

Claudia's eyebrows moved towards each other, creating a little wrinkle in the middle, but she nodded and pulled her arm from Lemon. "Your house. Your rules."

"Damn right." Ruby yanked Lemon by the wrist, and pulled her towards the kitchen, pushing hanging herbs out of her way. Nearly every surface of their kitchen was covered in little jars of simples, pressed flowers, crushed herbs, crystals and dirt from the tops of peaks. "What the absolute, ever loving fuck were you thinking?"

The jars vibrated with the force of Ruby's anger. She was never one to hide from a fight. Usually Ruby was in front, fists swinging, except when it came to Lemon. She wasn't sure if it was a byproduct of the way they had run away, the fear her father would follow, or if it was just sisterly love, but Ruby had never taken danger involving Lemon very well.

"You brought a vampire into the house," she hissed, grabbing ingredients at random. "A vampire, Lemon! An honest-to-god, motherfucking, cursed vampire. In our house. Without asking me."

Lemon's cheeks stung. She should have told Ruby. If things were reversed, she'd be just as mad as Ruby. She took the jar of crow feathers from her and sat them down. "You're right, but I talked to my mother. And she agrees. This is what witches do. We help people. I'll get to try real magic."

Ruby let out a low noise between a growl and a snort. "Real magic? Our magic is real. You just want more power. Since when? I've never heard you mention it more than in passing."

It was true that she had never given much thought to the things that led common witches to become the strongest of their kind, working their power like exercising muscles. But when it was set before her she found herself reaching for it. What would she do with that power? She didn't know, but she could nearly taste it. "Can you just talk to her for a minute? Get to know her. It's not like I'm in mortal danger."

"Until she pops open an artery like a coke can." Ruby drummed her fingers on the counter so hard Lemon worried for the finish.

"I'm sorry," Claudia said from the doorway. "I couldn't not hear, but..."

"What?" Ruby spun towards her and the lavender hanging above them shook.

There was a presence to Claudia, an air of calm strength, as though she could enact multitudes of violence, but only if she absolutely needed to. Her hand slipped into her pocket for just a moment, and the fire in her eyes died before it reappeared. "First, I apologize. I shouldn't have come into your home without your permission and I admire your protection of your sister. I would do the same for my brother. But..." She ran her hand through her hair, and it tangled in the thick mass. "I was a rare ingredients supplier. And I pissed off some powerful people who had a difference in opinion about what I was owed. I do not think I will become a monster like so many curses. I can feel the call of my old bosses. I don't know how familiar you are with myths, but like a siren in stories. I think that was the intention, to make me subservient."

There was clearly more to this story, but Ruby's fingers stopped their incessant tapping on the counter and she nodded. "You aren't a witch anymore, though."

"No."

"No powers." Ruby turned, grabbing a bottle of whiskey off the shelf. "I'll be on the porch. And I *do* have powers." She disappeared through the door, letting in the chirping of crickets for a moment before it swung shut behind her.

Thoughts raced through Lemon's head, books half read and even more forgotten, tales from childhood told on hikes and car rides. Curses were on the top of the bad-magic-you-should-never-mess-with list, but there were things beneath it, things that didn't snatch away all of a person, leaving them a snarling beast.

Those spells, potions, hexes, and terrors, all required things that Lemon had no access to or would never be comfortable getting, finger bones, eyes, innocent blood, just to name a few. And Lemon didn't know more than a few. She hadn't wanted to know. She spent her time learning the magic of the forest, of the rolling mountains, of the curling mists. She'd never wanted to reach into that dark pit, especially when she knew that half of her was Hathorne. Even if it didn't show, even if her mother's magic had won out, she never wanted to test it.

"I'm sorry. I'm asking too much." Claudia's hand was back in her pocket and Lemon wondered what was in there. Whatever it was she was rubbing her fingers on it. Some token, perhaps? Lemon didn't ask. Claudia deserved to keep some secrets.

"Are you sure it's a curse? This has all the trappings of a hex, and it would be much easier to remove." Hexes were not the deepest of dark magic. They were perpetrated by spurned lovers and angry teenagers. A crime of passion, not the dark blood magic of curses. And they could be called off more easily, just the right potion, a cleansing of rosemary. They would not need the blood of a Hathorne. She was certain she could handle a hex, some mountain snow, the feather of a dove, peonies crushed under a full moon. She was already devising a potion.

But Claudia shook her head. "My brother knows the man who did it. But you're right, perhaps it's not a standard curse, but where is the line? Magic is not black and white, but this cannot be undone with simple magic. But I think you're strong enough, and I know I can find whatever you need. You have a gift, don't you?"

At guessing the right ingredients. She was known for it in the town. Even the older witches would come to her. They'd bring her sick children, stubborn acne, whatever ailed them. Sometimes even Dr. Mills came to her aid. She could lay her hand upon something and know how to fix it. But how did Claudia know that? She could not believe that word of her powers had spread so far and she was not the only witch who could do it. It was not the rarest of gifts.

In fact, Lemon had so many questions she wasn't sure where to begin. "If you have a brother he must be a witch, right? Why didn't you ask him for help?"

Claudia glanced towards the ground. "I did. He's searching for the Hathorne and witch who did it." It wasn't the whole truth, not with the way Claudia was twisting her hands and Lemon's unease grew. There was so much hidden and yet she felt drawn to her, just as she had been at the spring. Something deep inside her told her that this was hers to fix, but she couldn't understand why.

Like a leaf in a stream, Lemon could not control where she went. She simply followed the pull of the woman before her. But she glanced towards the door, where the sticky smell of weed had wafted through, and Ruby was giving pointed coughs, clearly listening.

Claudia chucked. "This is so stupid. I'm sorry. I'm sorry I asked at all. Of course, you don't want to do this. There's been what? A dozen curses cured? Even with the blood... I just thought with your magic..." She started to turn and Lemon grabbed her by the shoulder. Claudia pulled her hand free from her pocket, and something fell out.

The photo floated to the floor, landing face up. Two children with chestnut hair, side by side in matching striped bathing suits on the beach. Twins. One was smiling, one was not. Both were deeply tanned, with golden skin and brown hair, tangled by the waves and wind. Claudia picked it up, rubbing her fingers over the frowning face. "That's my brother. We're identical."

It took Lemon a moment to put the pieces of what Claudia had said together in her head. "Oh." She watched as Claudia turned over the photo. Glued onto the back was another photo—both of them in the same poses as adults, Claudia in a bathing suit, her brother, muscled and smiling now, in trunks.

"Listen, I do want to help but..." Lemon moved forward, putting one hand on Claudia's cheek. She brushed her finger against her jawline and closed her eyes. Images flashed. A man face down in a puddle of blood. A black ewe with its throat slit. The roots of a tree she knew but could not place, overlooking a mountain. The wing of a bat. A pure white flower growing in the cracked rock of a cave.

The world seemed to sway and Lemon swayed with it, her heart pounding. Only Claudia grabbing her kept her up, and then they were so close. She could see the indents her incisors left on her lip, the odd amber of her eyes, the streaks of gold and red throughout her hair.

Those amber eyes darted to Lemon's mouth as she spoke, rendering her once again silent. The hands steadying her slipped to her waist, thumbs slipping under the fabric of her shirt. She lowered her head, brushing the tip of her nose against the column of Lemon's neck, breathing in.

Lemon snapped out of it. A fool for a pretty girl she may be, but she wasn't going to let a vampire sniff her carotid. She stepped back, pulling her shirt down and straightening it. She took in a deep breath, but the air seemed thin. "I know what I need."

Running her tongue over those dangerous incisors, Claudia smirked. "Do you?" She took a step closer, across the invisible barrier Lemon imagined between them, keeping her and her good senses away from the vampire. On this side of the line, Claudia turned Lemon's thoughts into those of tangled sheets and panting mouths. So she stepped back as well.

"For the magic. I know what I need for the magic."

"Sure." Claudia smiled.

Lemon rolled her eyes, pressing her thighs together, which honestly didn't help the problem. "But I'll need the blood of the man who did it. And a black ewe, the roots of a tree that I don't know where it is, a bat, and a flower growing out of a cave that looked incredibly treacherous."

Claudia smiled, all the flirt gone, only a strong woman, pale under the moon. "Okay. I can do that."

Who was she? What kind of person smiled like that when faced with such an impossible task? Lemon wasn't sure, but she intended to find out, because as far as she was concerned that vision was a sign. From the universe, from her ancestors, from whatever. She was meant to help. Like she'd been destined to do since she stepped into those woods and felt the call, the pull, towards the thing that made animals flee.

"I'll go," Claudia said, looking at her with an expression between hunger and admiration. "I need to call my brother, and I have a feeling your stoned sister is going to want a long talk."

"I can hear you." Ruby called from the porch.

"Am I wrong?" Claudia's voice was even, but she winked at Lemon.

The back door opened with a creak, and Ruby stood in the doorway. "Listen, I don't trust you, but if my sister is in, and obviously she is—she can't resist a charity case—so am I. So don't be glib with me."

"What about pithy?" Claudia's smile grew, but she turned and left, leaving the house, inexplicably, a little colder.

Chapter Five

Lemon settled into the old wooden swing on her porch, enjoying the creaking as it moved back and forth, a problem no amount of WD-40 could fix. It reminded her of childhood, of her mothers rocking her through troubled nights, of laughing with Ruby as they saw how high they could go.

"I know you think I'm dumb."

Ruby raised an auburn eyebrow. "I've never thought you were dumb. I think you're a helper. It's how you get roped into planning dances and working on committees. I'm just worried about you. There's a piece missing from her story."

"I know," Lemon said, taking the joint her sister passed and closing her eyes as she inhaled. She imagined flying as the swing moved. "She swears it's a curse and the counter-potion is the most intricate I've divined, but... it seems like a hex to me."

Curling her feet beneath her on the rocking chair, Ruby pulled the blanket around herself tighter as the autumn winds gusted. The wind loved Ruby, always following her. And sometimes Lemon thought it was because she was meant to leave, that this little town was too small for her sister, who deserved so many big things. "Does it matter? Either way, whoever did that to her meant cruelty and they're likely to come looking for her. A curse like that... he must have wanted to keep her around. He didn't make a beast."

"It'd be better, wouldn't it? Easier to find him if he came here."

Ruby chuckled. "I'd almost be interested in seeing the Hathorne who was bold enough to step into a witch town." Usually, they avoided them with amazing precision. There were entire websites dedicated to travel without entering one. The law enforcement in witch towns weren't in their pocket like other places, and they would be held accountable for their crimes. Sometimes the federal government would step in, but usually the charges were true, and there was little they could do. So they stayed away, in the vast freedom of the rest of the country, where they avoided punishment, as they had for hundreds of years.

Lemon put the joint out on the bottom of her shoe and stuck it in the empty flowerpot on the side table. Her head was swimming, and she thought of Claudia. "Do you think I'm…"

"Horny?" Ruby offered.

"Yeah, I guess that *was* what I was going for." She sighed, the ingredients for the counter-potion flashing through her mind. It would be tricky, hard to get, even harder to make. Brewing it would be more complex than anything she'd ever done. But if she was the one this had happened to… well, she knew exactly how much a witch's help could mean against a Hathorne. She voiced as much to her sister and a long look passed between them.

It had been years since they'd spoken of that night in more than whispers. Never in the last two decades had either of their mothers mentioned what they had done to Giuseppe Diggory—whether he was dead or alive. He had never contacted Lemon or her mother, as far as she knew, leading to certain conclusions. But her mothers still watched crowds, still spent almost all their time in the safety of Hecate's Hollow.

"You know, I haven't ever thought much about strengthening my magic," Ruby said, getting up from the rocking chair to sit beside Lemon. The night was growing cooler, and the wind pulled at loose strands of their hair. "It's like… why even bother? I never needed more magic. We aren't exactly fighting demons anymore. It always seemed unnecessary."

"Sometimes I think we'd all be stronger if the world was fairer. But they use it to punish us. *Look at this strong magic she did. Better watch out, she'll do more now.*"

It was hard to know the truth of anything with witches. When they'd been burning them at the stake, they'd also burned their spell books and for a long time few had spoken of their histories, scared of death. There was no amount of magic that could save you against an angry mob, or a blazing inferno. They had their oral histories, and plenty had been patched back together, but witch historian wasn't exactly the most popular career. It was still dangerous to do magic, no matter how many tourists flocked to the hills each year.

"I think it's all just working towards a goal." Ruby offered, draping her blanket over Lemon's legs. "I think it's like doing the splits. You gotta stretch and stretch and suddenly your ass is flat on the ground."

"I'd like to see you do a split."

Ruby made a low noise in the back of her throat. "I bet you'd like to see Claudia do a split."

"Big talk for somebody who spends her weekends at the Slipper Sip, looking for cowboys. The walls are thin, you know."

"Don't say cowboys. It's gross." Ruby put her head on Lemon's shoulder. "They're... mountain men."

The next day Lemon didn't see Claudia at all, but she did finally have to complete a shift at the Red and White Apothecary.

"I heard you were on a date with a girl." Elias Redwood wiggled his eyebrows as he sorted through the basket of tumbled rocks on the counter. "Took her home and everything."

Internally, Lemon cringed, remembering how quickly she'd invited Claudia over. Don't invite a vampire in—that's fantasy TV rule number one. But she preferred dramas—the soapier the better. Again, negative one for her lesbian street cred, but this was Hecate's Hollow where the streets were named after flowers and one of the only other gay inhabitants was looking right at her and wearing Wranglers. Plus she'd grown up watching soap operas on Lavinia's couch. "Is that why you're here?"

Elias had the decency to blush. "Well, I also heard, from several sources, that she's spooky. You got a spooky girlfriend, Leblanc?"

Lemon leaned her elbows on the counter, careful of the stoppered bottles of witch hazel she hadn't put away yet. "She's a vampire."

A muscle in Elias's jaw twitched and his eyes narrowed as he tried to figure out if Lemon was pulling his leg. "Of the Cullen variety, I hear. Rumor is she was nearly silver. Spell gone wrong?"

"Indeed."

"Well, you'd be the witch to find, yeah? Speaking of, my sister's baby cries all night, gassy little monster. You must have something for that."

"Of course." She led him across the shop, waving away incense smoke. "This one." She shoved a salve into his hands. "Directly on the stomach. And this one, a couple drops in the bottle. If the baby takes the breast, she can dropper it right into her mouth but it's a little bitter. Don't worry, it's mostly ginger and turmeric."

He held them up to the light, examining the yellow liquid inside. Lemon had always liked Elias. He was a year younger than her, but he'd been friendly since they moved in. Their houses had been on the same street and they used to ride bikes together, exploring the waterfalls outside of town and making grand plans they never got around to completing.

"My mom and Gran never mess with this stuff. They're all about elemental magic. Do you think I could do some of the potions? I've always wanted to try, but I was scared I'd blow something up."

"Honestly," Lemon leaned in conspiratorially, "a lot of potions are just herbs mixed together. Not all of them even require magic. Some do, obviously. You can't just mix mouse ears and orange peels together and cure a wart."

Elias pulled a face. "Thank heavens for that." He headed back towards the counter, balancing the potion and salve in one hand while he fished for his wallet. "But, seriously, the girl. Should we be worried? Don't get a lot of hexed women coming through the Hollow, you know."

Lemon froze. He was right; they didn't. And people had noticed, as they would keep noticing, that she shone under the moon. They'd notice animals in the woods drained of blood, and however much they liked witches, she doubted they'd be predisposed to a wanna-be vampire running through the town. She needed to say something. The townspeople didn't know Claudia, hell, she barely knew Claudia, but they trusted Lemon.

Would the truth work? Would the town be willing to help if they knew she was cursed? Would they care that a Hathorne wanted to bind her to him? Would they trust Lemon to handle it? Was she even qualified? What if it failed and Claudia killed someone?

"Jesus, Leblanc, you look like you've seen a ghost. You haven't, have you?" He glanced at the corners of the shop. Then, eyes widening, and kindness washing over his features, he put everything down on the counter and took a step towards Lemon. "Seriously, Lemon, is everything okay?"

She opened her mouth, not sure what she was going to say, and nothing came to her mind, so she closed it again. She was all big talk and blustering words. Since she was a child, she'd had almost no interaction with Hathornes. Sure, she was excellent at potions... She took a deep breath. She was good at potions. She could do this. "You'll keep a secret?" She knew Elias would, at least for now. He nodded, leading her to one of the chairs flanking the table they used for reading cards.

He sat across from her and shuffled the deck, the cards flew through his fingers. "You can trust me. You know that."

"She's... hexed." Lemon still wasn't sure it was a curse, whatever Claudia said, and she didn't want the town taking up pitchforks.

"Like a vampire." Elias nodded, setting down the cards. Their gilded edges caught the sun, making lines across his thick glasses. "Do you remember... Oh, what was her name? Bertie Edgewood?"

"Like a ghost!" Lemon said. She couldn't believe she had forgotten it, but she'd just been a kid then, preoccupied with middle school. But she'd been the reverend's wife, and she'd done... well, no one knew what she'd done and she left right after, but for a full week and a half Bertie Edgewood had been transparent. "Do you remember how they fixed her?"

"My grams did it. I remember her house smelled terrible, and she killed a goat for its blood. It was so nasty, but she said, 'Well, better the goat goes than Bertie.'"

Lemon pulled the card off the top of the deck. The Page of Swords. Relevant enough, she supposed. "I often forget how strong magic can be."

"Big words from one of the best witches in town. You'll have Doc Mills out of practice soon enough." But he stopped, concern back in his eyes at something he saw on her face. Gingerly, he reached across the table and put his hand on top of hers, the card trapped beneath them. "Lemon, is this worse than you're letting on? You don't have to do it. People can't just traipse in and demand things of you."

But even as he said it, she could feel the pull, faint and far away, the same pull that had called her from the spring in the woods. Some kind of thread ran between them, like the web of a spider, too fragile to pull, but felt all the same.

She'd never felt something like it, and she was too old and too jaded to believe it was some meshing of souls, some meeting of the beyond. But she believed in magic, in all the ways people were connected. She thought of the birds, the way she could call them when they flew above.

"No. Maybe. I'm not sure, but she's not demanding. She's just someone who needs help. You know how things can be...out there."

Elias nodded. He'd moved to Atlanta one summer, with the highest hopes, and come back that September. It wasn't that they didn't want the lights and life of a city. It was just when you'd been cradled in safety, brought up in a bubble, it was hard to leave. Unless, of course, you were see-through Bertie Edgewood, who swore off witches once she was corporeal again. "Well, if she needs help, she came to the right place. The Hollow's a family." He kept up a string of under his breath complaints about the treatment of witches and the hypocrisy of Hathornes. And then sighed. "I'm bummed you weren't on a date. I was hoping for some hot gossip. I love it here, but damn, it can be boring."

"A date with a vampire? Come on, Elias. What kind of girl do you think I am?"

He stood, offering Lemon his hand and pulling her up from the table, but there was mischief in his eyes that reminded Lemon of tenth grade and stealing his mom's Schnapps. She'd caught them drunk in his tree house and given them a thorough talking to—mostly about stealing her shit and how she was going to chop their fingers off—but she never told Lemon's mothers.

"Oh, I know exactly what kind of girl you are. Now ring me up so I can go make a bet with your sister on how long until there are fang marks on your neck."

Once he left, Lemon felt lighter, because Elias was right. Whatever happened Lemon wasn't alone. She had everyone in Hecate's Hollow. Even Lucille, who hadn't cared for her since they'd shown up to the first day of sixth grade wearing the same outfit, would have her back for this. And they'd have Claudia's back, the same as they had when Esther and Amaryllis had shown up decades ago. So many must have suspected the truth, but they understood the world and they'd never demanded an explanation.

Speaking of the devil, as it were, Esther showed up, her red hair in a ponytail and a box of office supplies under her arm. "Easier to get toadstool than copier paper in this backwards ass town." She heaved it onto the counter, avoiding everything breakable.

"Hey." Lemon came around the counter and wrapped her arms around her mom. Esther froze for a moment, no doubt confused, and then returned the hug, squeezing Lemon around the ribs. "I love you." Lemon didn't tell her enough.

"I love you too." She pulled away enough to look at Lemon's face. "Are you okay? I talked to Amaryllis last night. She told me everything."

"Sometimes I forgot how you saved me." She sighed, flashing back to that night, the headlights. Esther turned towards her, a smile forced on her face.

"Good," she said, rubbing Lemon's shoulders. "You don't owe me anything, honey. Now..." She tapped the box twice, and it popped open. Inanimate objects were always obeying her. She took out a piece of paper and pulled a pencil from behind her ear. "If you're gonna help this girl, it's gonna be a town effort. That's the problem with the world." She tapped the pencil on the counter twice and it was sharpened. "People rush to the cities. Who is gonna break their curse in New York? The bagel guy?" Lemon didn't think Esther had ever been to New York. She still ranted about Yankees sometimes. "No, the witch towns. That's where you get help. And I know your mama Amaryllis is nervous, and Ruby, well...anyway, I wasn't brought up in the woods to be scared of owls, you know. And you and Ruby would do well to remember it. We aren't going to cower in the Hollow, scared of some Hathorne when a girl needs help."

It was outrageous, of course. Amaryllis and Esther spent plenty of time in Hecate's Hollow scared of the phantom of a Hathorne. But Esther had also stood up to her father. She knew that whatever had happened, she was the ringleader, not Amaryllis. Her mother had always cowered until Esther relit the flame inside of her.

But a day in the shop had bolstered Lemon, reminded her of who she was, of who surrounded her. But one thing still frightened her. There'd been bloodwork and scientific testing—plenty done on the subject—but still she worried. "You don't think I have any of his magic in me, do you?"

Her mother looked up from the list she was making. "Who? Your father? Fucking Giuseppe didn't give you anything but thick eyebrows. Don't you worry about that. There's no anti-magic in your veins. It wouldn't make it past your heart."

Chapter Six

"What are you wearing to the festival?" Ruby asked as Lemon flipped an omelet over in the skillet. Ruby was sitting on one of the barstools, her legs dangling just above the floor. She had on a green sundress and her red hair danced around her shoulders, gilded gold and copper in the sunlight.

Their mothers had graciously, and possibly because they thought she was going to have a meltdown, told Lemon to skip working the booth that morning and to stroll the festival. Granted, she usually did anyway, everyone did, taking time to wander the rows of wares and wanna-be mind readers.

Even in a town like Hecate's Hollow, the Festival of Blessings pulled its fair share of charlatans, but there were also plenty of actual witches from out of town who'd come in, paying the booth rental fee and filling the town coffers.

"I don't know. I hate all my clothes." She plated the omelet and poked at it with her fork. Her mother's always looked so fluffy, hers looked... well, sad.

"Oh, bullshit," Ruby said, and she disappeared up the stairs, Athena at her heels. When she reappeared, she had a nearly too short black dress, a lacy shawl and a pair of boots. "It'll show your tattoo." Ruby grinned.

One of several, she had lemons tattooed right above the back of her knees on both legs with the words NOT SWEET written below. It was silly, but honestly her favorite tattoo. She liked it even more than the half sleeve of flowers and birds covering her right arm and shoulder.

Shoveling the rest of the food into her mouth, Lemon took the offered clothes and slipped into the laundry room to change, leaving her pajamas behind. Ruby had an eye for fashion that Lemon definitely didn't, and she did look cute.

Her sister set her down on the stool by her shoulders and started in on her, stringing earrings through her ears and swiping mascara on her eyes. Lemon sat still, her mind wandering, once again, to the things she needed to find for Claudia's cure. But she still hadn't heard from her, and they wouldn't get anywhere without the blood of the Hathorne. She didn't know how much they'd need, but at least a few drops.

"Done," Ruby announced fifteen minutes later. "We can walk together." As though there was ever any other plan. She'd probably walked into town with Ruby more times than without her.

The streets of the sleepy town had been transformed, gauzy silver fabric hung between lamp posts and signs, interspersed with jewel tones. A large banner reading Festival of Blessings hung from the rafters of the gazebo, and booths covered in the same glittering fabric filled the square. On the streets were vendors selling everything from balloons to churros.

But Lemon's attention was drawn to a lithe man standing at the end of their street, arguing with a taller man. Though his voice was raised, it mingled with the sound of the crowd and she could not make out the words.

Ruby froze beside her, neither of them sure what to do. Getting to the festival would require passing the two men.

The smaller man's voice boomed, loud enough for them to hear. There was something familiar about him, but Lemon couldn't figure it out, even as she wracked her brain. "I know exactly what you goddamn did, and you've got a lot of nerve coming here. Are you following me?"

The other man's mouth lifted towards a smile until the first's fist collided with it. He stumbled back.

"I don't give a shit what kind of magic you think you know. You're going to have a hell of a time doing it when I yank your arms out of their sockets."

The bigger man wiped the blood off the corner of his lip. "You've backed the wrong horse, Auberon. He'll come here soon, you know. And then what's your plan?" The attention of the crowd was turning towards them. "I'll give you a week."

"I'm not doing it."

The larger man turned on his heel, disappearing into the crowd while the other stood glowering and flexing his hand.

Before Lemon could react, Ruby rushed forward, a wide smile on her face. "I've got ointment for that at my shop." She caught his hand in hers, as though they were old friends. "It'll help with the sting."

The man's face moved through several emotions, landing on amusement. "It's not as bad as that. He was soft enough."

Lemon stood watching. She'd seen Ruby flirt a million times, but she was really putting it on now, using her recently freed hand to pull at the longest strands of her hair and smiling sweetly, as though she hadn't just watched him threaten someone.

"I'm Ruby Carmine."

The man's smile crinkled the skin near his eyes. "Fritz Auberon. You must be one of the inhabitants of this lovely town."

"I am. And what brings you here? I take it that it's not the festival." She ran a hand through her hair and Lemon leaned against the tree. Watching Ruby was as good as a nature documentary.

"Oh. I came to check on my sister."

And it clicked for Lemon who he was. She could see it now, the almost upturned nose, the sharp cheekbones, the thick chestnut hair. But his skin was tanned and so were his eyes, true brown—not amber. "You're Claudia's brother!"

Fritz turned towards her, noticing Lemon for the first time, and he chuckled in earnest. "You would know Claudia."

"Excuse me?"

He laughed again. "Nothing. Do you know where she is?"

"No, I haven't seen her in days." She tried not to roll her eyes as her sister mouthed how cute he was behind his back. She wasn't about to date a pair of identical twins with her sister. Not that she was dating Claudia. Jesus, what was wrong with her?

But she could see in Ruby's eyes that she would be taking a more active role in this now that Fritz was around. Not that she would have stayed out of it before, but now she'd be positively underfoot.

"Yeah, I own the apothecary up the way," Ruby lied. Their mothers had owned the building since they were children. "I can show you and then we can look around for your sister."

"There's two hotels in the whole town," Lemon said, catching up to them as they headed towards the festival. "She can't be too hard to find."

"Well, fate has shone on me today."

As it turned out, they didn't need to look far to find Claudia. She was in the middle of the square, looking over hand-beaded necklaces and holding a funnel cake. An extremely large hat shadowed her, and without the moon her skin was pale.

She smiled at the sight of Lemon, but it faltered when she saw her brother laughing with Ruby. "Fritz..." She moved towards him but stopped at the edge of the shadows provided by the trees, sucking in a breath.

Fritz paled, his eyes wide. "I'm going to fucking kill him, Claudia." He swept his sister into his arms, nearly smashing the fried dough into her chest, but she held it away.

"I missed you so much. And I found the witch we heard about." She beamed up at him.

"Orlo was here. Did you know that? I should have strangled him on sight but..." He glanced at Lemon and Ruby and gave a pleasant, if vacant, smile.

Ruby sidled up to Lemon, interest plain on her face. There was more to this than Claudia was telling and Lemon wasn't sure where that put her. She owed Claudia nothing, no more than she owed anyone else asking for help. And she wasn't sure Claudia owed her the truth. Did asking for help mean you had to tell your complete life story to someone?

But there was the curiosity of it all. Lemon wanted to see this through to the end. Partially because she wanted Claudia, had already imagined those sharp teeth against her skin, but also just for the mystery of it and the allure of being one of the few witches able to say they'd saved someone cursed. That she had come against anti-magic and won. Most of the successes she'd read about were witches like herself—those who could feel out the ingredients needed by touching a thing. She wanted to be on that list.

Claudia broke away from her brother and moved towards Lemon. The clouds shifted and the sun broke through the cloudy day. Hissing and dropping her food, Claudia jumped back into the shade of the tree, clutching her hand to her chest. "God damn it." She gazed down at the funnel cake. "And it tasted like shit. I'm so sick of this."

Ruby's eyes went wide and her fingers started to curl around Lemon's wrist, but her face softened and she released her. "It is bullshit."

"Come on." Lemon's eyes darted ahead, searching out a shadowed path towards the Red and White Apothecary.

She wrapped her arm around Claudia's shoulder and urged her forward. There were a few curious glances. No one else in the square had on quite as large a hat, and Claudia's jacket was nearly a cloak.

Fritz and Ruby trailed behind them as they walked. Claudia pulled her jacket tighter when the sun filtered through the trees and looked toward Lemon. "I didn't know you were all tatted up."

"You still don't know the extent of it." Lemon winked and pushed the door to the shop open. Amaryllis was inside, her face hidden by a curtain of thick blonde hair. She glanced up at the sound of the door, taking in all of them, but said nothing.

Lemon headed into the back, pulling Claudia by her undamaged hand while Ruby talked to their mother. Instead of the dried herbs, polished crystals, and stacks of tarot out front the back was full of raw ingredients. Piles of feathers and dead mice littered the shelves, still green herbs and plants laid across the tables and more hung from the ceiling. The air was thick with the smell of it, but to Lemon, the scent was home.

"What are you doing?" Claudia asked, pulling out a wooden backed chair to sit in.

"Making something for your hand." Lemon grabbed yellow root and comfrey, then mortar and pestle.

"How gallant," Claudia teased, but her smile seemed genuine enough to Lemon.

She finished her poultice and sat beside Claudia. Truly, there was no reason to involve herself in something that was clearly dangerous, probably much more than she realized, but as she dipped her fingers into the mess of crushed plants and ran them

61

across Claudia's skin, she knew she would. Claudia barely needed the help. Her skin was almost fully healed, smooth and cool under the pads of Lemon's fingers.

"I know what you'll need for your curse." Lemon grabbed a rag and wiped her hands on it. The voices of Fritz and Ruby drifted back to her, the bell of the store rang, but Claudia was looking at her like she was the only person in the world.

"You might help then? I know...." Her eyes strayed from Lemon's face to her neck and something flashed in her eyes. "You don't owe me anything."

Lemon's breath hitched in her chest. This was dangerous. Claudia was not the cursed beast witches were warned about, but that made everything more treacherous. How would she know when blood lust started to take over her mind? But she nodded, and tried to swallow but her throat was dry. "I'll help."

"You smell so good." Claudia leaned in, her nose tickling against the side of Lemon's neck, and against better judgment she moved her head back, granting her access.

With a groan, Claudia pulled away. "I can still control it, and I swear that I'll try to tell you if I can't. I should have a month, maybe two at the most. But I can feel it, Lemon. I'm drawn to the Hathorne who did this like a moth to flame. He means to control me."

"Will you ever tell me that story?" Lemon's head swam. The air was heavy and thick with magic.

"I will," Claudia said. "As much as I can. There are things..."

But Lemon didn't learn what those things were. The door opened, and they moved apart. Lemon could feel her cheeks heating and Ruby raised an eyebrow, biting her lip against the smirk on her face. "How goddamn long does it take to make a poultice? Fritz hasn't even had a chance to see the town and you're back here canoodling."

"Shut the fuck up." Lemon stood, putting out a hand to Claudia, and pulling her to her feet. The briefest of smiles passed over her lips.

"I should go. There's too much sun." She glanced towards her brother. "I've been staying at the inn down the street. We could talk for a bit." She turned toward Lemon and then looked around the room. Finally, finding what she was looking for, she grabbed a pen and a notebook and scribbled something on it. Ripping the paper free, she handed it to Lemon. "It's my number. Maybe you'll let me know what we need. And thank you."

"Come over after dark," Ruby said pleasantly, despite the firm set of her jaw and the straight line of her back.

Claudia nodded. "Very well."

"I'll bring pizza," Fritz added, apparently including himself in the invitation. The more the merrier. Lemon wouldn't stand by if her sister was cursed either.

"There's no good pizza for miles. Brings burgers from Duncan's and I'll get some beer. Can you drink beer?" She glanced towards Claudia.

"I find the higher the alcohol level the better it sits. Don't ask me to explain why. I'll grab something if I can make it before the liquor store closes. Everyone around here seems to be in bed by eight."

Ruby laughed. "Alright." She stood to the side, making room for Claudia to leave, and she did, with a last glance at Lemon.

Once they were alone, Ruby and Lemon stood in silence for a long time. "I've got to help her," Lemon said, feeling like a broken record.

"I know," Ruby said. "Just like you saved every broken-winged bird and cried when the tails came off of lizards. I should have just accepted it from the beginning, when she caught you on that mountain. Though I still think that was planned, it's a bit too Hallmark heroics for me, personally."

"You think she planned for me to stupidly fall down into a ditch?"

"She's undead, Lem. I'm sure she's committed worse atrocities." But Ruby was laughing, and she headed out of the storeroom, into the spring light pouring in from the windows at the front of the shop. "Come on, let's get back to the festival." She held the door open.

"Do not hit on her brother, Ruby. I fucking mean it," Lemon said, crossing the street back towards the town square. The smell of fried foods and spun sugar permeated the air. The town would smell like corn dogs for days. Speaking of... Lemon's stomach growled. "Swear it. Do not sleep with him, Ruby Carmine."

"Me?" Ruby moved her hand to her chest dramatically. "I don't know what kind of girl you think I am," she said, giving Lemon deja vu.

"Oh, I know exactly what kind of girl you are." She echoed Elias, wondering if everyone in the Hollow knew each other too well.

"The same kind as you." Ruby cocked her head to the side, one eyebrow slightly raised. Ahead of them was a woman in a billowing white dress, her silvery hair—that Lemon was almost certain was a wig—pooled in her lap while she ran her hands over a crystal ball.

Some of the festival was fantastic but some of it was so campy. But how would they prove who had magic? She suppressed a laugh, imagining throwing vendors into the lake and only allowing the ones who sank to sell.

"Seriously though, Ruby, don't mess with him. I want to..." She trailed off, realizing exactly where her thoughts were going, even as she glared at the crystal ball reader.

"Fuck his sister and that would make it too weird?" Ruby finished her thought, needing no help to figure that one out. "Fine. I won't flirt with him."

She headed towards a cart selling snow cones; Witches Blood

read the label on a dark red syrup. *Hilarious.* "Let's just focus on finding a cure, making sure a full-fledged vampire isn't running around the Smokies and not who we're gonna screw. Fair enough?"

"Aren't you curious as to exactly what happened? Judging by that argument, it's a good story." Ruby ordered a lime snow cone and paid for both of them.

"You have no idea." Lemon admitted. "I'm absolutely dying with the curiosity of it. It's a mystery novel. I feel like Agatha Christie. She is hot, but it's not that. I'd help either way. I can't help myself."

"Oh, I don't doubt it. I think mom still has our collection of Nancy Drew books up in the attic." She smiled, her eyes far away, and Lemon knew she was remembering their childhood—summers spent trying to eavesdrop when the sheriff would come into the shop and then solve whatever crime they invented before the police could.

They never accomplished it, not in small part because the crimes were almost entirely fictionalized by their excitable underage brains, but they'd had fun doing it.

"Come on." Ruby inclined her head across the square. "Let's go make some money off some tourists."

Chapter Seven

Heading into fall as they were, it was past eight when the sun went down, and later still when there was finally a knock on the door. Athena twitched her ears towards the sound, and then wove between Ruby's legs as she headed toward the door.

Lemon glanced around the sunroom, trying to see it as Claudia would, and wondering what her house looked like to outsiders. The sunroom was Lemon's favorite, stuffed full of plants, their vines running across the ceiling and walls. It was full of sun in the day, and even at night the wide windows let the moonlight stream it, casting a pleasant glow over the candlelit room.

Claudia and Fritz appeared. Side by side, she could see the resemblance. But Fritz had the shadow of a beard on his chin and a stronger jaw, square where Claudia's was sharp.

The main difference, at the moment, was their expression. Fritz was standing awkwardly, holding a bag that promised burgers and fries, while Claudia was grinning. Lemon wondered if that was what she had been like before the curse. Had she always been so bold, so full of life?

She flopped down onto the rattan couch, cradling a bottle of vodka like a baby while Friz spread out the food. Claudia sniffed and then scrunched her nose. "I miss being able to enjoy food. Do you know how hard it is to catch a rabbit?"

Ruby almost choked, but kept passing out the fries. "So, Lemon said you know who did this to you?"

"Okay." She twisted the top of the bottle and took a long drink. Lemon's stomach hurt just watching it, but Claudia didn't so much as grimace. "This doesn't necessarily paint me in the best light."

"As long as whatever you did isn't worse than turning someone into a mythological creature, you're probably fine," Ruby said around a mouthful of burger.

Claudia glanced towards her brother, but Fritz only shook his head and Lemon knew that look. She'd given it to Ruby a thousand times and her sister had done the same. It was the look of *I told you not to get us into this shit.* Yet, he was there, just as Ruby was, ready to face whatever obstacles they found to help his sister.

In response to his look, Claudia rolled her eyes and sat up straighter, legs spread apart. The bottle of vodka dangled precariously from her fingers between them. She took a drink, raising an eyebrow at Lemon.

And, if Lemon was being honest with herself, it was more than being a helpful witch, or a good person, that led her to want to help Claudia. She was gorgeous, unassumingly funny, and she captivated Lemon more than she wanted her to. And there were all the selfish reasons Lemon wanted to help; to be the hero, to save her, to kiss her and not feel sharp teeth. And, again, if she was being honest, she'd wanted it from the first moment Claudia had caught her in her arms and said she was looking for her.

She was only so strong, after all. "So what's the story?" She pulled a beer from the pack on the table and twisted the cap off with the bottom of her shirt, drawing Claudia's eye. She knew what she would find there, the fern leaves running across her hip bones.

The vampire's smile only grew as she dragged her eyes back up Lemon's chest to her face. Was there anyone else in the room? Lemon was sure there was, but she found it hard to look anywhere else, until Fritz cleared his throat and the spell between them—well, maybe it wasn't broken, but it wavered a bit.

"I worked for a man. Julian." She glanced again towards her brother, but he'd clearly heard the story before. He was busy shoving fries in his mouth. "He's very powerful among certain people. And I'm not trying to be cryptic, it's just it was dangerous and, well..." Her amber eyes found Lemon. "I don't want to put you in danger. Julian is a Hathorne, but witchcraft never seemed to matter much to him. He sourced and sold rare ingredients among other things. And I..." She took another drink of her vodka.

Lemon did the same with her beer. She was already finding this tale hard to take. Across the table, Ruby pulled out a joint and lit it. Fritz held his hand out.

There was something between them, she was sure of it, but she didn't have many thoughts left for what her sister was doing. Red-haired, blue eyed, and usually laughing, she always had someone interested. But Lemon looked back to Claudia. "You chose to work for him?" Her stomach did a flop, though she could have guessed as much, when Claudia nodded.

"Me and the man you saw in the square, Orlo. I was newer, much newer. Orlo had been working for him for years. But I'm... well... I'm hot, so I could finagle my way into places that Orlo couldn't. So we traveled together." Another drink, but this time she smiled and slid off the couch to sit on the floor beside Lemon.

Their thighs were touching, which wasn't important. But it made Lemon's brain scream. She watched the delicate curve of her wrist as she put out her hand to Ruby. Her sister was a bad influence, and she still wouldn't tell Lemon who sold her pot, wiggling her eyebrows and calling her a narc each time.

Claudia pressed closer. Lemon was sure she knew exactly what she was doing, but she wasn't going to get involved with a vampire.

Still, it had a certain Hallmark, big city girl comes to a small town vibe that she enjoyed.

She exhaled obnoxious smoke rings. Poor old Victorian house. It had taken a beating since Lemon and Ruby took it over. Though the sixties had probably been worse as far as smoke damage. "So I traveled with Orlo, which was awful. But he had this soft spot for my shows. The bad but binge worthy ones that I'm too old to watch." Again, a flutter of Lemon's heart. Bad TV was her passion. She wanted to ask her about Riverdale. "And it turned out he really liked vampire shows. Team Damon. So when we weren't working, we watched everything from True Blood to the 90s Dracula. Obviously a mistake. Too many vampire brides, I think."

"Should have taken a detour to the Globe Theater, got some oration tips, Claudy," Fritz said, pointing at her with a fry.

"That's in London. We went to Scotland that last time." Beneath the table, where the others couldn't see, Claudia's leg pressed harder, moving in just the right way to push the fabric of Lemon's skirt up even higher. But her face gave away nothing and Lemon wasn't sure what it meant, flirtation or just a way to steady herself against this tale.

Ruby put out the end of the joint in a vulgar ashtray and leaned back. "So what? You stole from your boss?"

Another long swig and Claudia's jaw tightened, her amber eyes darkening. "Yeah. I got separated from Orlo at the airport, and it wasn't just witch stuff, it never is. Drugs, jewels, counterfeit money—depended on where we were coming from. This time I had a bag of stolen diamonds hidden on me. It was a lot of money. Enough to start a new life. And working for him was awful. He's cruel, capricious, violent. You never knew when he would snap. So I thought I'd run off, hide. Hide somewhere like this. I really thought I could do it."

"But he caught you." Lemon didn't realize what she was doing until her palm was on Claudia's thigh, smaller than hers, lean and strong.

There was no indication that she noticed except a sparkle in her eye that no one else seemed to catch. And Lemon was in way too deep and it was too soon. She couldn't get involved with Claudia, there was no future but pain. And yet...

"He had some of my blood. That's all he needed. I woke up one morning, and everything was like this..." She gestured to herself. "Or something close. And I knew from the beginning what was happening because of a small off-hand remark of Orlo's about how nice being someone's sire seemed. It's like a pull. I know he wants me to come to him, and I don't think I'll be able to resist much longer."

"Oh, fuck that," Ruby said before Lemon could respond. "Listen, diamond thievery aside, I'm gonna assume this was an evil man."

"The kind of man who recruits college sophomores to their crime ring, if you need any more proof," Fritz said, reaching for a beer. "I've wanted to kill him for years."

"Yeah, so as I said, fuck that. Lemon's more the helper type than I am, but this guy sounds like a dick and I've always been very anti-dickishness." A trait inherited from Esther, who had wasted no time in dealing with her father.

"You seemed pretty anti-vampire as well." Claudia laughed. Actually it was a giggle and Lemon wondered if she was drunk. And her hand was still on her thigh. She finished her beer quickly. Oh, this was bad; even Ruby liked her.

"Eh." Ruby shrugged. "You did lure and snatch my sister in the woods."

"She's quite snatchable."

Lemon stood up, knowing weird words were pouring from her lips. Unable to stop them. "We need a mixer for all this vodka." She picked up the bottle from in front of Claudia and hurried to the kitchen.

Don't do it. Don't crush on a vampire. She hadn't had sex in six months. She could not end her dry spell with the cursed person she was supposed to help. She flung open the fridge. Not that she knew Claudia was trying to sleep with her. She probably just wanted her help. She said herself that being attractive got her places. Lemon grabbed a box of Capri Suns. Why did they even have these?

"Speaking of college sophomores." Claudia's voice made Lemon jump, and the box went flying. She caught it easily, like some sort of superhero, and looked at the box. "Mountain cooler? Really?" She stepped closer. Too close. She leaned across Lemon to put the box in the fridge.

And they were only a breath apart. The light from the fridge made her look even paler, but her lips were red, her eyelashes long.

"Have I told you how good you smell?"

Warmth rushed through Lemon and she made a little sound that made Claudia smile. "You've mentioned it." The air from the fridge was freezing her ass, contrasting with the heat inside of her. "We shouldn't."

"Oh?" Claudia reached up, brushing a piece of hair off Lemon's forehead. "I always wondered if I could pull off short hair. It looks good on you."

Lemon's brain was short circuiting. There wasn't a rational damn thought in the whole thing. It was all Claudia's lips, the soft fingers running across her jaw. Lemon's hands drifted down, resting on Claudia's hips.

Her tongue darted out, wetting her bottom lip. "Lemon, I..." She cupped Lemon's head with her hand.

Fritz laughter rang down the hallway and they jumped apart at his footsteps on the hardwood. Lemon spun around, pushing the fridge closed. "The only juice we have is Capri Sun, which I've been informed is juvenile."

"I didn't say that. I said college sophomore, that's halfway to a bachelor's degree. Slightly educated juice." Claudia had moved away, walking around the kitchen and brushing her hand against all the different herbs hanging to dry, or waiting to be crushed.

"Oh, that'll do. I mean, it'll be nasty, but it's better than running back to the store." Fritz's eyes followed his sister. "I mean, if you *want* us to get drunk at your house. We could definitely go drink at that hotel if you'd prefer. Or not drink at all. Or just leave."

"This is the south, man. If we wanted you to go we'd say 'we'll it's starting to get late.'" Lemon kept rifling through the fridge. There was grenadine stashed behind the mayo in the door. And if grenadine, Capri Sun and vodka were wrong... well, Lemon agreed with whoever said that, but it was better than nothing.

"You should have listened to me," Fritz said, and Lemon had no idea what he was talking about until she turned and found him watching his sister run her fingers over the vines of a pothos plant. They were quite a pair, and she once again wondered what Claudia must have looked like before, tanned skin, the same eyes, like fresh-tilled soil.

"I know, Fritzy. I've known for a long time. I can't even feel them now. I can't feel anything at all." Her voice held immeasurable sadness, so different from the woman who had just been pressed against Lemon.

It was hard for Lemon to imagine losing her connection to the conversations of plants, the flight of birds, the immense magic running through the current of the earth. It was in the wind and the sea, the same as it ran under her skin, two parts of a whole. To be cut off from that, and in such a grotesque way, infuriated her. Witches had to stick together. They were all they had. "I can make a list of what we need. It's not going to be easy to find. And we'll need Julian."

Fritz ran a hand through his shaggy brown hair. "I worry he'll come soon, anyway. But if he doesn't, I can get him."

Thinking about a Hathorne in Hecate's Hollow made Lemon's chest tight. Was this safe? Were they being foolish? But then she thought of Claudia dropping a funnel cake she couldn't even eat as she burned in the sun. She had to do it.

She pulled a piece of paper across the counter as Fritz began mixing drinks. Ruby and Claudia drifted towards her, looking over her shoulder as she wrote what they needed. *Blood of an ewe. Tree roots. Bat wing. White flower. Hathorne blood.*

"Do you know where all of it is?" Claudia asked and Lemon was glad to work with someone who knew potions, who knew rare ingredients. She would understand how important getting it right would be. They could not substitute a magnolia for the flower she had seen growing out of a rock.

Lemon shook her head. "The tree is a sourwood and I know I've seen it before, but I can't remember where. I've hiked so many places."

"How about this one?" Ruby pointed to the black ewe. "Something like that is usually less specific, no?"

"I think any ewe will do and it should be easy enough to find around here." A chill ran through her. The potion and the spell would contain her magic. She'd seen it hundreds of times when she summoned up visions of ingredients for people. There was no way for a witch to separate herself from her magic. And everything on the list surrounded Lemon. It was all wound up in her life—her safe life in Hecate's Hollow.

The realization stirred something—something that her slightly stoned, slightly drunk brain could not fully grasp. Why was Claudia sniffing her out? Why did the magic want her? Her heart screamed

73

that it was her undeniable connection to Claudia, that they were meant to find each other. But this wasn't a Hallmark movie. This was real and dangerous and she could get hurt. She could get killed.

"I'll call around tomorrow. Someone has to have some." Ruby took her drink from Fritz, her fingers brushing over his, eliciting a smile.

And the sidekicks, her brain said. She tried to quiet it with a gulp of her own drink. It was predictably awful. Sidekicks; every good movie had them. She'd clearly spent too much time watching tv. It had addled her brain. Lemon chanced a look at Claudia and found her looking back.

But Ruby was drunk and wanted fun. She grabbed Fritz and Lemon by the arms, pulling them towards the living room. This was what Ruby had missed growing up here. She wanted people; she wanted clubs and parties and dancing. She wanted to sing and laugh and clung to anyone who showed up with a promise of that. It had only been a matter of time before she came around to Claudia.

Gorgeous Claudia, who looked like she belonged on the back of someone's yacht, and her equally gorgeous brother. Lemon started to protest, but what more could they do tonight? Was she going to go hike through the woods in the dark?

As if in answer, thunder cracked. She glanced at her sister, but it didn't seem to be her shenanigans, just a real storm. And what plotting was there? They'd get the things in time or they wouldn't. Then it was just getting the Hathorne and some of his blood. Was Claudia nervous? Lemon couldn't get a read on her.

Fritz and Ruby were blasting music through her bluetooth speakers, their heads bent over his phone. Before Lemon could contemplate Claudia further, the sorta-vampire's eyes caught on something behind her and grew wide. Lemon spun, but it was just Elias, his glasses sprinkled with raindrops.

She turned back to her sister. "Are you trying to have a party?"

"Elias is hardly a party."

"Ouch." He flipped off Ruby as he headed into the kitchen, taking stock of Fritz as he passed. She should have known Ruby would not simply invite people over and call it a night. And she couldn't exactly go to the local bar. She'd exhausted most of the selections—and they were bleak to begin with.

But a vampire party? As if on cue, Vampire Weekend started playing through the speakers and she couldn't help but laugh. "Y'all are stupid," she yelled over the music.

But Claudia was smiling. How long had it been since she'd felt okay? They met in the woods, after all, and she could barely go out in the sun, whatever size hat she wore. And maybe, just maybe, if Lemon was willing to admit it, Ruby knew how to cheer people up.

"Live a little," Ruby whispered in her ear, twirling Lemon around the living room and scaring the shit out of the cat. Her voice lowered even more. "Besides, she'll want to stay the night now."

"Who?"

Ruby leveled a look at her. "The tooth fairy. The hot vampire you've been making eyes at. Come on, you have every Sookie Stackhouse book under your bed. This has to be a dream come true."

"Shut up." She was going to smother Ruby in her sleep.

"You had a poster of Lestat, and you're a lesbian."

"Well... I mean, it's close enough." She laughed. "You're so embarrassing."

"I'm your sister. It's my job." Ruby kissed her cheek. "It's a shame the hottest guy in the Hollow in years is her brother."

"What's that?" Fritz asked, walking up behind her with a box of crackers and making Ruby scream. "Can I eat these?"

"By themselves? I think we have some cheese. Come on." She led him back to the kitchen with a wide smile on her face and maybe for tonight, surrounded by friends, just being happy was enough.

Later and much drunker, under the deep cover of night, Lemon stood outside on the porch. She could smell the dirt, wet with rain. She could feel the life it would give to the trees and flowers. Bats flew overhead. Getting a wing of one would be easy enough, they might even have some in the storeroom.

Her head was swimming after drinking more than she had in months. And it might have been the drink, or cursed vampire abilities, but she didn't hear Claudia until she was beside her.

"Your sister is a gem," she said, amber eyes glassy, pupils blown wide in the dark. Her dark hair was messier than usual, and her entire outfit was mussed. She twisted the rings on her fingers. "And I'm thankful, Lemon. I really am."

Lemon turned, leaning her back against the railing. What could she say? She'd always been a sucker for anything in need. She'd nursed countless birds, baby squirrels, and raccoons to health. She gave all her money to panhandlers. She watched people's kids so they could have nights off. Lemon was a helper.

She was also very gay and not even the slightest bit blind.

Elias appeared in the window, giving her two large thumbs up. What would she give for friends who weren't entirely embarrassing? Nothing actually. She loved them, stupid brains and all. "She's hot," he mouthed, inexplicably.

Lemon refocused on Claudia. "You need help. And..." She cleared her throat. "Well, I'm pretty much useless against beautiful woman who literally sweep me off my feet." Might as well, the sloshy drunk part of her brain urged.

Claudia laughed, throwing her head back. The sound rang through the night. "Shit. You know, well, this is sad, but I don't think I've ever had friends beside my brother. I guess I used to, but then I started working for Julian and there was no time for friends. So I just watched TV or read books. And then this happened and there was no one to ask for help. I'm a fucking witch and I have no witch friends. I don't even have human friends"

"Then you came to the right place. The Hollow doesn't seem to understand strangers. You probably could have asked anyone here, and they'd help you."

"I noticed." Claudia grinned, leaning on the porch beside Lemon so their arms brushed against each other. "I walked into the bakery and Lavinia said she'd never seen me before, so I got a free muffin and then she walked me to the inn, at night, mind you, to help me book a room. I should have just asked where you were."

"Someone would have driven you."

Claudia laughed again. Then, once silence had fallen, leaving nothing but the sound of an owl somewhere far away, she turned. "I'd like to finish what I started in the kitchen."

And Lemon did too. God knew she wanted to. She wanted to taste her, to run her hands up her back, over the swell of her breasts. But she was cursed. And she'd done things, the kind of things Lemon couldn't imagine. Jet setting with a criminal, getting ingredients to do who knew what. Most definitely for dark magic.

Claudia was literally a jewel thief. And she was still bound to that horrible man. It would be foolish to get involved, to put her heart in any more than it was.

She had never been more grateful to Ruby than when the door swung open. "Come on," she said, nodding towards both of them. "We're going to use the ouija board."

"I swear, Ruby Carmine!" Lemon rushed inside before her sister summoned a demon.

Chapter Eight

The next day Lemon's head pounded with each heartbeat, which seemed a big enough problem until she realized someone else was in bed with her. Luckily, a quick appraisal revealed it to be Elias, the covers thrown completely over his head.

She was pretty sure she hadn't told him to sleep in her room, but she didn't mind much either. She peeled back the edges of her floral quilt to make sure he was still breathing, and he was—each breath like the inside of a brewery.

She pushed herself up on one arm and rifled through the contents of her bedside table—a journal she didn't keep up with, enough pens to last a lifetime, tangled necklaces, and finally a nasty brown looking tonic that she downed quickly. Her headache eased.

She grabbed her robe and frowned at her reflection. Could Claudia see her reflection? The perfect wings of her eyeliner seemed evidence enough that she could. Ruby's laugh floated up the stairs and, with a final glance at the still sleeping form of Elias, Lemon went downstairs.

It was raining, and the lights cast long shadows over the house, but in the distance she could see the sun shining in the fields. Ruby then, her magic keeping the sun away from their vampiric party guest. "Showing off, huh?"

"It's a neat trick," Claudia said, looking up from a glass of what was, unmistakably, blood. Lemon's stomach did a flop. "The weather thing is pretty rare." Her smile faltered as she followed Lemon's gaze down to her cup. "Rabbit. I went out last night."

Lemon pulled her robe tighter. She couldn't blame her. What should she do? Starve. But she couldn't imagine a romance either—well, she could, easily enough. But not if she went further than hands tangled in sheets, pounding hearts. She couldn't see a future beyond the physical. And how selfish was that? To fix her because she wanted to kiss her, to run her hands through her dark hair, to watch the light catch and turn it golden. She shook out her head and headed for the coffee.

"Be nice." Ruby hissed in her ear, handing her mocha creamer.

Lemon shot her a look. She'd been the one hesitant at first. When she didn't answer, Ruby put her hand on her Lemon's elbow and led her outside, the gentle rain on the tin roof blocking any sounds from inside.

"What is that look on your face?"

Lemon shrugged. "I can't stop thinking about kissing her and then I think about her *drinking blood*."

Ruby's mouth set in a hard light as she fought against the laughter shaking her shoulders. "Oh Lemonade, of course you have a crush on a vampire. You've been waiting for it your whole life. You had that Kate Beckinsale poster until what, last year?"

"Shut up." It was still in her closet. "Better than Bieber."

"Obviously. But you gotta quit looking at her like... I don't know, like your face is about to fall apart. It's *weird*. You should just fuck her and get it over with. You'll feel better."

Always Ruby with the sage wisdom. Lemon rolled her eyes. "She's a *vampire*."

"Not technically."

"What if she wants to drink my blood? And what? One night of drinking and you're all team Claudia? You're supposed to tell me to be responsible."

Now Ruby did laugh in earnest, so hard she gripped the damp porch railing and held her stomach with her other hand. "Oh, I love you so much. Fine. Get none of the perks. And you're always responsible. You're too responsible." She shook her head as she straightened. "A decade of writing fanfiction and now you won't even jump at the chance." Her head was still shaking as she went inside.

Lemon imagined kicking her right in the ass, watching her sprawl across the antique rug and into an even more antique vase. Apparently, her instinct to protect Lemon had been overridden by her desire to do every reckless thing she could. When she headed back in, Fritz and Elias had come downstairs and their heads were bent near Claudia's, looking over the list of potion ingredients they would need. Somewhere between karaoke of The Avett Brothers and the Jonas Brothers, they had filled Elias in on everything. His eyes had gone all wide, and then he'd taken off his glasses, sighed and said he would help.

"It looks like a lot of hiking," Claudia said, sipping at her cup of blood. "Like, it's all hiking."

"You find rare ingredients for a living. You must be used to hiking." Lemon poured a cup of coffee; lots of sugar, less creamer.

"Yeah, but these mountains are no Tibet."

"Hey!" Elias and Lemon yelled in unison, Elias backing away and crossing his arms.

"Never talk shit about the mountains, especially not when you've got a group of mountain people trying to cure you." Lemon sat her mug down on the counter. "But it is going to be a lot of hiking, and unfortunately, I don't know where most of it is. We can ask our moms to help divine some of it, at least send us in the right direction. Hey, what about y'alls mom? She's a witch, right?"

Fritz and Claudia both laughed, and Fritz shook his head. "No. My mom's a waitress at a diner between New Orleans and the middle of nowhere. She didn't even know our dad was a witch, considering she barely knew him at all. We haven't told her about this. She's got enough to worry about."

"My mom can ask the birds," Elias said. "If you don't mind me telling her. Whatever details you can get about the sourwood, I'm sure the crows have seen it."

Elias's mom had a huge aviary. Lemon hadn't visited in a while, but she used to spend hours there, bringing her all the birds she found and Mae would nurse them back to health. But her pride and joy was the murder of crows that all but lived in her yard, perching in the low-hanging branches of the giant oaks.

"See," Lemon said, adding more sugar to her coffee. "Did anyone in Tibet help you find the things you needed?"

"Well, yeah." Claudia drained her glass and rinsed it in the sink. "But not like this. Thank you." She smiled, one side going up further than the other. "I really appreciate you all. I don't want to be some mindless drone for Julian. The years I worked for him were enough."

She sighed, and her eyes lost their sharpness. She was somewhere else, imagining Julian. And Lemon could see it too, Claudia years ago, fresh and young in college, some handsome Hathorne pulling her under his wing, promising a poor girl more money than she'd ever had.

"We should get started soon," Lemon said, looking through the fridge for something to eat and settling on a toaster strudel. "We don't know when your draw to him will become too strong."

"I can't today," Ruby said. "I have to work. I've been blowing it off too much lately. But I can do some research while I'm there. I'll see what I find on breaking curses so we can brew a potion that works."

Glancing towards the window, Claudia sighed. The sound was heavy, and it pulled Lemon's heartstrings. Everything inside of her that led to helping baby birds and volunteering at soup kitchens mixed with everything inside of her that was horny and hasty and wanted to make out on the kitchen counter. "Want to go for a drive? I know where we can get the blood of an ewe."

Claudia opened her mouth but didn't answer. She ground her teeth together, her eyes still on the faraway sunlight. It must be getting worse. She'd met Lemon in the woods a week ago, but she'd also burnt her hand in the square. Would she be able to travel without Ruby's cloud coverage?

"My windows are tinted," Lemon offered, pulling out her strudel and spreading on the icing. "My mom can make them darker."

"Oh, have you seen her car?" Elias's brown eyes lit up and Fritz roused from where he'd curled up near the window reading the paper.

In the garage, they all oohed and ahhed and Lemon would be lying if she said she didn't love it. Her '57 Thunderbird, still painted the original dusk rose, stood shiny and pink in the middle of her garage. It was her pride and joy, her baby, the thing she'd spent the most money on in her entire life.

"Fuck," Claudia said, watching her brother run his long fingers over it. "I do want to go for a drive in this thing. It's hot."

It absolutely was hot and Lemon always felt like the baddest bitch on the planet when she got out of it, pulling her leather jacket straight and running a hand through her hair. She loved her car. Bernadette, she'd named her the moment she'd seen her for sale. She'd drained her savings and spent way too much money keeping her in perfect condition. But she was worth it.

"So, a drive?" She locked eyes with Claudia, imagining the window down, her arm out of it, wind streaming in her dark hair, dusk on the horizon. She thought of her legs on the dash, shoes kicked off, the ghost of a laugh on her lips. And, the way Claudia looked back, well, she thought maybe she was thinking the same things.

Fritz cleared his throat, looking absolutely anguished to leave the car behind. But he put his arm around Elias's shoulder. "Why don't we go see what your mom can do about those birds?" He leaned in close, whispering something, and Elias laughed as they headed back into the house.

Something had happened last night, drunk and lying around, throwing popcorn into each other's mouths, seeing who could jump the furthest off the porch ledge, laughing in piles when they slipped in the grass. They'd become a group. A unit. They were all going to do this dangerous thing because the world sucked and someone had to give a shit.

Now it was Claudia's turn to run her fingers over the pink paint, to peer through the windows at the leather seats. And it never got old, but fuck, there was something stomach clenching about seeing a hot girl do it. "I'm sorry if I was too forward last night."

"Oh," Lemon squeaked. "No, you weren't. You, uh, definitely weren't."

There was no blush on Claudia's cheeks. In fact, she rarely looked ruffled. She was smooth, a still lake, but she smiled, turning and leaning on the car, her round ass pressed against the door.

Lemon's brain was going to explode. It was too good. She wished she could take a picture, Claudia's long legs crossed at the ankle, her hair brushing her waist. Lemon's goddamn pink car shining. "We should go. If we stop by the shop, we can darken the windows."

A quick trip to the Apothecary and Lemon's windows were safe for Claudia. Esther tapped a finger, and the glass obeyed, darkening to keep out the sun. Secretly, Lemon thought Esther's gifts were the best. Amaryllis's gift was tracking, but she almost never did it. Lemon suspected the irony of it was too much after they'd run away.

Claudia looked spectacularly hot in the passenger seat of Lemons car as she drove through the winding mountain roads. Few words passed between them, but a small smile stayed on Claudia's lips.

There were a few farmers who raised sheep, ewes, all manner of animals and by now they were used to witches coming and asking for strange ingredients. Most of them would sell whatever was needed, though Lemon had failed to think about how they were going to get Claudia into anyone's house. She prayed the clouds in the distance would blow closer and cover the sun.

"Do you have any money?" she asked, over the sound of Dolly Parton on the radio.

"You gonna rob me?" Claudia turned towards Lemon, her eyes crinkled at the edges with amusement.

"Yeah, haven't you figured it out? That was my plan all along." She pulled into a viewing area and reached into the back for an atlas. This deep into the mountains, her GPS was useless and while she had a decent sense of direction, she couldn't remember exactly which turn to take. She ran her finger along the route trying to find where they were. "No, if we want him to bleed one of his animals we're going to have to pay him."

"Yeah. I'm flush." Claudia looked at her, emotion flashing in her eyes. And then she did it—straight out of Lemon's dreams. She kicked her shoes off and leaned back in the seat, feet up on the dashboard. "It really is beautiful here."

"Yeah," Lemon agreed. "Can I have your hand?" She had an idea, though she wasn't sure if it would work. It was worth a shot. After all, she needed Claudia out in the sun. With her strength and agility she'd hurry along the process of finding the ingredients.

"Absolutely." Claudia reached out her hand, palm up.

Her skin was smooth, her fingers soft. Lemon closed her eyes and wrapped them in her own. Claudia smelled of summer, ripe berries and bright green grass. Just as she hoped, things flashed through Lemon's mind. Calendula. Valerian. Winter soil. They kept flashing and when she finally opened her eyes, Claudia had the most curious expression. Her mouth was slightly agape, there was a little line between her eyebrows. She looked soft, the kind of woman that begged to be held in your arms, protected. So different from her usual sharp edges.

"My magic was similar," Claudia said, her hand still in Lemon's. "Not like this, but I could feel things, whatever I needed or wanted. It would have been easy to find all of this. I was like a human compass. What did you read?"

"It won't be permanent, but I think, once we get back, I can protect you from the sun. You'll probably need to drink it often."

"Really? I could kiss you." Claudia pulled her feet from the dash and flung her arms awkwardly around Lemon in the small space. At first the hug was full of excitement and gratitude, but it changed. Claudia lingered, pressing her nose to Lemon's neck. She pulled away slowly, her fingers touching the short hairs at the base of Lemon's skull.

How was Lemon going to do this? Sometimes she forgot why she fought it. But what if she didn't succeed? What if Claudia became hopelessly caught up in the servitude of a Hathorne? Better to keep her heart guarded than get it broken completely.

Another car pulled up beside them, a minivan complete with a family of four who poured out of the doors, the children rushing towards the guard rail to peer into the valley below. Their screams of excitement broke the spell between them, and Claudia pulled away.

They continued to drive, and Lemon's wishes came to fruition as the clouds that had lingered above the tallest peaks rolled in. Lemon was used to the roads, winding like snakes down the sides of mountains. She'd learned to drive on these roads, though it had been her mom's Corolla and not her boat of a vintage car. Claudia wasn't used to it, and apparently Tibet had not prepared her, because she gripped the edge of her seat until her knuckles were white, letting out little squeaks and leaving Lemon wondering what the rest of her involuntary noises might sound like.

"When I cure you we'll drive with the top down." The road flattened to farmland, and a creek wound its way beside the road, full of rocks smoothed by the endless pour of water and slick with moss. Claudia kept her seat pushed back, away from the lesser tint of the windshield, though the sun was threatening to leave for the day, replaced by a fine mist of rain.

Silence grew between them as they headed deeper into the rolling farmland, but it was companionable. Claudia was like a caged animal. She could not hold still for long, always moving, twisting in her seat, watching Lemon as she drove.

"Lemon?" She waited until she glanced over before continuing. "Why'd you decide to say yes? I'm like this absolute disaster. Before all of this happened, I don't think I would have helped. You barely resisted."

Lemon shrugged, but she gripped the steering wheel tighter. What could she say? It was all terribly embarrassing. She settled on a bit of the truth, pretending she couldn't feel the heat creeping up her neck. "Well, firstly, because you aren't the only one of us who loves vampires. Then, you made a good first impression. And..." She cleared her throat. The big truth, and she didn't know why she was spilling it except that Claudia had been forced to spill her secrets.

"My father was a Hathorne. He would have killed my mother if Esther didn't force us to leave and I... well, I haven't seen him since. I don't know if there's anything to see, even. So I thought maybe this could make up for that."

Darkness flashed in Claudia's eyes. Every witch had a story about the way some Hathorne had terrorized them. And then they were accused of ungodliness, of being heathens, as though they could go to church with someone who hated them preaching from the pulpit. As though they chose any of it. "Good for Esther."

The silence grew again, and was broken again by Claudia as they drove through the gates of the unnamed farm. Ostriches stared with their horrible, black eyes on either side of the driveway, giving Lemon the creeps. "Do you like it here? In Hecate's Hollow?"

"Yeah," Lemon said, without thought. She did. She saw Ruby gaze at the horizon sometime, watched her google vacations, but her tiny town and its inhabitants were enough for Lemon. Sure, she'd like to travel, to see a few things, but Hecate's Hollow was where she wanted to land.

"Maybe I could stay too," Claudia said, but it seemed more to herself than Lemon. "I don't know what I'd do, but it might be nice."

The door to the farmhouse opened as Lemon put the car in park, pretending like her brain and stomach and maybe even her heart weren't switching places, doing somersaults, screaming at her. What if Claudia stayed?

Claudia pulled her hood up. "Maybe I could be a waitress," she said, and got out of the car, grinning at the farm's owner, Mr. Robbins.

"Hey, Mr. Robbins. I've got an odd request."

"You witches always do." He hooked his thumb under the straps of the overalls. "What is it?"

"I need the blood of a black ewe." Lemon toed a divot in the ground.

"Sure thing. Wait out here a moment." He turned, pushing chickens away with his boots and went back inside.

"Do you think I'd look cute in overalls?" Lemon whispered and was rewarded with a slight creeping of red across Claudia's nose.

"I'd need to see you with and without to make a proper comparison."

"I'll see what I can do."

Inexplicably, when Mr. Robbins returned less than three minutes later, he had had a jar of blood with him. "Now don't you go lookin' at me like I'm the one making weird requests." He shoved the jar into Claudia's hands. "You witches… Well, you're always up here for some kinda blood, so I've started keeping it in the fridge. Almost gave my wife a heart attack but this is witch country, I told her. She was convinced the police were gonna think we were murderers. I told her if they're police who don't know about spells, they have no business on my property."

"Try telling them that," Claudia said, pulling a wad of cash out of her pocket.

"I sure as hell will tell them that," Mr Robbins said, his mustache fluttering in indignation. "That's why I moved here. Tired of their bullshit, lots of people are tired of the bullshit. If a man can't see through that anti-magic propaganda, he needs to get his damn eyes checked, I always say."

"Well, I appreciate the blood."

"And don't worry, I wouldn't bullshit ya. Black ewe. She was old, ready to be out of her misery." He looked at the two of them, his eyes settling on Lemon. "Your mamas still run that Apothecary?"

She nodded. "Always will. You thinking of coming by?"

As though it was a normal thing to have, he pulled a business card out of the front of his overalls. It had a cartoon green tractor in a wheat field with his name across it. "Listen, I meant what I said. I want to keep working with the witches. It's good business. I've got my greenhouses set up for the things you need, mushrooms, herbs. I've even imported some seeds. I'm expanding my farm and I'd love to talk to your mothers about it."

Claudia made an excited noise and reached into her pocket, pulling out a cream-colored card. "Most of this is irrelevant now, but the number's good. If you need any help, I've got a brother looking for work. I've got my own things to finish, but I have one hell of a green thumb and I'll need a job in a few weeks."

A hearty grin broke across the farmer's face. "I told Mary Ellen taking on her father's farm was gonna be good business, and look at it, driving in. Your brother strong? Tell him to come by, and I'll see what I can do for him. There'll be more money to pay you if you keep sending witches my way."

"Of course. Yes, sir."

Lemon wanted to hug him. "I'll pass this along to my moms. We're always looking for good suppliers for the Apothecary."

"I look forward to it." He tipped an imaginary hat. "Y'all have a good day. Drive safe."

Claudia lit up when they were in the car, the bottle of blood between her knees. They were both damp from the rain, and Mr. Robbins had quickly hurried inside. "We did it. We fucking did it. One thing down and, god, I really do love it here, Lemon. People actually give a shit."

The thing inside of Lemon twisted again as she put the car into drive and started down the road. What if Claudia stayed? What if she cured her and she stayed? She glanced at her. Claudia had secured the blood, wrapping it in an old hoodie of Lemon's left on the floorboard.

Lemon didn't give herself time to think before she pulled off the road. Claudia was still radiating happiness, and Lemon thought of the first time she had seen her in the woods, the leaves as a backdrop, the water under their feet. A vampire. She giggled and Claudia looked slightly concerned, her lips parted, eyebrows raised.

"What are you doing?"

"Kissing you." Lemon moved across the bench seat. She leaned forward, but Claudia was faster. She grabbed Lemon by the back of the head and kissed her. Her tongue darted into Lemon's mouth and the weight of her pressed Lemon down into the seat. Claudia seemed to touch all of her at once, sparking something inside of her that threatened to grow into a roaring flame.

She wound her hands in Claudia's chestnut hair, twisting the silky strands around her fingers. Rain beat gently on the car's roof and Lemon moved her hand to Claudia's hip, pulling her closer.

She deepened the kiss and Claudia's tongue swept through her mouth and she could taste it—the coppery tang of blood.

She stilled and Claudia pulled away, her pale face red, her hair tangled. And, fuck, Lemon wanted to kiss her again, to keep kissing her, and let them sink down into the vintage leather. To touch every inch of her.

But it was blood. And she wasn't sure she was ready for that. All the other reasons for keeping her distance came back. And they weren't fair, not a single one of them. But she also knew there was so much between them, so many things Claudia wasn't telling her, a whole criminal enterprise. Despite that, she smiled, gently, teasingly. "Soon," she promised, hoping it was true.

And like an answer to her prayers, the sun peeked out between clouds, forcing them to hurry home.

Chapter Nine

"So you kissed her?" Ruby still smelled like the apothecary, incense and herbs and something else Lemon couldn't put her finger on but that reminded her of their mothers.

Instead of a reply, Lemon buried her head further into her arms, nearly upturning the plate of grilled cheese on the counter beside her.

"So you finally got your Kate Beckinsale and—"

"Selene was a vampire hunter, Ruby. She was super fucking powerful and she didn't need anyone's help. Jesus Christ, do you live under a rock?"

Ruby ignored her outburst, but Lemon could practically hear the thoughts moving around in her head. "So first, that movie came out like twenty years ago, so maybe take it down a notch. Second, what's going on with you? You insisted on helping her, you *clearly* like her. What is even happening in that pretty little head."

"I don't know." Lemon groaned into the countertop. "I want to help her. She's funny and gorgeous, but once I do she's gonna leave. Whatever else she says, I know she's going to leave."

"And? You've fucked tourists before. *Oh.*" Ruby slid into the seat beside her and rubbed a circle on her back, no longer smelling like the apothecary but cheap cheese slices. "You *like* her."

Lemon made a noise of agreement. She'd kissed her. Oh, God. She'd actually kissed her. And she'd tasted like blood. An international thief with sanguine kisses. She'd stolen from a mafioso Hathorne and Lemon had kissed her. "I want to have her stupid, blood sucking babies."

"Well, let's not be dramatic. Can you look at me?" Lemon shook her head. "Well, okay. So, you kissed her and then you freaked out."

"I know that."

Her response was lost in a knock at the door and Elias came in. Something rustled near Lemon, prompting her to finally raise her head. It was a map. She grunted at it.

"Whatever is wrong with you, this should cheer you up." He grabbed the remnants of her grilled cheese and took a bite. "It's three locations of where your tree should be—assuming it's located around here—which is a big assumption since Claudia isn't from here. However, looking at the rest of the things it seems like they're all local. It happens, I guess." He looked Lemon over and then scrunched his nose and wiped his thumb across her cheek. "Mayo, I hope."

"She kissed the vampire," Ruby explained and Lemon wished looks could kill.

"Oh, well... Was it bad?"

"No." Lemon pushed back the chair and stood up. "It's just...this is all so weird and she's like..."

"Like what?" Came a voice from the doorway and Lemon thought she might actually liquify and drip through the hardwood beneath her feet. Claudia looked great, her cheeks nearly rosy, her hair shining, a wide smile on her face.

"I realize you were invited in but knocking is still a thing, yeah?"

Claudia raised an eyebrow. She'd put on fresh clothes—a pair of deliciously tight jeans, a crop top and a cardigan. Lemon was in the pajamas Ruby had bought her for Christmas last year: pink with pictures of Athena the cat on them. At least she'd showered. "I visited your apothecary. It was closed, but your mom saw me in the window, and gave me what I needed for that sunblock spell."

"Perfect. I've got a list of places to get the tree roots," Elias said, grabbing the map Lemon hadn't even had a chance to look at.

Okay, so maybe this was all in her mind. Or was it? Was it really illogical to not want to get involved with a cursed woman who was slowly being enthralled by the criminal who had cursed her? A woman who couldn't go out during the day, who she might not cure. Claudia would hate her if she didn't finish this—if she had any thoughts at all. But she didn't seem like she was losing her mind, she seemed mostly normal, except the teeth and the skin and the way she liked to sniff Lemon.

Thinking of sniffing turned her mind to kissing, the feeling of Claudia under her fingers. Her cool skin and long hair. And maybe Claudia could smell her now because she looked up from the map, her amber eyes locked on Lemon.

But Lemon didn't know what to say. That she couldn't kiss her because she tasted like blood and she was absolutely fucking freaked out? It was selfish. Claudia must be a million times more terrified than she was.

"What do you think? We could go look for things tomorrow if I've got the sunblock."

"I have to work," Lemon said, which wasn't a lie. She'd only worked two shifts so far that week and as cheap as it was in Hecate's Hollow she still had bills to pay.

"I've got you," Ruby said, giving her a very pointed look. "I can buy the groceries this week."

Elias must have felt the tension in the room because he looked into the cloth bag Claudia was holding and smiled. "Oh, we do something similar in the summertime. I can totally help you with that." He led Claudia away, towards the sunroom they used to brew potions.

"What the fuck?" Lemon asked. "After everything I told you?"

"Do you want me to do it? I'll be happy to. Of course, I didn't see the tree so I'll probably have to dig them all up. Or would you rather wait? I *told you* it was a bad idea from the start but now you've agreed to help, and there's an unchangeable timeline."

"I'm just…"

"Freaking out. Yeah, we can all see that. And I'm sure it's weird because it's incredibly weird for me too, but you said you'd help her. And you're right, she is nice. I mean, a hardened criminal, but in a charming way."

"But what do I do? I can't keep kissing her." Lemon looked down at her slippered feet. Why Claudia kept trying to kiss her, she couldn't imagine.

"Well, if you ask her to stop I'm sure she would. She's not kissing everyone else so I don't think it's compulsive. Also, Lemmy, sometimes two people just want to kiss each other and it doesn't have to be a *whole thing*." Ruby dumped the rest of their food into the trash.

"I know," she groaned. She knew exactly how dramatic she was being but she didn't know how to stop. And the thing about the kissing was that Lemon didn't actually want it to stop. Sure, when she thought about it logically she knew she should, but she also finally understood the longing in all those romance novels. She ached, she pined, she had the dirtiest thoughts. "This is not good for my heart."

"Oh, for sure not." Ruby picked up a dish rag. "But, live a little, Lemon. You'll either fix her or you won't and she'll either stay or she won't. And when she's gone, would you rather miss her or regret not even trying?"

Lemon scrunched her nose. "It's so annoying when you're right."

"Must be a constant feeling for you then."

Her house was slowly becoming *the* place to be. Even as she worked late into the night, finally figuring out the sunblock potion, she could hear the creaking of the porch swing outside and the gentle snores of Elias on her couch. Ruby had gone to bed hours ago so she could wake up early, but assured them they wouldn't wake her.

Lemon carefully laid an old necklace into the solution she'd made, trying not to get any of it on the clothes she'd changed into. There was too much danger in missing a spot if Claudia had to spread the solution on her skin, plus it was hard to make. She was hoping to imbibe the necklace with the solution. She'd done it with a few other things, protection spells, fertility potions, but never anything so dire. She couldn't really test it until the sun was out but she thought it was going to work.

She closed her eyes, holding her hands over the solution and muttered a few words. The wind outside picked up and images of the ingredients flashed through her mind. *Come on.* She opened her eyes and the citrine stone was glowing. She picked it up, grinning, and slipped it into her pocket. *Take that Hathornes.*

With a final glance at the prone figure of Elias, she headed to the porch, where Claudia was already waiting, a lit cigarette between her fingers.

"I quit years ago, but I figured, can't die."

Lemon laughed. "That can't be true. The immortal part." No one had magic strong enough to keep away death.

"No, I'm sure it's not. Haven't tested it though. I never actually stopped, but now it's only when I'm really stressed." She put the cigarette out under her shoe and sighed. There was a tension between them that Lemon knew she had put there, landing them firmly in the what-the-fuck-is-going-on-between-us territory.

She still hadn't made up her mind about what she wanted after her conversation with Ruby. No matter how many times she imagined all the ways she'd like to get naked with Claudia, the fact was, she barely knew her. Lust was driving her, which wasn't exactly new for Lemon, but usually it was some femme laughing at the bar, who she knew would be gone in a few days.

Not this. Not the woman who laughed in the rain with farmers. Not the woman whose hair was currently silver tinged in the moonlight, the dark shadows seeming to pool in the hollows of her pale face. And Lemon couldn't figure out what to do.

She'd had relationships but nothing lasted very long. The town was small, she knew everyone who lived there and the tourists didn't stay. She'd never intended to be a spinster, but she'd never really planned on settling down either. She had the Victorian and Ruby and her town.

But when Claudia had asked about a job something had shifted in her. The faint whisper of a future. And maybe it was nothing. A month from now she could be looking back and realizing they were anything but compatible. Or she could be looking into a news camera as she explained exactly why vampires were now a thing. Or she could be looking at the dust flying up from Claudia's tires as she got the hell out of this tiny mountain town.

And she couldn't ask. Not when all Claudia could be thinking about was the cure. Not when that was much more pressing. It would be so fucking obnoxious to ask her to stay when she barely knew her. And even more importantly, there were all the things Lemon didn't know. She wasn't naive enough to think Claudia had told her everything about her life before Hecate's Hollow. She didn't even know where the man from the festival, Orlo, had gone.

And that was another problem. The way horniness was winning out over clear thought. But what was there to do? She had an idea of where she'd land, but she hadn't come to terms with it yet, so she shoved it back in her brain.

"I really appreciate what you're doing for me, Lemon. And I hope..." Claudia's voice trailed away. "Well, I hope for a lot of things, but just being a person again would be nice." She pocketed the cigarette butt and sat on the swing. The hinges creaked as it started to move and Lemon hesitated, unsure if she should sit beside her. "I finished the necklace." She pulled it from her pocket and held it out. "But be careful when you use it. I can't test it."

She held it to her chest. "Thank you. This is a real chance to start over, and I'm not going to waste it."

Curiosity won out and she sat beside Claudia, leaving inches between them. Crickets chirped and in the distance she should see the outline of the mountains, a dark shadow against the night sky. "I know you can't tell me everything."

Claudia leaned her head back and her hair cascaded down the back of the swing. The moon glinted off her elongated canines and once again Lemon had to remind herself that Claudia wasn't an immortal creature; she didn't walk through history. She was just a woman, not much older than Lemon. And she was hopelessly adrift. "No, I can't. But I can tell you one thing. This place...even as I am now, I can feel it's magic. And I have traveled a lot of places, seen a lot of people, but the minute I set foot here it was like it had always been here. Waiting for me."

Lemon scooted closer, and hesitated for only a moment before she let her head fall onto Claudia's shoulder. "Some people say these mountains are one of the places magic comes from. That it used to bubble beneath the surface of the world and then it burst through here. That there are other spots, not all mountains, but spread throughout the continents. There's no way to know if it's true, and so many witch towns claim the same, but it does feel like home."

"I don't want to go back. I shouldn't have robbed him," Claudia said, her voice soft. "Maybe I will work for that farmer. I already told Fritz." Her fingers traced the curve of Lemon's ear and then found her hair. "I don't know why I'm telling you all this. I barely know you."

"Sometimes it's easier that way, when you don't know someone, I mean. Why did you do it, then? Would he not let you leave?"

"No, he wouldn't have, not easily. Working for Julian was for life. But still, he wouldn't have cursed me like this if I hadn't robbed him. But the way I grew up, we were so poor. And then I wasn't. I was first class in planes, I was buying Prada and Louboutin. My clothes didn't come from a rack, my food wasn't microwaved. I helped my mom. I paid off her house. I would have bought her a new one but she refused to move. I was afraid to go back to how it was. Where would I work? Some diner like my mom?"

Lemon wasn't sure what to say, so she snuggled in closer. She knew, without a doubt, that from the moment she had agreed to help their lives had become inexplicably linked. Maybe even before. Claudia had heard about her. Claudia had come looking for her. It felt like the cosmos wanted them together, to find each other.

And, Lemon thought, breathing in the smell of her, metallic and earthy, no matter what they did they would always be in each other's orbits. Sometimes you make choices and it changes everything. Just as Esther had once changed everything by falling in love with the mother of her daughter's best friend. By attacking her husband and stealing her away in the night.

"Have you ever been to Charleston?" she asked, enjoying the feel of Claudia's long fingers on her scalp. "It's where I'm from."

"Yeah a few times. I liked to walk along the battery and imagine owning one of those houses right up on the edge of the water. Then I learned about the hurricanes and put that dream to bed." She hesitated, her fingers stopping their slow stroking. "You left because of your dad?"

The crickets sang their songs in the distance. Somewhere above Ruby slept, as did Elias even closer, and Lemon was surprised to find how peaceful she felt. "Yeah. My Hathorne bastard of a father."

"It's funny how witches end up caught up with them so often. You'd think we would learn."

"It must turn out okay sometimes. They're just people too. It has to be like witches, some of them barely practice. It's not like the world needs witch hunters anymore."

"It never did."

Lemon looked up. Full lips, high cheekbones, her strong, straight nose. She thought of kissing her, the way those lips had felt against her own. The sharp bones of her hips. But there was something she wanted to know, something she could not figure out. "Why can you smell me?"

Claudia chewed on that tantalizing bottom lip. Then she shrugged. "I honestly don't know, Lemon. I wish I did. I keep thinking about it. What kind of magic could it be? But when I saw you in those woods... I'm glad it was you."

"You could stay after. You said you don't really have roots anywhere." She sat up straighter. Lemon was aware of every inch of her skin that pressed against Claudia's. The way her smooth legs felt against her own. She didn't know her, only that she was beautiful and mysterious. She kept saying it to herself, trying to keep her distance, to protect her heart. She wasn't one to fall quickly, in fact she rarely fell at all.

But she'd never had a hot vampire sweep her off her feet in the woods either, and it seemed to have short circuited every rational part of her brain, and replaced it with a cartoon lobster singing "Kiss the Girl."

An owl called out and Claudia stood up. "I do want to stay. I do. But then I think about everything. I think about you and that ridiculous pink car and I...I get too scared. Scared it won't work. Scared that I'm going to be too far gone to save. That I'll leave Fritz behind. And it's my fault. I made all the wrong choices and they're catching up to me." Her amber eyes had gone wild and she paced the porch.

"Hey." Lemon stood up, catching her in her arms. She pulled Claudia into her chest, and something settled there—the knowledge that she had done the right thing. She'd watched Esther and Amaryllis the entire drive into the mountains, with Ruby sleeping beside her and she'd known, even at eight, that if they hadn't left her mother would have died. And she'd sworn she'd be as good as Esther one day. That she wouldn't be Amaryllis, scared, too afraid to act. Not that she had blamed her mother, she understood her fear. But it was Esther she'd wanted to be. And it had led her here and somehow, on the porch in the middle of the night, under the shadow of the mountains, she didn't regret it.

She was terrified, cataloging everything that could go wrong, second guessing every choice she'd made, worrying she wouldn't find the cure in time. But she didn't regret the choice to help. Without the help of witches she didn't know where she'd be. Without Lavinia and Elias and Esther and everyone else in the Hollow, who would Lemon be, raised under the cruel hand of a Hathorne, hating her own magic?

"The universe led you to me. And I'm going to fix this," she promised Claudia.

Claudia stilled, her shoulders tensing even as she nodded. "I'll make this all up to you. I'll figure something out. I promise."

Lemon was glad to see headlights coming up her driveway. Fritz parked in front of the house. "Hey, I couldn't find—" He stopped, hand on the door, looking at the two of them, wrapped in each other on the porch. "Claudia."

And there it was again, the tone, the actions that Lemon couldn't make sense of. The secret hidden between the two of them, that she so desperately wanted to know.

He hurried up the porch, smiling gently at Lemon. "Come on. We should go." When Claudia nodded he walked her to the car and tucked her into the seat with the care of a mother. Then he returned to the porch.

"Do you think you can do it?"

"I think I can." She looked into his brown eyes, trying to imagine them in Claudia's face. "I'm no fool. I know there are hidden things. And maybe they aren't my business, but is it something I need to know?"

He glanced toward the car with a quick jerking motion. "I thought she was full of shit when she first said she needed to find someone. She kept saying it was like a string, and she knew help was on the other end. And then she found you, and—"

Lemon held up a hand. "Fritz, is it something I need to know?"

He sighed, scrubbing his hand over face. "Lemon, I've spent the last eight years terrified for her, waiting by the phone, convinced my sister would be dead. You're the first hopeful thing in a while. But I don't know all her secrets. She kept me at arms length while she did god knows what. She used to laugh about Orlo, what a pain in the ass he was, but sometimes she'd praise him. She'd talk about how they liked the same things. I ate dinner with him. So don't ask me where the danger lies. I barely know her at all, but I want to."

It wasn't really an answer but she knew she wouldn't get a better one. And how would she feel if she'd spent years terrified for Ruby, a constant eye on her phone, worried the next message would be horrific? "Once we fix her, you'll be safe from the Hathornes as long as you're here."

Fritz laughed, cold but not unkind. "That's what I keep hearing. Listen, thank you, Lemon. You're a good person. You really are." And he headed back to his car.

She hoped she was a good person. But there was such a deep pool of guilt in her over the way Ruby's wings had been clipped, stuck in this tiny town. She would have been one of those barely practicing witches, she would have had a huge life. But she was here, because she had loved Lemon, because she had stuck up for her. Claudia felt like she could ease some of those feelings. Lemon could point to her and say, 'Look, look at the bad things that happen to witches in the world. Better to hide.'

But maybe she was clipping her wings too.

Chapter Ten

The necklace worked. Lemon had been nearly certain it would, but she was still excited to see Claudia, arms thrown wide, twirling in the sun. Take that Hathornes. She'd always known their magic was bullshit, and she hoped that they'd over reached with this little stunt.

"Are you sure you're fine?"

"Hell yeah. Movie magic coming through." Claudia shifted the bag on her shoulder. "I love my daylight necklace."

There was also the nagging voice in the back of her head. She could find all the work-arounds she wanted, but the magic in Claudia's body was still growing, urging her towards Julian. It got worse every day, the faraway look in her eyes and frequent glances towards the horizon.

"Okay, but tell me if you start feeling weird. I packed some of the salve as well. This isn't actually a tv show and I'm not using some ancient curse breaker. It's sunscreen."

But the necklace might have not been necessary at all. Fat gray clouds had started to roll in. She wondered if they should head back, but they were hours up the mountain, still on the way to the first sourwood tree the crows had whispered about to Elias's mother.

Only the two of them had made the hike, so she decided to ask the question she'd been thinking about since the night before.

Anything to keep their minds off their aching legs and the fact that they were most likely going to die in a mudslide sometime soon. "You felt drawn to me before. Do you still feel it?"

Her long ponytail swung, and she turned to look at Lemon, a muscle in her jaw working overtime as she thought about it. "The draw is to Julian. It's constant. Have you ever smoked? Or really wanted a piece of cake? You know when your brain can't stop thinking about something? It's like that. With you, it's different. It's like I always know which way to go to get towards you. I could always find you."

"But why?" She didn't understand it and she wanted to. *Why?* There had to be a reason a woman she'd never met got cursed and came looking for Lemon.

Claudia paused, her eyes once again towards the horizon, and the view of a valley spread out beneath them. "Fuck if I know. I think they messed up the curse. Orlo had certainly never done it before, but he'd known before I stole from him that Julian liked me better. He wanted to take away something I liked. The one thing we had in common. And what a stupid thing it was."

It was common with curses—if you could call the bastardization of malfeasance and anti-magic common—that something went wrong. Someone would try to turn their lover into a snake, and they'd turn into something between a salamander and a bird. Stories told of the scorned turning their unfaithful lovers into bears that ate them whole. There was no guidebook for it, no spell book. It was cruelty personified. And maybe, once again, it had just gone wrong.

Thunder cracked overhead, and Lemon looked towards the sky. April showers bring May flowers and all that, but it was October so could it stop raining long enough for her to get some things done? "It's going to rain before we can get back to the car." She could smell it in the air. "We could head back, but either way we'll be caught in a downpour."

"Well, shit." Claudia stepped back from the cliff side. "What a fucking way to go." She grinned. "So, Calamity Jane, what do we do?"

"Keep going and try not to die, I suppose." Could the mountains give her a break? She tried to map it out in her mind, picture where they were. But she was further from the Hollow than she usually was, and she didn't know this area well. "We might be slightly fucked."

"Fun." Claudia winked, taking Lemon's brain off of the task at hand. She'd worn shorts, tiny little ones that hugged her thighs. Another crack of thunder and a large drop of rain fell right onto Claudia's nose and she jumped.

Lemon laughed. "Come on." She grabbed her hand, interlocking their fingers, and took off through the trees. This was her domain. She'd figure it out. She racked her brain for memories of this place, and prayed her feet would lead her where she needed to go, but they were running blind as the rain poured.

She slowed, better to get soaked than to break their ankles on slippery soil. And she was a witch. She looked up and found a pair of beady, black eyes looking back at her. *Help.* The squirrel seemed to understand. Thoughts of a cave floated into her mind. Not far from here. They'd be soaked by the time they got there, but they could avoid any hazards.

"God, I miss magic," Claudia said, watching her.

She couldn't imagine. She'd never gone a moment without it. "Once I fix you, I think we find this Julian and we punch him right on the nose."

"I never want to see him again," Claudia said.

The rain had turned to a downpour, and she could hear the tumble of a stream over rocks. Unspoken words hung between them, the thing they didn't discuss. They had to find Julian. The blood of the Hathorne was required. It was the reason curing curses always failed. But there was hardly time to think of that right now as the sky continued to darken.

They broke through a line of trees, and Lemon could see the cave. She prayed it was empty. "There."

"My savior." Claudia's legs were muddy, her shirt and hair were soaked. Both of their shoes were ruined.

Lightning struck nearby and Lemon jumped, losing her footing. Her feet went out from under her and she tumbled, crashing sideways into a tree. Its bark caught her bare shoulder, ripping into her skin. "Fuck."

She pushed herself up, palms skinned and aching. "Graceful."

"You're always falling." Claudia pulled her up, and they headed towards the cave, moving more carefully.

By the time they made it, she was absolutely soaked and her entire right side was aching. The cave was barely more than an overhang, but she was thankful it wasn't deep. There wouldn't be any other inhabitants.

Gingerly, Lemon pressed her fingers to the cut. It wasn't deep and the pouring rain had washed most of the mud away. "Do you think—" She stopped as Claudia made a strange guttural sound.

Her hands were braced on the opening of the cave, her knuckles white. Her eyes were wide, pupils blown out, lips red and parted.

"Oh," Lemon said, her fingers were coated in blood and her heart missed a few beats. And for possibly the first time since she was a child, Lemon was genuinely afraid. A real vampire or not, Lemon could see the blood lust etched on her face. "Claudia."

"Hush." She stepped closer, every inch of her body tense.

Lemon's brain screamed to flee, to do something, to get away, but her body wouldn't move. Even as Claudia came closer. Her fingers clutched Lemon beneath the chin, nails digging into her skin. She kept her eyes on Lemon as she turned her head.

And she lowered her mouth and licked the blood. "Fuck," she moaned. She looked up, pupils still wide. "Lemon."

Lemon's heart was doing something widely erratic and the rest of her body burned with want. She breathed out and Claudia slammed her into the rocky wall of the cave, clawing at her clothes, seemingly trying to touch every inch of her at once. Lemon kicked off her pants as they fell to the floor, and pulled at Claudia's top. She was gorgeous, soft and smooth beneath her hands.

Her mouth found Lemon's. The kiss was harsh, but it only stoked the fire raging inside of Lemon. She cupped the swell of her breast, rolling circles over Claudia's nipples with her thumb until Claudia was panting.

She caught Claudia's lip between her teeth and bit down. The resulting moan washed away any fear left in Lemon and she grabbed her, pulling her close. She needed to touch all of her, find every spot that would make her squirm.

Claudia moved to her neck, sharp teeth scraping the surface but not breaking the skin. "Let me fuck you," she whispered, warm breath on Lemon's ear.

Desire ravaged her body. "Yes," she said, not letting her doubts in, too turned on, too full of ache and need. Their limbs tangled together, and they crashed to the floor, no thought to her bruised body.

Claudia was above her, her mouth back on her collarbone, making the most tantalizing sounds Lemon had ever heard. She pulled at Claudia's shorts, finding her wet and ready beneath them. She ground into Lemon's hand, but it was only a moment until her body shuddered and she righted herself. "I need to taste you."

"Okay." Lemon let her knees fall apart as the ancient rocks dug into her back.

"You're beautiful." Claudia trailed kisses down her chest until she was between her thighs. She paused and looked up, amber eyes blazing. She spread Lemon with two fingers, not taking her eyes off of her until her head fell back. Lemon tangled her fingers in Claudia's hair, urging her lower.

She buried her face between Lemon's legs, wrapping her arms around her thighs and holding her tight. The world tightened to a pinpoint. There was nothing but Claudia. Her sharp teeth and soft mouth. Lemon squirmed, but Claudia held her tight and pulled her closer.

She ran her nails down Lemon's legs and she screamed her name into the sounds of the storm. It was not long before she found release, her whole body shuddering, her nails scraping the rock.

Claudia crawled up to Lemon's chest, and for the first time in a long time, Lemon's mind was quiet. But then she opened her eyes and found Claudia looking at her, her face flushed and Lemon wanted more. She didn't want this to end or to go back to all the shit the world held for them. She ran her finger over her cut and brought it to Claudia's mouth. "It's my turn."

The storm did not give up easily, and it was longer still before they found themselves spent and sticky, laying on the floor of the cave. Lemon wondered how they'd hike any more today. She wasn't entirely sure her legs still worked.

Part of her never wanted to stop, and she kept tracing circles on Claudia's skin, wanting to coax more orgasms out of her, watch her writhe and moan. To let Claudia do the same to her. But they would have to get back, and vampire or not, it would be better to do it in the daylight.

Still, neither of them was inclined to leave, tucked into one another, their limbs tangled together. Claudia brushed her fingers over the short hairs of Lemon's undercut as the sun began to shine, illuminating the rock walls, the floor damp with rain and sweat.

Claudia's necklace was tangled on the ground beside her, discarded for its own safety. It sparked when the sun hit it, shining with the faint glow of magic.

Claudia pushed herself up on her elbow, the fingers of her free hand trailing from Lemon's neck to her shoulder. She smiled playfully. "This is a memory to cherish, but I worry when I'm cured I'll look back on the blood in horror."

Lemon laughed. "Well, as someone who is not even remotely a vampire, I assure you it was hot. And I'm not even into that."

Her fingers continued their path, running over the hardened peak of Lemon's breast. "Not into blood play or vampires?"

"Blood play. Everyone's into vampires." She caught a strand of her cascading hair, watching the sun change the brown into gold and copper.

"Hard to have one without the other." She lowered herself again, her head on Lemon's chest, her breath cool against her skin, making it pebble.

"Yeah, but it's hot if it's a vampire, weird if it's just some dude drinking your blood." Claudia inclined her head towards Lemon, one impeccably groomed eyebrow raised. "Don't look at me like that. I'm not kink shaming, I'm just kink... questioning."

"And the difference is?"

"Okay, maybe I am a little bit." She brought Claudia's hand to her mouth, kissing her knuckles. She was full of satisfied joy. Though she wasn't sure if there was something real between them or just some magic of the shallow cave, she knew she'd pour every bit of herself into curing her. "We should go, check out at least one tree before we head back."

The crows had been the most hopeful about this one and the path did seem familiar to Lemon. Another ingredient down. But she had always known it would not be the finding of the things that would be difficult, it would be the blood. How would they get it?

Despite her staunch beliefs about bodily autonomy, she'd always thought it ridiculous that they could not force a Hathorne to give even a vial of his blood. It would prove his innocence. But the church had created them and though they no longer claimed any official brotherhood, their ties to the government went deep.

They cited laws about forced testimony, about the fifth amendment. All it came down to was that when their blood cured curses, it would have been proof of their misdeeds and the federal government could not allow it. The Hathornes were governors and congressmen. Most no longer practiced. Their anti-magic was an antiquity, but they did not want cases of their guilt piling up. So they stacked the courts, and the witches continued to burn hundreds of years later.

Their bags were by the cave entrance, their clothes laid wherever they had been flung, and the sun continued to sink lower in the sky. Lemon tried to move from beneath Claudia, planning to get her bag and try to come up with a plan, but Claudia groaned in protest, wrapping her arms around Lemon.

"We probably need to check the area. You said the white flower was in a cave. It could be nearby." Her fingers slipped between Lemon's legs.

"Caves do not travel in groups." But her eyes fluttered closed, nearly against her will. She forced them open. One of them needed to think clearly, though it was hard. Claudia was staring at Lemon. Her red lips were swollen from kisses, her eyes heavy. Lemon kissed her hard, biting down on her lip, and when her limbs slackened in surprise, she used the moment to slip from underneath her.

Leaving her standing over the prone, naked figure of the most beautiful woman she'd ever seen. Why exactly was she leaving this cave? In answer, a ray of sun broke through, falling over Claudia's thigh and she hissed, twisting away to grab the necklace. Lemon rushed for their bags, all the realities of their situation coming back

.

Birds flew overhead, swooping and cawing as they made their way slowly down the wet, muddy trail. Lemon could feel their excitement and it raised her own. She could do this. She *would* do this. Julian was a criminal, not a member of Congress. Could it really be that hard to get just a touch of blood from him?

She knew the answer was yes. Lemon had barely ever been in a fight, not since Sarah Mack had stolen her gel pens in middle school. But Claudia was fast and strong and they didn't need much. It was possible.

The trail they were on was narrow, rarely used. Claudia kept brushing herself against Lemon, though they'd barely spoken since they left the cave. They came to a break in the trees, and a drop down the side of the mountain opened before them. Claudia grabbed her wrist and Lemon stopped.

"I like you," she said, adjusting her hair, now back up in a high ponytail. "I know I don't really know you, but ever since I saw you dripping wet from that spring, I wanted you. And now I've hung out with you, and I like you. I just thought you should know."

Lemon cupped Claudia's head in her hand, running a thumb across her cheek. "Do you want to do something tonight? I'm sure I'll be starving and we could get a drink. Pretend we're normal people for a day."

Nodding, Claudia's gaze swept across the curve of Lemon's neck. Lemon allowed herself to wonder what it would feel like for sharp teeth to pierce her skin. The thought made her flush, heat rising between her thighs.

Claudia reached down and took Lemon's hand in hers. This was new, and despite everything, made Lemon hopeful. It had been a long time since she had felt this way. She hadn't been lonely. She had the town and Ruby and her friends, but this was nice too, filling a hole she had forgotten was there. Even with all the obstacles, all the reasons this was likely to end in tears, it was exhilarating to feel flutters in her stomach once again, to remember the warmth of a beautiful woman's hand in her own.

Hand in hand, they continued on the perilous path, right at the edge of the mountain, and it felt like a precipice in so many ways. She couldn't help stealing glances at Claudia, clearly enjoying the sun on her skin, so she didn't miss it when she froze, her mouth agape.

Birds squawked as she turned, and the sourwood was before them, grown precariously on the edge of the mountain. Its spindly leaves fluttered in the breeze, some of them still shiny with rain.

"I knew it!" Claudia said, dropping Lemon's hand to throw her arms around her neck. She smelled of rain and blood, incense and sex. "When I started asking around, there was a woman at a head shop and she said there was a witch in the mountains with one of the rarer gifts. And then I started looking for you and I realized you were the person I felt drawn to, the only thing tugging me away from Julian and I knew you were going to help me." She kissed Lemon hard. "And I was right. You are incredible, Lemon Leblanc. Just incredible."

Unfortunately, there was still the matter of extracting a root from a tree growing from the side of a mountain, and while Lemon had a reckless streak, getting splattered on rocks would not be her preferred way to go.

Lemon couldn't think of magic to help them. She didn't know of any spells to allow her to walk on air or to move the tree to a more manageable position. They pulled garden trowels from their bags and stood side by side, looking at the tree.

"It's going to be growing on this side," Claudia said after several long moments of silence, filled only with bird calls and the rustle of leaves.

"Yeah, but we'll have to dig deep to get to anything we can pull off." She continued to stare at the tree as though it would tell them its secrets. When it revealed none, they got to work, digging out from the base. It was slow, tedious work. Several long minutes into their task, Lemon scraped her knuckles against a gnarled root and Claudia stiffened.

"That was the first human blood I've drunk," Claudia said, so quietly the wind almost swept away her words.

Lemon's breath caught in her chest and the cadence of her heart increased, missing beats as adrenaline flooded her veins. "Do you need more?" She forced her hands to continue digging. The roots were growing thinner, not long until they could break one off.

But Claudia wasn't moving, and the forest had gone quiet, once again recognizing the danger that lurked within. The birds left their perches, high in the sourwood's branches, flying off into the sky. When she spoke again, it was not an answer to Lemon's question but she understood it all the same. "This won't be forever. It can't."

Lemon put down her trowel, covering Claudia's hand in her own. "It won't. I swear it."

The look Claudia gave her was strange, laced with more than just longing, full of deep sadness and regret. "Look," she said, turning her amber eyes towards the mountain soil. "That one will work. Look at all the little roots coming off of it. That will be enough, won't it?"

Lemon pulled her hand away, wrapping her fingers once more around the cool handle of the trowel. "It's perfect." She looked up towards the tree, hoping it understood her thanks.

They packed the root into Lemon's backpack, wrapped in towels. She hoped she was right about the ingredients, though she was never wrong.

The descent was easier, and Claudia grinned as they passed the gouges in the soil where they had run for the cave and Lemon couldn't help but smile in response. She'd fucked a vampire, and she'd survived. They had hiked through woods that felt like home and held hands under the hickories and oaks. Soon it would all turn to shit again, so she tucked those moments away in her heart.

Her car waited at the trailhead and she threw her bag into it, turning to find Claudia blocking her path back to the driver's seat. Her skin was washed in the pinks and oranges of the fading sun. Claudia settled her elegant hands on Lemon's hips, pushing her back until the door handle dug into her ass.

The kisses were slow, as though they would have all the time in the world, as though they were not covered in mud and dust and sweat. When Claudia stopped kissing her, she nipped at Lemon's earlobe before stepping back.

"Will you tell your sister?"

"Will you tell Fritz?" She trailed her finger down Claudia's damp shirt, between her breasts.

"Of course. He'll need to know where I am tonight."

Lemon laughed, startling the chirping bugs nearby into silence. "Awfully cocky Ms. Auberon."

"I always have been."

Chapter Eleven

Freshly showered, Lemon felt like a whole new woman. She took stock of her injuries in the mirror, running her fingers over the wound on her shoulder, and cringing when she heard her mother's voices through the walls of her Victorian.

She had twenty minutes until she was supposed to meet Claudia. She fixed her hair, pulled on a v-neck and jeans, a couple pieces of jewelry and tried to sneak down the stairs.

Athena screamed at the sight of her, dashing quickly towards her food bowl. Her mothers were cooking something meaty and the smell of it filled the house. She rolled her eyes at the cat. The bowl was nearly full. "Greedy little goblin."

But part of her was jealous. As a teenager, she'd never gotten a familiar, just anxiety and her mother's hips. Athena seemed to love both of them, though, possibly even preferring whoever had fed her most recently.

"Darling, daughter." Esther appeared in the doorway to the kitchen, a dish towel thrown over her shoulder.

Ruby appeared behind her mother in a cloud of red hair, wiggling her eyebrows and making vulgar hand gestures. "Went upstairs awfully fast. Did you find anything?" Her voice faded, but she continued mouthing. *"Was it good?"*

She should have known that trying to sneak into and out of her house would never happen. She pushed past her sister, aiming an elbow at her side, but Ruby jumped away, tongue out.

Amaryllis smiled from the stove. "I assume you'll come back to work, eventually. You're staying for dinner, right?"

"I... uh... can't." Her fingers strayed to her shoulder. "I have a date."

As one, the three women's heads turned to look at her. Ruby was grinning, but their mothers' mouths were open in identical round Os. She tucked a wayward strand of hair behind her ear.

"Oh, darling, with who? Doctor Mills's girl?" Amaryllis asked.

"Tabby? Is she gay? And no."

Amaryllis looked up from the stove again. "She did cut her hair."

"Oh my god." Lemon scrubbed her face with her hand. "You're lesbians and you both have long hair. Jesus Christ. No. With Claudia."

"The vampire!" Amaryllis clutched her throat.

Ruby dissolved into such intense laughter no sound accompanied it, just the shaking of her shoulders. Lemon hoped her lungs collapsed.

"She's fine. It's fine, mom. I'm fixing it."

"Oh, Amy, calm down. Claudia's finer than frog hair and Lemon's been walking around in a daze since she showed up."

"Finer than frog hair?" And Ruby exploded back into laughter.

Lemon grabbed her wallet off the table and shoved it into her pocket. "I love you. Goodbye. I hate you all."

✦

Widow's Peak Bakery was empty when she showed up—too early for the drunks to get hungry, too late for coffee—but Lemon hadn't eaten anything since that morning. She ordered a sandwich and sat by the window.

The bell above the door jingled. Doc Mills walked in and Lemon had to duck her head, thinking of her mother's earlier comments.

Luckily, his daughter, Tabitha, wasn't with him. Probably off shaving her head.

"You been good, Lemon? I've heard you're helping that new girl staying at the bed-and-breakfast."

"Oh, yeah. I've been great Doctor Mills. How about you? How's Tabby?"

"Oh, she's good. Going back for her masters in the fall."

They chatted about her, about the town and the upcoming Founders' Festival, and Lemon relaxed back into the seat as he went to order donuts. There was a faint hum to the town, people walking by, couples canoodling in the square, and running through it all was the thrum of the mountain's magic.

She was picking at her sandwich when a chill spread through her. *Danger.* The man—Orlo—who had been arguing with Fritz was walking by, his arms crossed across his chest. She tried to fade into the shadows, but she was too late. He saw her and smiled. Lemon pushed herself to her feet as he slammed open the door.

"Where is she, girl?" His voice boomed through the bakery.

"Lemon, hun, is everything alright?" Lavinia pulled off her apron and hurried around the counter..

"She's fine," Orlo said, taking another step towards her.

"I'd hear it from her, before I hear another word from you." Lavinia stood a head shorter than him but she put her hand on her hip and jutted out her chin in defiance. Still, it was Dr. Mills who slid himself between them.

"You got no business here, son. This is Hecate's Hollow, not whatever godless place you hail from."

"It's okay, Dr. Mills," Lemon said, but even she could hear the way her voice shook. Not just from fear, but the knowledge that Claudia's secrets were connected to the man in front of her. She thought of him traveling with Claudia, the way he had learned what she loved, and turned it against her. "Or do you plan on cursing me too?"

Lavinia let out a strangled gasp, and shadows appeared in the doctor's eyes. He was as human as they came, but he'd never shied from witches and he'd spent his whole life in the Hollow. "You can leave now, or I can get the sheriff, and like I said, this is The Hollow. We don't take kindly to violence against witches."

Orlo laughed, but his eyes stayed on Lavinia, and Lemon wondered if he'd heard the rumors about her. Several dead husbands and not a hint of fear anywhere on her.

Finally, he turned towards Lemon. "You tell her he's coming. He's tired of waiting, and that if she doesn't tell you, I will."

Lemon wanted to say something, to grab him and demand he tell her what he knew, but he was out of the shop before she forced air into her lungs again.

The doctor helped her to her chair, and Lavinia brought her a sweet tea. "Well, he was a horrible little man. No wonder the poor girl needs help. Cursed is it?" Lemon nodded. "I didn't notice at first. It's quite unusual."

"Well, she's come to the right place," Dr. Mills said, keeping his eyes on the door. "I'll tell the sheriff to keep an eye out for dangerous types."

"And I'll get Gunter to pull all the library books on unusual curses. I heard about a girl once, kept living her life, but danced instead of walking. They never found out who did it."

Lemon sipped her tea slowly. "I'd only heard of monsters."

"After everything your mama went through, we never wanted to talk to you much about curses. We were so scared one would happen to her," Lavinia said.

"You knew about my mom?" No one ever had ever said a word about her father to Lemon. They'd been welcomed, brought more cornbread and casseroles than their freezer could contain, but no one had ever asked.

"Of course we knew about your dad, you goose. We aren't here to judge a woman from running off from an evil man."

"No one ever asked me about it."

Dr. Mills chuckled, fogging his glasses on the exhale. "Of course we didn't. The two of you were just little girls, and it wasn't long before you were smiling and laughing. Why would we bring up that ugliness?"

She wanted to know if they knew what happened to him, if they knew the details neither of her mothers had ever told her, but she was too afraid of the answer.

The bell on the door jingled again, and Lemon jumped. It was Claudia, in a tight red dress that was certainly by some designer Lemon couldn't name. But she sent up a prayer of thanks for whoever it was, because good Lord, they deserved it.

The doctor clapped her on the shoulder. "You be good now. You have my number if you need it."

"Honey!" Lavinia wrapped her arm around Claudia's shoulder. "You should have said you had someone bothering you. Especially with you staying just a stone's throw away from the bakery. And you know, I live just off the square."

Confusion clouded Claudia's face, but she didn't shrink away from Lavinia. "What?"

"Well, some horrible witch man just came threatening sweet Lemon. I assume there's a Hathorne buddy of his on the other end of his threats. But this is Hecate's Hollow, and you landed in the right place, baby. We'll take care of you here. You're working on a cure, I assume. We all know what the tricky part is, but I'll tell you, getting blood from a man's not as hard as some people make it out to be."

Red creeped up Claudia's neck, turning her cheeks nearly the same color as her dress. "Oh. Okay. Well…" She glanced at Lemon.

"Oh, Lord have mercy. Y'all are on a date, aren't you? Get on out of here!" She took Lemon's tea even as she reached for it. "But don't be afraid to holler if you need anything."

Claudia's eyes were wide as they left the shop. Lemon scanned the streets and the town square, but she didn't see Orlo anywhere.

"Lemon…" Her face was flushed and memories of her naked and moaning her name only hours ago flooded Lemon's brain.

The sun had set, and the stars were shining—little specks of light above the dark shadows of the mountains. Lemon focused on them as she held up a hand. "I need a drink." She wasn't a drunk. She'd go weeks, even months without it, but tonight she needed one.

Lemon didn't live a life that led her into danger. She'd gotten enough of it as a child. She had never yearned for it the way some people did in their adolescence. And Orlo had shaken her to her core.

"Alright, let's get you one."

The sign swinging above the bar needed a coat of paint, but the words could still be read. Dionysus Dive. They loved their Greek gods in Hecate's Hollow. What could she say? She loved her town, weird quirks and all. The inside still looked the same as it had when it had been built in the seventies, including the smell of smoke that clung to the wood paneling, despite the fact indoor smoking had been banned over a decade ago.

The carpet was an unpleasant orange color. It might have once been cheerful but years of spilled drinks and dirty shoes had done their damage. It wasn't very late into the night, but Dionysus was already half full and the first person to notice Lemon was her neighbor, Betta McCray, who abandoned her barstool, jumping up. "Lemon! Fancy seeing you here!"

It took a few minutes to extract herself from Betta's red curls, but once she did, she ordered whiskey on the rocks and gulped it down. Beside her, Claudia ordered a glass of wine and wasn't much slower.

God, Lemon hadn't wanted it to go like this. It had been eons since she'd been on a date she actually gave a shit about. But it couldn't be fun and easy, no matter how it had seemed in the cave, with the rain separating them from the rest of the world. There was too much at stake, too many secrets between them.

She took a long drink from her second whiskey and turned in her seat. Claudia was gorgeous, all long legs, flowing hair and red lips against her pale skin. And the dress was a masterpiece. But all the good things were overshadowed now. "He said if you didn't tell me, he would. Tell me what, Claudia?"

Claudia drained her glass, and then reached for Lemon's, taking a sip and making a face. She inhaled deeply, and Lemon wasn't sure she was going to answer at all. "Julian gave me a date, it already passed, but he said he would be generous. I have until Saturday and then he's going to come here. And the pull towards him is so strong. I don't know if I'll be able to resist if there isn't half a continent between us."

"Orlo already told me that Julian was coming," Lemon said, scraping at a burn mark on the bar with her fingernail.

Claudia ran her hand through the hair that Lemon loved so much, her fingers catching in the tangles. "I've done so many bad things, Lemon. I've hurt people. I've acquired things I knew would be used for evil." She stopped the bartender with a raised hand, ordering a gin and tonic. "Before I stole from him, he was going to send me here. You're right about the mountains. They are full of magic. He wanted to know about the witch towns. I was supposed to infiltrate Hecate's Hollow, find out why your magic is so powerful, befriend you, and... I don't know. He didn't give me specifics. I barely ever even saw him, but a few times a year."

Lemon stood, feeling the need to pace, and brought her drink with her. There wasn't much room to walk in the bar, no dance floor—the only open space was full of pool tables, but she had to do something, so she stood against the wall.

What if Claudia had come like that? Lemon would have been putty in her hands, though she didn't know what she would have been able to tell her. But there were secrets, the spring in the woods, the hidden places where powerful things grew. Her mother had always told her it was where the blood of the gods had once fallen. She'd never believed it, but it was still their secret. And Claudia had planned to steal those things and hurt people with them.

Claudia finally joined her, twisting the straw in her drink. Lemon knew the eyes of the bar patrons were on her, like a pressure at the base of her spine. It was a small town. They wanted to know who the new girl was.

"I'm sorry, Lemon. I really am. I'm sorry for so many, many things."

The truth of what she said was etched on every inch of her face. Sorrow and remorse twisted her features.

Lemon took a step closer, her shoes peeling off the sticky floor. She wanted to touch her, to put her hand in the space where her waist curved, to tell her everything was forgiven. But she couldn't bring herself to do it.

"So that's how you knew about me?" It shouldn't shock her. Her father had been a Hathorne. He used to talk about towns like this, about the sins that happened and the way they were overlooked, as though his own weren't.

"He made a list of witches with your power. It'd be a valuable tool for him to have in his corner. There are a lot of witches on his side, but none of them can divine ingredients like you do."

"And now? When I change you back?"

"Now nothing, Lemon!" Her face was strained with the effort to keep her voice lower than the country music playing over the speakers. "I was already going to leave. I just needed help. And I didn't lie about being connected to you and... and that I can't explain." She reached out, taking Lemon by the hand.

Lemon didn't know what to say. She wanted to be mad, to be furious, but the anger bubbled and then dissipated at Claudia's touch. Instead of screaming, or walking away, or any of the things she knew she should do, she grabbed her by the face, kissing her so desperately that they collided with the wall behind them.

The man beside her whooped, and they broke apart, both red faced. "I want to be so fucking angry with you."

A flash of emotion crossed her face that Lemon couldn't read. She didn't know if she'd ever be able to understand all the depths of Claudia. She didn't know if she'd ever get the chance or where they'd be in a week. She didn't know what to do or how she would ever trust her, but she wanted her, and for right now, her head swimming with whiskey, it seemed like enough. At least for tonight.

She was about to ask Claudia if she wanted to leave when her eyes caught on something over Lemon's shoulder. Lemon turned to look. Fritz was coming in, flanked by Elias and the librarian, Gunter Greyson.

"Well, look who came out of that creepy house," Gunter said. His sandy brown hair was cut into what could only be called a fashion mullet, and he had on a pink leather jacket. Smiling from ear to ear, he looked Claudia up and down. "Well damn, I guess I can see why Lemon hasn't been at the shop lately. This your sister?" He turned towards Fritz, who nodded.

"The one and only. She's usually got a bit more sun, though." He winked at Claudia.

Who would have imagined Hecate's Hollow to have such a thriving bar crowd, especially at nine on a Monday? Still, the three of them together warmed something in her heart, especially since she knew Elias had been carrying a torch for Greyson for years.

She ordered another drink, dousing the flame of irritation and fear inside of her with whiskey. There would be tomorrow. There would be time to be mad and frustrated and fucking freaked out beyond belief, but today she'd slept with the hottest woman this side of the Mississippi and she just wanted to bask in it for a moment.

"Is Ruby coming?" Fritz asked, pushing his way to the bar beside her and ordering the same drink as his sister.

"I'm sure she will if you text her." Lemon looked him up and down. He was hot, she supposed. "Go ahead."

He grinned. "Claudia pinched me when I talked about her the other day."

"Good." Lemon smiled. It was... well it was weird. Siblings dating siblings. Always absolutely weird. But she wanted Ruby there, too.

And twenty minutes later she was, her red hair wild, curls of it falling in ringlets around her face. The urge to tell her everything that had happened was nearly overwhelming. But Lemon was pretty deep into her drinks now, and Ruby, despite being possibly a little stoned, was sober. She knew she'd go find Orlo the second she mentioned it, and do something more than a little illegal.

So instead, she watched as she joined Fritz in a game of pool. Behind them, Elias and Gunter were tucked away in a booth with peeling leather seats. The hanging light above them swung, casting strange shadows across their faces.

An arm snaked its way around Lemon's waist and Claudia leaned into her. "I've never been a part of a community. I wish I'd tried. You have people here. Roots."

Roots indeed. Roots that encompassed the whole town. There was so much to lose here. Her mothers were here. And suddenly, she realized where she'd seen the cave and the white flower before. But it had been years, and she didn't know if she could find it again. Or if her mothers would remember either. They had explored so many places.

And thoughts of ingredients only brought her back to the same place. No herb, flower or animal was going to be what stopped them. That had never been the hard part for Lemon. She watched her sister laughing, throwing masses of hair over her shoulder, Fritz's dark eyes gleaming, and she wasn't sure she could make the next words come out of her mouth, to say what she needed to say, to bring danger here.

"Kiss me," she said, instead. And Claudia obliged, her nails digging into the skin left bare between her shirt and pants. She tasted like gin and blood and Lemon wrapped her arms around her.

"This place needs dancing," Claudia said, wobbling on her feet.

"We do our dancing in the street. Next week is the Founders'—fuck. Claudia, you believe in this place?" When she nodded, Lemon dragged her outside by her hand, past Betta laughing and playing pinball with her enormous husband, and into the balmy night air. "Look around. Hecate's Hollow is special. You can have a fresh start." She needed her to understand. Lemon would help, they would all help. But Claudia needed to change, too.

She headed for the gazebo, needing to feel the spirit of Hecate's Hollow, to remember that she was home. That the land would protect her, and that maybe the town had found a new daughter to protect. Maybe whatever magic built these mountains had called Claudia here. Maybe she hadn't been following Lemon but the embrace of mother nature.

Or maybe Lemon was drunk. Either way, she plucked a flower from the bushes surrounding the gazebo and put it behind Claudia's ear. Footsteps crunched the acorns on the sidewalk and her heart swelled at the sight of Gunter, amid her other friends.

He must have read it on her face because he stopped, the color of his jacket washed out by the streetlamps. "Listen, I don't know exactly what's going on, but I can see she's cursed and I've seen that creepy man around a few times. So, I can leave, but..."

"Elias..." Ruby turned towards him. "You told."

"It wasn't hard to figure out.." Gunter shrugged. "It's a small town, and she's a freaking vampire."

Claudia snapped her teeth at him.

"Alright." Lemon steadied herself on the street lamp. Apparently, a night for forgetting all her problems would not happen. Instead, she was compiling a rag-tag Scooby gang... which honestly seemed right. She grinned at them. "Ruby, do you remember that time we went camping, and you threw up everywhere?"

Ruby glanced at Fritz, whose lips were a thin line, though laughter danced in his eyes. "No."

"Yes, you do. You threw up in the car, and then we pulled over, and you threw up more, and it made that little kid at the rest area throw up too. And it turned out it was because you ate some plants in that cave."

"Yes, obviously, I remember that. But it wasn't really a cave, was it? It was behind a waterfall with..." Her eyes lit up and she bounced on her toes. "Oh! With the flowers! The flowers I ate. Oooh, Claudia, this potion might be rough."

"What is happening?" Claudia leaned her head on Fritz's shoulder.

"I know where the flower is. Well, kinda. My mom might know. It's not too far. Definitely driveable. Do you remember, Ruby?"

"We were going to spend the night somewhere, Asheville maybe, and we didn't make it far. Our road trips always took forever because our moms stopped for ingredients constantly."

"I want to come this time," Fritz said. "Y'all shouldn't have all the fun."

Claudia and Lemon exchanged a look, and Lemon could feel her ears heat. None of it was helped by Ruby elbowing her in the ribs. "Yeah, let us come with you."

"We wouldn't even all fit in a car," Claudia pointed out.

"Gunter has a van!" Elias said, absolutely crushing Lemon's dreams of getting fingered behind a waterfall.

"Fine. As long as Ruby promises not to barf anywhere."

Chapter Twelve

Lemon's arms ached from carrying boxes into and out of the storage room of the Red and White Apothecary. But she had to do at least one shift before she took off again. Her mother was bent over the counter, marking places on the map where the waterfall could be. Unfortunately, she remembered the vomiting more than the location.

Elias's mother's crows had been little help. They did not fly far enough to know the place, and Lemon was not hopeful of finding it on their first shot again. But after that it would be the wing of a bat, which she already had in the shop and then Julian's blood.

And he was coming. She didn't know what she would do. Magic did not work on Hathornes, with few exceptions—potions that were really just archaic medicine or things like Ruby's gathered clouds that would still hang over them. But spells and enchantments? It was impossible. Sheer force might be their only option, but even in a town like Hecate's Hollow, holding a man down and cutting into him was illegal. And she understood it. She really did, but she didn't see many other options.

Amaryllis pushed her reading glasses up her head and looked at Lemon. "I hope you know I'm proud of you."

"Really?"

"Of course. You're braver than I ever was. Whether or not you succeed, I'm proud of you."

Lemon's thoughts strayed to when she was a child, all the screaming, her mother's bruises, broken glass and fear—so much fear. There had been times she'd been angry with her mother, blamed her for not leaving, but as she had grown older she'd found forgiveness and understanding.

Because her mother had gotten out, which was more than so many people managed, and she had created something beautiful. She pulled her mother into an embrace, breathing in the scent of her Dior perfume. "I'm proud of you too, mama."

Amaryllis pulled away enough to look at her, and she smiled. "Oh Lemonade, please be careful with all of this. And let your friends help. Don't shoulder all the burden. Know, you have generations of witches before you who have undone wrongs that were not theirs to carry, but they did it all the same." She took Lemon's face in her hands. "You are good and strong and you make our ancestors proud. You are the reason we were given magic—to help and to heal. I love you so much."

Lemon blinked away the tears in her eyes as her mother let her go. Outside of the shop, the sun was shining and people milled about in the square. She had a home, she had friends, and maybe she had found someone she could love. She tried not to think of the obstacles, of how they would get the blood they needed, of what Claudia would do once she was cured and didn't need Lemon anymore.

But the last thought stuck, refusing to be pushed away like the others. What would Claudia do? Would a woman who had traveled the world ever be happy in a small town? Lemon knew she could not leave. This was her home. It always would be.

She shook out her head, no use worrying about the future before it came. It never changed anything. So she busied herself in her work until Esther came, dried lavender, mugwort and sage in her arms.

"You've got yourself quite a little curse breaking group, huh?"

Lemon laughed, putting a hunk of tourmaline back on the shelf, a price tag now affixed with string. "It kind of snowballed."

"Good. Witches thrive in groups, and so do hikers. They're all at the house. I sent a little something to your bank account, in case it takes a few days. I'd rather you stay in a hotel than get eaten by a bear. Now get out of here and try to have some fun." She winked as she shooed her out of the store.

As it turned out, Gunter's van was less of a van and more of a mini-school bus. The thought of driving through the winding mountain roads in it gave Lemon heart palpitations.

"I swear I can do it," he insisted. "I've been driving it for years."

Longingly, she thought of her own car, tucked away in the garage. But it only fit two people and somehow this had turned into some kind of gay witch quest. She glanced at Claudia. The two of them could be whipping down mountains, the wind blowing their hair. Instead, she had friends—which was fantastic, of course, but less ripe for fantasies. "If you say so."

"Lemon LeBlanc, I am not going to kill you." Gunter still had remnants of his drag makeup around his eyes, and he'd bleached his hair white-blonde since she'd seen him last.

"Come on, live a little." Elias appeared from the back of the van. His face was red from the exertion of dragging all their bags into the back.

"I'm not scared of living. I'm scared of driving off the side of a mountain in this thing." She eyed the teal van suspiciously.

"Come on, baby, people drive RVs around here." Claudia kissed her cheek. She had on a sundress and a wide-brimmed hat.

The use of 'baby' made her heart do a strange little dance, and she took a deep breath. She threw her hands up in defeat as Ruby came out of the house, Fritz following behind her, his muscular arms loaded with bags. His hair was unusually mussed and Lemon raised an eyebrow, but Ruby pretended not to notice.

"Do you ever imagine what it would be like if we had met in some normal way?" Lemon asked.

"All I think about is being normal. But to answer that question I'm thinking movie marathons, ice cream, I'd teach you how to sail."

"You sail?"

Claudia grinned. "Wouldn't you like to know."

She would. She wanted to know so many things. To learn about the woman behind the vampire and find out if they were really as compatible as she hoped. "We'll go sometime. After it's done."

"It's a date."

It wasn't long before they were all loaded up. Elias leaned over the seats, putting down the windows and letting in a cool breeze. It was a gorgeous day; the sky dotted with fluffy white clouds that blotted out the sun at intervals as the wind blew. The air was fragrant and thick with all the smells Lemon associated with home. As they drove away birds chirped happily, wishing them well on their way.

"Okay, so I've got it all mapped out. Places to look and then places to stay the night that have actual restaurants in them. This could take a few days, depending on how fast we find it, but I'm hoping with four witches we can divine something."

"I'll read leaves tonight," Ruby said, making her way up the aisle as they drove out of Hecate's Hollow. She plugged her phone into the aux cord. "I made a playlist."

Mitski came over the crackling speakers as Claudia turned in her seat. She propped her chin on her hand, her elbow digging into the yellow leather. The bus was probably the tackiest thing Lemon had ever seen. The outside was teal, the seats were yellow, and the inside was hand painted in bright neons like something out of an 80s nightmare. "Have I told you thank you lately?"

Her skin was even paler, and dark circles had formed under her eyes. Lemon could practically see the strain in the lines of her face, but she smiled, and Lemon didn't want to bring it up if Claudia didn't. "What can I say? I'm an incredible witch."

Elias pushed down the last of the stubborn windows and made his way back up the aisle, taking the front-row seat to the right of Gunter. Lemon glanced around the van. Ruby had returned to her seat, and was bent over something Fritz was holding. She let out a bark of laughter at whatever it was, but Fritz wasn't looking down. His eyes were on Ruby.

And good lord, this was going to be a long trip. Three couples, or at least three wanna-be couples, which was undeniably worse. It hadn't even occurred to her before. What kind of back-woods, gay couple's retreat had she gotten herself into?

"We could jump out the back door, take my car," she whispered to Claudia. "Hey, are you okay?" Her eyes were closed, and she held her head in her hands. Lemon moved from her seat to Claudia's and put a hand on her leg.

She opened her eyes at the contact and glanced at Lemon's hand on her bare leg, smiling. "Yeah. It's hard sometimes." She pulled a pill bottle out of her purse and tipped the contents into her mouth. "Fritz made this. They help take the edge off."

Resolve steeled itself inside of Lemon. They'd find the flower. They'd get the blood. Julian had already threatened to come. She wrapped her arm around Claudia and she leaned into the touch, resting on Lemon's shoulder.

She stroked her hair as the van continued to wind up the mountain roads, miraculously not driving off the edge. Lemon held Claudia while her friends laughed in the front of the van and Claudia finally opened her eyes when Ruby lit a joint.

"That smells like shit."

Ruby scoffed. "Well, some of us are backwoods hillbillies, not fancy jewel thieves, so we take the drugs we can get."

"Fair enough." Claudia stretched her body across the leather seats. "When in Rome..."

They were all laughing by the time they made it to the first spot they intended to search. Lemon stretched as she got out of the van, but the trailhead stirred no memories in her. But she'd been smaller the last time she had been there, and her memories could be wrong, but still, her hopes were low.

The ascent was an easy hike and fairly deserted for the time of year. She knew as she made it higher she wasn't in the right spot. More than the view, she had remembered the feeling of the magic running through that place and she felt none of it as she made her way up the hillside.

But it was soothing to be with her friends in the autumn air. Claudia was terrible at hiking and Gunter wasn't much better. They grumbled the whole way up, and their complaints kept startling the animals before Lemon could divine their thoughts. But what did it matter? Each day they didn't find the flower was a day together, unburdened and away from the Hollow and the threat of Orlo. Out in nature, it was easy to forget that she'd gotten herself tangled up in something dangerous. This was what she wanted from life—a group of friends, her sister happy, days spent outside.

When they made it to the waterfall, everyone stopped to stand in awe. The midday sun caught in the water and glimmered across the wet rocks littered with leaves. Behind it was an open space, and Ruby made it first, the light of her flashlight reaching into depths the sun could not, but it was just bare rock.

"Well, what were the chances of it being the first place, anyway?" Elias said, slipping off his shoes to cool his toes in the pooled water between the rocks.

So they sat on the shore, the water misting over them, and ate the cheese and crackers that Gunter had brought with him.

Coming back from behind a tree, where she'd snuck away to take a piss, Lemon caught Fritz's eyes on Claudia. She had stretched out across a rock, warming herself in the sun like a lizard. Lemon couldn't guess what Fritz was thinking, but her own heart swelled, glad she could help her live in the light again.

Before she could make her way to her, Claudia stood, stretching her arms above her head, bringing the hem of her sundress dangerously high. She winked at Lemon, then turned to Gunter. "Okay, I'm ready." She darted across the rocks to the other side of the shore in a blur—faster than any human ever moved.

Gunter let out a whoop of satisfaction. "That is so fucking cool."

Claudia bowed. "I'll be right back." She was still grinning as she disappeared into the woods. Lemon watched her retreating figure before heading back to her friends.

"Where do you think she was going?" Ruby asked.

"Well..." Lemon glanced towards Fritz and he wiggled his eyebrows.

"Oh, fuck." Elias chuckled. "That is nasty."

"It's not so bad," Lemon said, picking up a slice of pepper jack.

Elias's laughter was loud enough to startle the birds in the trees. "Lemon LeBlanc, you saucy minx! You dirty dog."

"Okay, what the fuck is going on?" Ruby glanced towards the tree line

"She, uh, needs blood." Fritz ran a hand through his chestnut hair, cheeks tinged pink. He hadn't shaved that morning, and there was stubble on his chin. He looked like he belonged in the mountain town, more than Lemon thought Claudia ever would.

"What does that have to do with Lemon?" Ruby asked and Gunter cleared his throat, eyebrows raised. "Oh... oh! Oh!" Ruby stood up and then sat back down. "Well, butter my biscuit," she finally said, and Fritz's eyebrows disappeared into his hairline before he exploded into laughter.

And all in all, it was an excellent day. One of the best Lemon could remember, excluding the day they had found the sourwood, and the hour spent in the cave there. They loaded back on the bus, headed for wherever Gunter, bopping his head along to Taylor Swift, had planned for them to stay. Lemon's cheeks hurt from laughing and Claudia, looking better now, sat beside her.

She lifted Lemon's legs and put them in her lap, rubbing her calf. There was a piece of twig caught in Claudia's hair, and Lemon leaned forward to pull it out. Claudia caught her mouth in a quick kiss. It was over before anyone else noticed, but it still made Lemon shiver down to her toes. "Share a room with me tonight?" she whispered.

Composing herself, Lemon nodded. Whatever was growing between them felt real. She hoped Claudia was feeling it, too. Once she had returned from the woods she had laughed along with the others and sipped from her brother's flask. Claudia was bright, effervescent, and Lemon wanted to bask in her glow.

Right now the thing between them was small, but just like a seed, Lemon hoped that if the relationship was tended, it would grow and spread its branches wide.

"Okay, queers and Ruby, do we want a small town vibe or more rural country vibe?" Gunter asked from the driver's seat, yelling over the rumble of the tires.

"Small town. I want a restaurant, not a weird bar, where I get hit on by rednecks who are mad about it," Elias said, stretching his legs across his seat. He crossed his arms behind his head. Lemon remembered him as a child, full of anxiety, tiny legs pedaling as they flew through the streets on bicycles. He still held some of that anxiety now, but he had become a man who was content with who he was.

Ruby seemed content too, though she kept sneaking glances back at Lemon, as though Claudia might snack on her in the middle of the van. Her fingers played with the hairs at the back of Fritz's neck, absentmindedly. Lemon didn't think they'd gone very far. Ruby hadn't mentioned anything about it to her and Ruby was always one for kissing and telling. And Lemon was coming around to the idea of something between them, or at least the beginnings of it. Though she hated to admit it, even to herself, if either of the twins was going to stay in the Hollow, she would put her money on Fritz.

Sometimes people came to the Hollow, on vacation or passing through, and they just never left. They fit in, making friends, falling into the rhythm of life in her town, until it seemed like they had always been a part of it. Fritz was that kind of man.

"Any counter arguments?" Gunter asked, and when none came, he took a turn and the bus began its descent down the mountain.

The town was small, with a cheery little main street lined on both sides by stores, most of them closed for the night. A quick glance around told Lemon this was a witch town, though possibly not as full of magic as Hecate's Hollow, and she breathed out a sigh of relief.

The dinner was decent, and the company was better. But the motel at the end of the street had seen better days. It wasn't dirty, but the carpet was matted down, and the paint was faded. The girl behind the counter looked up at them as they walked in, taking stock. She must have liked what she saw, because she smiled. "Welcome to Arbery's Inn! What can I do for you?"

"We need..." Elias turned towards them, wheels obviously turning in his head, "four rooms?" Gunter shrugged and his mouth twitched towards a smile. "Unless you two want your own rooms," he asked Lemon and Ruby.

"She's... uh... she's good." Claudia rubbed her hand along the back of her neck.

"Alright, four rooms." There was a chuckle in the counter girl's voice as she typed on her computer. She pulled out four room keys. "I'll let you divide these amongst yourself. B3-6."

The rooms were better than the lobby, but not by much. And Lemon could most assuredly hear Fritz on the other side of the wall, then the creak of a door and the laughter of Ruby.

"Well," Claudia put her bag down, as sounds came from Gunter's room on the other side. "Should not have picked a middle one."

Lemon nodded her agreement and kicked off her shoes, falling back onto the bed as a shriek of laughter came from the direction of Fritz's room. She glanced towards Claudia, who was looking back at her.

"Are they?" Claudia mouthed and Lemon shrugged. She climbed onto the bed with Lemon, laying on her stomach. Her sundress rode up her leg, brushing just above the delicious fullness of her ass.

"Interesting hiking attire, by the way," Lemon said, keeping her hands to herself, despite her desire to do anything but. She was not going to have sex with every friend she had in earshot.

"I am nothing if not vain." She rolled onto her side as Fritz's low voice came through the wall, words that rose the color on her neck and widened her eyes. "We can hear you, you disgusting perverts! "

"Since when is that happening?" Lemon asked. Apparently, her earlier assessment of the state of their relationship had been incredibly off.

"I have no idea." She lowered her voice, keeping her whispers inside the thin walls. "He's always so secretive about these things at the beginning. Not all women are understanding. I think he'd rather not tell me about the hate he gets sometimes."

For a second, Lemon found it hard to believe. Lean and muscled with thick brown hair and deep brown eyes, who would turn down Fritz? And then she thought of the picture she had seen and a streak of white-hot anger at everyone who'd ever made him feel less than for being trans shot through her. "It's kinda weird, our siblings, huh?"

"Yeah, but it's kind of nice, too. When I can't hear them," she yelled the last words and two sets of laughter came from Gunter's room. "It's gonna be a long night. Want to go get a drink?"

"I do!" Elias yelled from next door.

"Jesus, Mary, and Joseph." Claudia sighed.

Chapter Thirteen

Gunter and Elias walked ahead, through the narrow, brick-building lined main street, searching for a sign of life. The street lights reflected off of Gunter's snow white hair, making him look like a specter. "With every step, my hopes for booze in this place diminishes."

"It can't all be the Hollow." Elias glanced back at Claudia and Lemon. He looked so happy. Lemon wished she could bottle the look on his face. It would fly off the shelf.

"Speaking of small towns," Claudia started, shoving her hands in her pockets. She'd switched out of her sweaty sundress, into a pair of yellow shorts and a gauzy blouse. "I was thinking, if we pull this off, maybe we could go see my mom sometime. I think you'd like her, and road trips are kind of our thing."

Their thing. The words warmed Lemon better than any drink, rushing through her veins. She nodded, following Elias and Gunter around a seedy-looking building and onto a new street. "Yeah, that would be nice. Really nice."

"Excellent. Another date." Cool fingers closed around her own and squeezed, the frail thing between them growing a bit stronger. Lemon's eyes were on Claudia, the strong line of her nose, the soft curve of her lips, so preoccupied she ran into Elias when he stopped short.

He caught her by the shoulders, glasses askew. "I'm getting, like... real bad vibes." And since his power was divining tragic events no one argued. He read it on their faces. "Not like that, just regular human bad vibes. This is all residential anyway. I think there's some tequila in my suitcase."

"Oh, you think?" Lemon teased. "Got us out here walking in the dark."

"Now, now." Gunter wrapped an arm around Elias, and the tips of his ears turned blazing red. "As I recall, we were all trying to avoid hearing your sister get banged. I'm a librarian. It's hardly appropriate." He kept a straight face, but his eyes sparkled with mischief in the moonlight.

"I've seen what you read." Lemon countered.

"Lemon! I put on children's programs. I am a pillar of this community and all my erotica comes from Amazon, so..." He stuck his tongue out.

"You're all avoiding the important conversation we need to have." Claudia looped her arm through Elias's and Lemon's and turned. "Where are we going to drink the tequila, because obviously the hotel room is out for at least another half an hour?"

"There's a viewing station at the train depot. I saw it when we were coming in. We can act like a couple of vagrants, if you want. And I'll check hotel reviews on whatever Gunter has planned for tomorrow." Elias offered.

"Rude but valid." Gunter said. "Let's go."

The plan was solid and walking through the town had revealed almost no human activity. The threat of getting caught and arrested for public intoxication seemed fairly low.

The bottle of tequila wasn't large, and already partially gone, but the night was cool and the sky was clear. The crisp air wrapped around them like a second skin, making the train depot feel like it carried its own bit of magic.

Claudia laid across the old wood, her long limbs sprawled, gilded in moonlight. Lemon was in deeper than she should be after only weeks of knowing her. She watched Claudia as the others talked and tried to imagine her as she used to be.

Claudia picked her up head when Guther mentioned drag queen story hour, her dark hair a pool beneath her pale skin. "The parents don't mind?"

"They love it," Elias said, passing the bottle to Lemon. "And so do the kids. They dress up too sometimes and it's hilarious."

"I'd love to come sometime." She laid her head back flat, the beginnings of a smile pulling at her lips.

"Planning to stick around?" Lemon asked before thinking, bolstered by alcohol. Both Elias and Guther turned, almost imperceptibly, but the night was quiet and Lemon could hear their shoes scrape across the wood.

"Well, I never planned on it, but yeah, honestly. I am." Her amber eyes bored into Lemon. "Wow, okay, I'm drunk, so I guess I'll say this but I don't think I've had friends since I was a teenager. Not real friends."

"Well shit, that is a sad story." Guther pulled the bottle from Lemon, who was struggling to find words. The world expanded before her, laying out possibilities she'd never dared dream of. "So, what is your deal? It has to be a good story." He took a long drink and handed the tequila to Claudia, as the rumble of a train upset the quiet of the night.

The racket covered the arrival of Ruby and Fritz, and Elias jumped when Ruby finally spoke, greeting them. "Yeah. Let's hear it, vampy." She sat on the ground beside Fritz, and curled into his side.

"Well, Fritz and I were really poor," she started, and her brother grunted in agreement. "Our mom isn't a witch and our dad wasn't around, so she didn't know what to do with us really, though she tried her best. I wanted more from life, so I went to college with all these big dreams. But it turns out a shitty backwoods education doesn't lend itself to stellar grades in college. So I started, uh..."

"She became a criminal on the side." Fritz lifted the flask in salute. "Because she never learned to listen."

"And I got all jumbled up with Julian—he's the guy who did this. And I knew he was in love with me, but he didn't meet any of my criteria." Her eyes slid to Lemon. "And you know, men never take that well, so he started sending me away to get all the illegal goods he thought a pretty girl would be better at smuggling. It was just Orlo then and you've seen him, gruff and all that, so he attracted a lot of attention. It worked. They'd search him and I'd slip through. But where Julian was infatuated, Orlo was absolutely not. Everything was fine at first. We found ways to get along. But he thought I was young and silly and when I started getting better jobs than him, he got furious. He threw my signed Anne Rice into the Pacific when I came home drunk once, and that was kind of the end of us even attempting to get along. He wanted what I had, and the fact that I didn't even want it made him hate me."

"I tried to get her out." Fritz interjected, and his voice was strained. Lemon could imagine how she would feel if she saw her sister getting deeper and deeper into something dangerous. A literal criminal organization.

She slid closer to Claudia, longing to touch her, as the train continued to rumble by, and she was grateful Claudia couldn't hear her murmuring of sympathy.

"And I wanted out. But I had an overworked mom, and I knew Julian had started to sniff around Fritz. I couldn't let him get mixed up in that life too. I thought maybe I could sweet talk Julian, give him some of what he wanted and he'd let me go. He asked me to marry him." Lemon tensed. She hadn't heard this part of the story before. "I stole from him instead. He wanted to hurt me, control me.

So he did this." She gestured to herself. "It was all Orlo's idea, I know it. We'd watched all those stupid shows together at the beginning. So I got this whole sire thing. And I can feel him. There's this pull. I can feel how mad he is, how he's looking for me. I knew Orlo would show up before Julian did. He always sends him first."

Elias blew out a long breath. "That's fucked. Like, that's really fucked up. I'll tell you what, I never want to live in the real world. I know how people talk about the witch towns, but I can't imagine anything else."

"It's all about control," Ruby said, her eyes locked on Lemon. Her jaw was set in a hard line, her emerald eyes sharp enough to kill. "That's how we ended up here, too."

Lemon didn't want to tell that story, the way she used to cower, her mother screaming, nose bloody. How she used to pretend it wasn't happening because she never actually saw the blows land. But everyone was looking at her. "But you saved me. And we'll save Claudia too."

"Thank God for witches," Gunter said. "And I'm only a little jealous." He gazed at his own hands, wide and human, then back at the train as its graffitied sides rolled past. "Do you know what happened to your dad?"

No one had ever asked her before, as far as she could remember. She knew her mothers must have talked to the police, but this was witch territory and her mom had still been bruised when they showed up. She shook her head. "I don't know if he's even still alive."

Claudia's fingers found her knee, gripping tightly. Lemon didn't talk about her father any more than she had to. She kept memories of him locked in a little box inside her mind, and while she sometimes looked at the box, turned it over, examined the edges, she never opened it, afraid of what she'd find inside.

"He was a Hathorne. I used to worry it was in me, too. That I'd hurt somebody or hit puberty and stop being able to do magic. I don't know of anyone else like me."

"You aren't alone," Gunter said, handing the bottle back to her. It burned going down. "And the magic usually wins out, unlike in the real world. Out there, there's not much to be done, magic doesn't work on them. But usually, when it comes to babies, the witches win out." He looked around at them. "What? I'm around books all day. I know things."

"Well, since we're talking about it. We get this flower and then what are our chances of getting the blood?" Fritz asked, pushing himself up from the ground. He walked to the railing of the depot, watching the end of the train disappear into the night. "I'll cut the bastard myself if I need to."

Claudia sat up fully. "I don't want you in trouble, Fritz. I couldn't stand it, not for me." His returning look was burning, as though he'd do more than that for his sister. "Please."

"We know he's coming here. Let the inevitable fight happen. Self defense is a good defense," Elias offered. The street lights reflected in his glasses. "If he's trying to hurt Claudia, or trying to hurt anyone, we're well within our rights to protect her, and if he bleeds in the process, well..."

They were all silent for a while, contemplating. Ruby stood up and began to pace until she finally came to stand beside Fritz. "I'm not arguing, but I hate this."

Claudia made a small noise of discomfort. "I'm sorry, Ruby. I really am. I'm sorry I brought all this trouble to your doorstep."

"So am I. But it's not you I'm mad at. It's the world."

Lemon thought Ruby had always carried a little of that anger with her. Ever since grade school, the way she'd fought off bullies and shrieked at anyone who tried to hurt Lemon. She'd been born mad at the world and growing up had done nothing to dispel it. For

145

all of her laughter and jokes, there was a kernel of hate inside of her that Lemon couldn't blame her for. In fact, she was thankful. That anger had saved her more than once.

"Maybe we can make the world a little less shitty. Isn't that what our ancestors who founded these towns were trying to do?" Gunter said. "It's what we're celebrating at the Founders' Festival."

"Yeah," Ruby said, running her hands over her arms. "Somebody's gotta try."

As the moon rose in the sky, the others eventually left, staggering back towards the motel through the deserted streets until it was just Lemon and Claudia left in the depot. The night was quiet, only the sounds of nature to keep them company, the chirping of crickets, the song of the wind through the leaves.

Claudia was thoroughly drunk, her face slack and smiling, and Lemon wasn't far behind her. Humming a song Lemon didn't recognize, she scooted across the ground until they were face to face.

"Lemon." She said her name like she was tasting it on her tongue. "You know, I barely know you."

She couldn't argue. It had only been weeks—though it felt longer since her life had been simple, going to work, dinner with Elias, family night with her mothers and Ruby. "It's kind of abnormal that I agreed to help a stranger."

The single light in the depot stuttered, throwing them into darkness. Lemon couldn't see the lips that pressed against hers, gentle and brief. "I'm so glad you did." She heard movement—the slither of fabric against wood—and then Claudia was pulling on her arm. She stood, and they walked out of the darkness, back into the silvery moonlight.

They walked towards the motel as another train rumbled up the tracks, their fingers linked. Lemon could feel the bats overhead, the tiny zing of her magic connecting her to them.

But the shiver that ran down her spine was something else entirely, a different kind of magic. And Claudia must have felt it too because she turned towards Lemon, outside of a florist shop, bathed in blue neon from the closed sign in the window. She cupped Lemon's face in her hand, her fingers soft and uncalloused. "Things might get bad soon, but I need you to know this is real. I can't explain any of it, but the second I saw you, I knew. "

Lemon grabbed her by the waist, pushing her into the doorway. For a moment they just stared at each other, and then Lemon captured Claudia's mouth in her own and she grasped at her. Her fingers dug into Lemon's back, pulling at her shirt.

And then she was at Lemon's neck. Sharp incisors scratched over thin skin and Lemon's whole body was on fire. She fisted a handful of Claudia's hair and bent her head, exposing her neck. Claudia's breath danced across her skin and she trembled in her arms with restraint.

"Do it." Lemon breathed into the thick night air.

"I can't." But she ran her tongue from the base of Lemon's neck to her earlobe, nipping at her flesh.

"I'm a witch. I'll heal." Lemon grabbed her by the back of the head, pressing Claudia's mouth into her skin. If she would feed, let it be from her. She bit back a scream as Claudia's teeth sunk into the skin of her collarbone, and her toes curled in her shoes.

Her blood flowing from her, Claudia warm and squirming against her, was the most intense thing Lemon had ever felt. Claudia's free hand slipped down the front of Lemon's jeans and she did not care that she was on Main Street as her magic surged and the neon light exploded behind them and the street went dark.

Claudia moaned as her fingers plunged inside of Lemon, fast sharp movements, hindered by the fabric of her pants, but Lemon's body responded, and it was not long until she was panting, her nails digging into Claudia's neck, lost somewhere in white, hot ecstasy.

And her blood continued to flow. Claudia pulled her closer, breathing her name, bringing Lemon to the edge. She sank another finger into her, her palm grinding between her clit. This was dirty, public, and she savored every moment, committing her disjointed thoughts to memory as best she could.

"Please," she moaned, and as she came Claudia pulled away, dragging her tongue over the wound and collapsed against the window, panting, and Lemon did the same. It was fast and intense, a moment over almost before it began, as all her time with Claudia seemed to be.

"Oh, fuck," Claudia said as her breathing calmed. The sides of her lips were tinged with blood and even under the moonlight, her skin was brighter than Lemon had ever seen it.

Running her fingers along her neck, Lemon murmured a spell, feeling the itch of healing begin. "That was…" She trailed off, unable to find the words to express anything she was feeling, and surprised none of it was shame. Though that might change if someone stuck their head out of a door to yell at them. "We cannot tell *anyone* we did that."

Claudia barked out a laugh. "I'm rethinking this whole cure thing. God, Lemon, you are delicious." She brought her fingers to her lips, licking them slowly one by one, and Lemon was pretty sure her soul was going to leave her body.

She was definitely sure she would never recover, that nothing that ever happened for the rest of her life was going to compare to the last few minutes. She had certainly peaked. She ran her fingers over the wound on her neck again, her heart still pounding.

But the blood loss and booze were not mixing well, and she was lightheaded. Or maybe it was from getting fingered by a vampire in the middle of the night on Main Street in a strange town. It was hard to say. But either way, she thought eating something was probably her best option.

She pushed off of the wall, but instead of walking away, she found herself tangled up in Claudia once more, her fingers in her silken hair. Her blood was still on Claudia's tongue as it swept through her mouth. She ran her hands up her thighs, cupping her perfect ass.

And then she stumbled and almost fell, stopped only by Claudia's swift vampire reflexes. "Okay, we should get you laying down."

"God, you're gorgeous." She tried to kiss her again, but again she stumbled.

Claudia swept her into her arms, one under her knees, the other on her back and carried her down the street.

"You are fulfilling like every dirty fantasy I've ever had right now," Lemon said.

Claudia grinned. "Tomorrow we're getting a room with thick, thick walls and then we can talk fantasies."

It wasn't long before they were back at the motel. The lights in the rooms on either side of them were off. Claudia put her gently on the bed and grabbed a juice from the mini fridge, forcing her to drink it despite her protests at what it would surely cost.

Next she peeled off Lemon's clothes, then her own, and crawled into bed beside her. It was the first time they'd slept together, and Lemon was aware of every spot where their bare skin pressed together. But the excitement of what had happened was wearing off, blood loss and a long day catching up with her, and she found herself exhausted.

So she pulled Claudia close, breathing in the sweet, deep earthy scent of her and closed her eyes.

Chapter Fourteen

The next day Lemon kept waiting for shame to come, but it never took hold. Instead, she would look at Claudia, and want to yell at everyone else, demand to know why they had insisted on coming on this trip. She wanted her all to herself. She wanted to make her squirm against wet rocks on the side of the river they were following. She wanted her spread against the foliage, screaming Lemon's name loud enough it echoed through the mountains.

But she was stuck, listening to Fritz and Gunter argue about some movie she'd never seen, and trying not to respond to the looks Ruby kept sending her way.

Her sister broke her away from the group as they crossed a narrow bridge. It seemed steady enough, but Lemon still felt fear rush through her at the thought of walking across the aged planks. "What did you do?" she hissed.

"About what?" Lemon feigned ignorance.

"At the train depot?" Her eyes locked on Lemon's neck. The wound had healed, but there was a red mark that any witch could identify as something quickly and magically healed.

"Mm-hmm." Lemon agreed, like the lying liar she was. As if everyone in the motel hadn't heard her sister and Fritz.

Ruby slowed her pace, grabbing Lemon by the wrist, and she had to resist the urge to shove her. The last thing she wanted to do was dawdle on a rickety bridge. She couldn't resist looking down into the river and rocks below and, just as she suspected, it was a mistake, making her heart race.

"She's never going to stay," Ruby said, lowering her voice. Claudia was well ahead of them, walking with Gunter, but Lemon could tell by the way her shoulders tightened she had heard them. Still, Ruby continued. "I'm glad to help her. She didn't deserve any of this, but I don't want your heart broken, either."

She took the final steps across the bridge, and almost bent down and kissed the ground. "I'm not a teenager anymore, Rubes. I can manage my own heart." She wanted it to be true, but she knew she was falling too fast, opening her heart without any promises.

Her sister's lips thinned. "It's like me and Fritz. You just take it a day at a time. Don't pour your heart in."

"Oh, you're so full of shit," she scoffed. "Your heart and your vagina are on the same wavelength, and they always have been. Stop trying to give me the advice you should be giving yourself."

Ruby rolled her eyes. "So, we're both fucked."

"Maybe they'll stay. And if not, fall is coming. The tourists will be in soon. We'll keep our beds warm." Lemon didn't want to talk about this, didn't want to admit how entirely broken her heart would be by a woman she'd only known a few weeks.

"I'll make sure The Shop 'N Go is fully stocked with Rocky Road." Ruby smiled. "Really, I'm just a proud sister, watching all of your little vampire fantasies come true. I can honestly say I never thought I'd see the day. I mean gay and blood sucking. What were the chances?"

"All vampires are gay." Lemon hurried to catch up with the others as the trail widened at the curve of a river. "They're going to live forever and never even try it?"

"Hear, hear," Elias called out.

"Okay, so by your own admission, you'd fuck men?" Ruby asked, digging in her backpack and bringing out her water bottle. "You, who has been gay since fourth grade?"

"Hell, yeah. All kinds of men, too. Mark it down. If I make it to a hundred, I'm sucking dick. Having an orgy. "

"Jesus fucking Christ," Claudia muttered, but she was laughing and she slowed to walk beside Lemon. "Vampire shows. We have that in common."

"What else, do you think? How about empanadas?"

"Love 'em. Anywhere good to get some in Hecate's Hollow?"

"Oh, absolutely not." Lemon laughed. "Plenty of barbeque, though."

"I also like barbeque, but not as much as empanadas. Favorite color?"

"Yellow, obviously."

The bit of mountain they were on was gorgeous. The hike up had been rough-going, but it had evened out to a slight incline. They were higher than anything around, granting them gorgeous views. The river rushed by, heading quickly down the mountain, and when the wind picked up a cool mist sprayed over them.

"We're almost there," Gunter said, glancing at his map.

Lemon felt hopeful. Something about this place was familiar. But the knowledge that they might soon have another ingredient tightened like a vice around her heart. Soon she would meet Julian, soon she would do something violent, and her life had not been one marked by violence.

They came to a set of rudimentary stairs carved into the mountain face and the rush of water grew louder. Elias was the first to head up, gripping onto protruding roots as he ascended.

"I'll stay if you still want me after all of this," Claudia whispered, then, before Lemon could answer, she followed Elias up the stairs.

Once again, Lemon was left wondering where the lies began, because she knew they were there, lurking in each story told, but she could not find them, could not separate them from the truth. Or maybe she was paranoid, maybe Claudia only worried, just as Lemon did, that without the curse and a mission between them they would find they were two people who barely knew each other.

She followed the others up, letting the fresh mountain air clear her head. All of those worries were for another time, and dwelling on them wouldn't change the outcome. The rocks were hard and uneven under her shoes and the roots of the plants tried to tear at her palms as she grasped them, but she made it to the top.

She knew immediately she was in the right place. She could feel it in her soul in a way she could only explain as magic. This was it, another piece of the puzzle.

The waterfall was enormous, crashing onto rocks and then pooling, before turning into the rushing river they had been following for hours.

"Wow," Fritz breathed, and they all stood by the crude staircase, taking in the scene, afraid to break the tranquility of the scene before them.

"Indeed." Gunter agreed. "These mountains are the soul of Mother Nature."

Lemon couldn't disagree, taking in the withering blooms of mountain laurel, the smooth pebbles at the bottom of the clear pool and the pointed leaves of the maples growing over them, giving the spot a sharp woodsy smell.

"This has to be the spot," Elias echoed what they were all thinking, finally breaking out of the trance and taking a step closer to the waterfall.

The rush of sadness in Lemon's chest was unexpected, but not surprising. She rarely left Hecate's Hollow, and she was enjoying her time away, laughing with her friends, pretending Claudia was just a new girlfriend, that everything was normal. Just a road trip.

She took a deep breath, intending to steady herself, but a glance at Claudia had her remembering fangs against her neck, the rush of blood from her veins. But all the same, she felt ready.

The space behind the waterfall was nearly a cave, possibly deeper than the cave they had found looking for the sourwood, but these rocks sparkled in the sunlight, like it was full of crystals. And there was the flower. A single white flower, nearly buzzing with magic. Green vines crawled across the rock face and curled around the entrance until they disappeared outside.

Behind her, the others entered the cave, making noises of astonishment, but sadness and fear kept their grip on Lemon's heart. The last ingredient was a bat wing. Her mother had ordered a dozen for the apothecary.

Still, she gave Claudia's hand a squeeze. She was staring at the flower with such intensity her face was almost frightening.

"We did it," she whispered, then even quieter, "He's coming." She strode forward, wrapping her delicate fingers around the stem of the flower, and plucked it. The vibrating magic grew stronger, filling the alcove, and buzzing through Lemon's bones.

The magic faded and Claudia stood with the flower cupped in her palm. She let out a gasp and trembled so violently that Gunter rushed forward and grabbed her.

She clutched the front of his shirt, taking several deep breaths, and as she straightened her eyes found Lemon's, amber locking onto blue. "Fritz." She handed him the flower, and he wrapped his arm around her, ushering her back into the sunlight. Lemon could hear their murmured voices on the other side of the waterfall, though she could not make out the words.

The others stared at her. They had done it. They had found what they needed, nearly as easy as ingredients for an acne paste. And

155

now, they were inviting danger to their town. A Hathorne in the Hollow.

Elias was the first to speak. He pulled off his glasses and wiped them on his hoodie. "We've got the whole town on our side. It'll be fine." His voice echoed on the stones.

"Is this unhinged?" Gunter asked, glancing towards the opening between the falling water and the stone. "It seemed fun, but suddenly it's real. Are we really going to do blood magic?"

"Stop it!" Ruby said, glaring at all of them. "We aren't doing blood magic. We're reversing blood magic. Does she seem like a demon to you? Do you think she deserves to live like that? And no one made you do this, no one made you come. You all chose to be here and you're all free to leave. But we aren't going to make Claudia feel bad."

Lemon nodded, pushing down the fear. When she emerged into the sun, it was clear that Claudia and Fritz had heard every word. "Come on," she said, taking her by the hand. She led her to the stone steps and began their way down the mountain.

"You said he's coming." The way down was easier than up, and she did her best to put space between herself and the others. Claudia showed no sign of strain, held back only by the pace Lemon could keep. "He said Monday, but I'm guessing he isn't bound to that. What do you know about Julian, Claudia? Any tips to stop him?"

She shook her head, glanced back at the others and grabbed Lemon. She pushed her against a tree and kissed her. Fangs brushed against Lemon's bottom lip and she sucked in a breath, but they did not pierce her skin.

She could feel the wildness beneath the surface of Claudia. There was no peace in her eyes. She was a woman unsettled. "Is it... is your desire for him getting worse?"

Claudia nodded. "You're all that quenches it, however brief." Her eyes strayed towards Lemon's collarbone, sending a shudder down her spine. Quickly, she started walking again. "I feel like an animal trapped in a cage. Like I could rip my skin off. I'm hungry and... Oh, God. I just need it to end. He knows I won't make it much longer."

It was hard to watch her like this. Finding the flower had set off something in her, or perhaps it had been the explosion of magic, the reminder of what she no longer had. But there were deep shadows beneath her eyes. The glow of the night before was fading, leaving her pale. She held the necklace, rubbing it between her fingers before letting it drop against her chest.

Lemon followed behind her, wishing she could do more. Even if she wasn't Claudia, even if she wasn't beautiful and funny and mysterious, she would want to help anyone in such a state. But it *was* Claudia, and that made it all the worse. The woman who had shown up literally sweeping her off her feet, and turned her whole life upside down.

She thought of what she knew of the town, the people who had welcomed her when she was a child, and never treated her as anything but special. A town that held the magic she had always known existed in the mountains. A place that called to those who needed it and wrapped them in its embrace.

Julian was not just showing up for Claudia. He was coming to Hecate's Hollow, and she had to believe that it meant something, that she hadn't gone through all of this just to end up imprisoned on an assault charge.

Lemon had to jog to catch up to Claudia. She was muttering to herself and chewing her lip. "Claudia. Claudia! You're going to be okay." Lemon grabbed her by the arm and she spun towards her, eyes still wild, and for a second Lemon thought she was going to lunge at her.

"Oh, Lemon. I'm sorry. Don't forget that. I'm so sorry."

"I'm not." She glanced over her shoulder, but the others were still out of earshot. "You were right when you said we barely know each other, but I've never felt this way before. I feel alive for the first time in years, ever since you touched me. I don't regret it. Even if it's not the same for you. Even if Ruby is right and you leave, I..." She intended to tell her she'd still help. That Claudia could swear she would leave the second the curse was lifted, and Lemon would still do it. She'd probably stop having sex with her all over the state, but she'd help her.

But Claudia cut her off before she could speak. "Of course she isn't right! God!" She raked her hand through her hair.. "But..." she grasped at her chest and Lemon worried she was having a heart attack, but she straightened, grimacing. The footsteps of the others were drawing closer. "Why did that happen in the cave?"

Lemon shook her head. How could she know? So she offered a guess. "There's magic in the world, you know that. Sometimes it just sparks up." She'd felt it before, thunderstorms that left her fingers glowing, food that made her float. "When you plucked the flower your body must have remembered the magic that once flowed through it."

She laughed, cold and sinister. "And in a horrible burst of irony, it only made my connection to Julian stronger. I'll go to him soon, Lemon. I swear I will, just to stop the screaming in my head. You are all that helps, and I can't ask that of you."

The others joined them, stress and worry obvious on their faces. Fritz came closest, his brown eyes kind, and he took Claudia's hands in his own. "I'll call him. We'll end this."

"It's the Hollow, honey." Ruby wrapped a comforting arm around Claudia's shoulder. "No one's going to arrest us for taking an itsy bit of blood from a Hathorne. You know, it only takes three drops." She led her further down the mountain, continuing to talk about the town, all the ways she would be safe there, how they were going to win.

The look on Fritz's face as he followed Ruby was one that Lemon wasn't sure she'd ever seen before. It made her think of paintings, knights who wanted to win the favor of a princess, but the princess was Lemon's sister. He had the expression of a man so close to love he could practically taste it—devotion to the woman who was calming his sister, the storm maker who stilled the storms in others. She didn't think Claudia had ever looked at her like that.

Elias and Gunter walked on either side of Lemon, and Elias reached out, squeezing her hand. There was understanding between them, the kind that only comes with years of friendship. The skin around his eyes crinkled and his mouth broke into the goofy grin she loved so much.

"You know you owe me so many details about fucking a vampire, right? I mean, despite your stupid proclivities for team Damon, we did watch every episode of The Vampire Diaries together, so you totally owe me."

"Well, Damon was the obvious choice," Gunter said, adjusting his fanny pack and looping his arm through Lemons. "And I know we're not as close as you and Elias, but Mama would love those details as well. I mean, this is a once in a lifetime smutty story. You cannot keep it to yourself. Now we just have to save her, and this is your own Hallmark movie."

"I'm not sure Hallmark has many vampire stories," Lemon said, but the horror that had taken up every inch of her chest had subsided into something more manageable.

"Yeah, and even fewer lesbians."

"Am I stupid?" Lemon asked, keeping her eyes on the stream, all the leaves in the water flowing away as though they were never there. "I agreed to help her, and I didn't even know her. I agreed even though I knew it was dangerous."

"Half the town showed up without knowing anyone. Not everyone has a support system, that doesn't mean they don't need help. Sometimes you just have to help people, even if they have nothing to offer you."

She nodded, knowing it was true, that it was the same advice she'd give anyone who asked, and again, the vice around her heart loosened. "Am I stupid for letting her bite me last night?"

"You know, I think we'd have all tried it." Elias glanced towards Gunter, who pretended not to notice. "Was it really at the train depot?"

Lemon snorted, ducking her head into the crook of her arm to try to hide it, but coming up unsuccessful. "No. God, I wish it had been the train depot." She refused to answer their prying questions as they hiked, instead watching the back of Claudia, wishing there was more she could do.

But there was no way to change the past. Instead, she made an inventory in her head of all the things she would need for the potion. It was a week until the full moon. She'd need a few more witches, but those were easily found in the Hollow. She'd need a few crystals, some herbs she had in her cabinet.

On the drive back they were silent for miles, the only sound Phoebe Bridgers crooning over the bus's barely working speakers. Gunter kept his eyes on the road, and Fritz kept his eyes on his sister, with Ruby snuggled beside him, half asleep.

"It's the Founders' Parade tomorrow," Elias said, breaking the thick silence.

Claudia snapped out of her trance. She stretched her arms above her head and rubbed her eyes, gazing around the bus. "I'm sorry I freaked out. Thank you all."

"Don't worry about it. You're more than entitled to a little panicking. We do need some kind of plan." Elias twisted in his seat.

"I'll call," Claudia said, looking at Lemon. "Better to get Julian here when we know he's coming than have him show up on his own time. And then…"

"I'll start a fight," Fritz said, whispering so as not to disturb Ruby. "It'll be easy enough and the festival should help. It'll be crowded, it shouldn't get out of hand. Just enough to get some blood."

"My mom—Esther can lift it from your knuckles if you hit him hard enough." Lemon thought of her mother. The one who had saved them so long ago. She would help.

"Okay. Well, that's the plan. Claudia, you set up a time. We'll all meet in the square."

And they lapsed back into silence. After a few minutes, Claudia pushed herself up from the seat and walked back to Lemon. Without a word, she sat in the seat beside her, pulling her feet up and curling into Lemon's side.

She wrapped an arm around her, stroking her hair until her breathing settled and then Lemon fell asleep, her face pressed against the cool glass of the window.

Chapter Fifteen

It was a perfect day for the Founders' Festival. The sun was shining, a gentle breeze kept the temperature pleasant and Lemon kept momentarily forgetting where the day would lead. Fried foods and floats kept her mind occupied between bouts of panic.

Presumably, once upon a time, the festival had honored the families whose homesteads started the town, and though their names would still be prominently displayed, the festival had changed into something else, celebrating the town itself. Usually Lemon was more involved, dressing up like a frontiers woman and memorizing a script to read out to tourists and town folks alike.

This year she pulled on a pair of black shorts and a ratty Ren and Stimpy t-shirt she'd found at the thrift store while Ruby watched her from the vanity. She'd wrestled her red hair in a ponytail and was half heartedly putting on mascara.

"I am straight up freaking out, Lemon." She grabbed a tube of eyeliner, opened it and then closed it again.

"You and me both." All the ingredients were sitting on her dresser in little tupperware containers, mixed amongst her crystals and a dried rabbit's foot. "Breaking a curse is a big deal. Like... I mean, you know. It's a big deal." She pulled on a pair of purple Doc Martens.

The doorbell rang, and one of her mothers moved down below. Both sisters froze, staring at each other.

"We're going to be fine," Ruby whispered. She picked up a tube of red lipstick and swiped it on.

Fritz and Claudia knocked on Lemon's doorway before entering. Neither of them looked like they had slept much the night before. Lemon hurried forward, pulling Claudia into her arms. She grabbed her face, trying to memorize every inch while her heart pounded in her chest like it was trying to break away.

"I'm going to go first," Fritz said. "Your mothers will come with me. We can stake it out, see if there's anyone I recognize. You two need to look like you're coming alone."

"Okay, I'll walk you out." Ruby took a last look at herself in the mirror and stood.

Lemon opened her mouth, but no words came out, so she just nodded and let Claudia help her to her feet. Words continued to evade her as she looked at Ruby. Nothing needed to be said. They had talked about it all night. They were doing this. It was too late to back out, and despite their fear, neither of them wanted to.

Still, Lemon's stomach threatened to empty as she watched her sister walk downstairs, her pale hand held firm in Fritz's tanned one. He'd keep her safe. Her mothers would keep her safe. And besides, she wasn't Julian's target. But she worried if their plan didn't go correctly, he would see Ruby with Fritz and know where his leverage lay. She balled her fist so tightly her fingernails bit into her skin.

The pain calmed her. Fritz would scout the festival out first. Everything would go like they planned. She pushed the door shut and walked to Claudia. She kissed her, swift and fierce, then pulled down the collar of her shirt. "Drink."

"I can't. It's okay. I won't need to soon." But Claudia's face was pale and her hands shook at her sides.

"You said it helps, right? It helps with your... desire for him." Her mouth was dry, and the words were thick on her tongue.

"Lemon, I never should have. It's not right. It's not natural."

"Of course it isn't. This is dark magic. But..."

"No." Her voice was nearly firm, if not for the fear beneath it. "I never should have done this to you. Lemon, please forgive me."

"There's nothing to forgive." She bent her neck. "Claudia, he's going to be here. You need to be strong." And she grabbed her by the back of her head, forcing her face to her neck.

There was a gasp, hot breath on her neck. Sharp teeth pierced her shoulder and Claudia's arms wrapped around her. Her hands found their way beneath the cotton of Lemon's shirt, and dug into her sides.

Lemon breathed against the pain, closing her eyes and fisting a handful of Claudia's hair. Visions came to her, as they had in the spring, Claudia hunting through the woods, the home they had left behind in Charleston, the first snowfall blanketing the mountains. She could make no sense of them. Claudia moaned, bringing her back to reality.

With a lurch, she pulled away, blood dribbling down the side of her mouth. She wiped it with her thumb, licking the remnants, and Lemon groped for the healing tonic on her nightstand. It was harsh going down her throat, but she didn't want to waste her magic on a healing spell.

"We should go," she said, but she kissed Claudia once more, sweeping her tongue through her mouth, claiming her as though she may never kiss her again.

The town was in full festival mode, full of outsiders, though the parade was already over. Lemon had known she would miss it, but even with everything else going on, it stung a bit. Though she needed to limit her time in the square so Julian couldn't sneak up on them, she loved her town and usually she loved the festivals.

Even Claudia smiled at the children running by, dressed as little frontiers men or wearing dresses best suited to Little House on the Prairie. Against their better judgment, they'd walked together, though they kept their distance. To an outside observer they were just two women who had come to the square at the same time. Lemon leaned against a tree, scanning the crowd. Gunter showed up, in full drag, wearing what could only be described as Scarlett O'Hara meets Ru Paul and headed for Claudia.

He extended a hand, tipped with bright pink fingernails. "Emily Dick-in-Some at your service."

"Oh, I needed that." Claudia looked across the square, past the vendors and tents, to where her brother, Ruby, Esther and Amaryllis waited at intervals on the other side. There was a bench near the edge of the square, under the shade of an ancient oak.

"Welp. Time to be bait." Claudia forced a smile onto her face, but it looked more like the grimace it was.

Words and phrases sprang to Lemon's mind, but they all seemed wrong. None of them could convey what she was feeling. She wasn't sure she could name her emotions if she had a hundred lifetimes. It wasn't terror, not exactly, nor anticipation, but whatever it was, it made the hair on her arms stand on end.

There was fear under Gunter's heavy makeup. "Be safe. I'll be around." He air kissed her cheeks and then pulled bubbles out of his pocket, calling for the children. "It's me, Emily Bookinson!" He winked at Lemon.

She kept her eyes on the crowd, trying to look at anything but Claudia. If she looked at her, she wasn't sure she'd be able to let this happen, that she wouldn't grab her by the hand and drag her far away from here. But that would only extend her torment.

She thought of the farmer with the black ewe, the way Claudia had looked in the passenger seat of her car, the way she had looked that first night, in the shadow of the oak tree, just as she was now. She had fit so easily into Lemon's life, like a puzzle piece she hadn't realized was missing until she saw the picture completed.

And she had said she wanted to stay. So it was just this, this day, this man, this gripping horror, keeping her from a future she'd not dared to dream of. She'd always known Hecate's Hollow would be her home, that she would live and die within its boundaries. And maybe things wouldn't work out with Claudia, maybe this was a fling, based on lust and shared goals, but maybe she'd find someone besides Ruby to wander the trails with. Someone to swim with her in streams and listen to the whispers of the woods. She wanted to take her to the vision spring, the place where it had all begun. She wanted to speed down the streets of the valley with ice cream in the summer. To watch the leaves fall in the winter and drink cocoa under the stars.

She vibrated with the effort not to go to her, to sit beside her and remind her she wasn't alone. Instead, she headed for her sister, because whatever happened, however this ended, she'd have Ruby.

Her mothers hovered close by, and Fritz stood, his hands in his pockets, faking a casual feeling that Lemon knew none of them felt. She moved closer to him without making eye contact.

"He's scary, but he's just a Hathorne," Fritz said without looking up. "Your magic won't work on him, but force will. He's just a man. Remember, we blame the Hathornes, but they couldn't curse anyone without witch magic. We're going to be fine."

Ruby kept her eyes straight ahead. "But be careful, okay?"

"You worried about me?" He smirked. Don't worry about me, Ruby Carmine. I don't worry about myself when I know I'll have you to tend my wounds."

Lemon tried to sink into the shadows, an interloper on this moment. But she was happy for her sister. Fritz looked at her with reverence, as though she were the only woman in the world.

"Well, I don't want to tend any wounds. I want you whole and safe." She brushed her hand over his arm.

"Well, however I am, you have me." He briefly touched her hand before she withdrew it and stepped back, and they settled into silence.

Lemon saw him before Fritz did, but she knew the moment he spotted Orlo from the way his body tensed. She didn't think he even thought before he reached over, his fingers closing around Ruby's wrist. But Orlo was alone, a container of candied pecans in his hand. He scanned the crowd, but his face was placid.

Without thinking, Lemon moved towards Claudia. It was Amaryllis who stopped her, moving from her spot on the sidewalk to stand in front of Lemon, a too cheery smile on her face.

"We need him to show."

Anguish ripped its way through Lemon. "But she's scared."

"Of course, but we're going to help. You've always been so sweet, but you have to hold back and..."

The rest of her mother's words washed away on the wave of charged magic as Fritz blew by her. "Oy!" Lemon glanced over her mother's shoulder. The man he headed towards was blonde, his light gray suit impeccably cut. And there was something familiar about him. "A lot of nerve showing up here!"

A hush had fallen over the crowd, everyone turning towards Fritz. Lemon realized with a jolt she barely recognized anyone. These were all strangers, not townsfolk. The man only chuckled, still heading for Claudia.

Beside Lemon, her mother gasped. "Oh. Dear god."

"Fuck." Esther pushed Amaryllis behind her, reaching up in a smooth movement and plucking a twig from the tree. In her hand the twig grew, becoming a club.

Lemon didn't understand what was happening, even as Ruby pulled at her. She planted her feet on the ground, refusing to move, watching as Claudia stood from the bench, and Fritz continued to yell at the man. He swung, and the man ducked gracefully. He was an older man, but tall and muscled, not yet out of his prime. And beside him Fritz suddenly looked small.

As he righted himself, the man's eyes fell on Esther and his grin turned into something sinister. "You sneaky bitch." He sidestepped Fritz and headed for Esther. Amaryllis joined Ruby in pulling on Lemon, but her words were too punctuated with sobs to understand.

He came closer, and then he paused as Esther raised the club in her hands. His eyes locked on Lemon.

No.

No.

"Lemon..." His voice was softer.

Memories rushed into her, making her stumble back. Her mother crouched against the wall, the man looming above her. And then others, the same man, pushing her on a swing as she laughed. The man on a phone call, screaming into the receiver.

"Lemon, please." Ruby begged, pulling at her.

But it couldn't be. Her father was not Julian. His name was Giuseppe. And then behind him appeared Claudia's face, contorted in sorrow, tears streaming down her face. And Lemon screamed.

The man, her father, pushed through the crowd. Sparks reigned down, the power of a town of witches meeting his anti-magic.

"A Hathorne." Someone yelled.

He paused and turned towards the voice, webs of darkness snaking up his arms. "Leave." The woman who had spoken trembled, but she shook her head. "Fine, watch." He turned back towards Lemon.

No. This could not be happening. Claudia could not have been working with her father. She could not have drawn him to the place. Except she had, and suddenly all her apologies made sense. *She had known.*

Esther moved closer, her club still raised, her shoulders squared.

"Not this time, witch." Julian sneered. He lunged forward and Esther jumped back, raising her club. She swung as a child ran by, and Gunter screamed. Esther stumbled, thrown back by the weight of not completing her swing, and grunted as she hit the ground.

Lemon stopped screaming, her voice raw. Her father. Only feet from her. "Stop."

"Not this time." He reared back his foot, kicking towards Esther, but she scrambled back, her club growing. Lemon needed to move, needed to do something, but she was frozen between her mother and her sister. Esther scrambled to her knees, raised her club and swung, but she was too low. It bounced off Julian and he grunted, but still stood. This time, his kick landed, sending Esther reeling.

And then Lavinia was running for them, her small body moving faster than Lemon thought possible.

Something changed in Julian's features, the realization of where he was dawning. "Lemon."

"Fuck you." She spat on the ground.

"You're coming with me." He grabbed her by the arm, yanking her.

The self-defense class Ruby had once dragged her to flashed through her mind. She drove her elbow into his stomach and rammed the back of her head into his nose. In his shock, he let go and Lemon raised her arms. "Fuck you," she repeated. A crowd was closing around them, but Lemon could only see her father's face.

He frowned and then turned and ran. She wanted them to grab him, for someone to stop him. And though she had always believed in the people of the Hollow, they let him pass, horror and confusion keeping them paralyzed.

She needed to check on Esther, but her body refused to move and it was Ruby, and then Lavinia, who got there first, and pulled her to her feet. Esther brushed off her clothes, grimacing. At the sight of her standing, Amaryllis came back to life, her whole body shaking with sobs. She wrapped her arms around her wife, kissing her and wetting both of their faces with her tears.

And still, Lemon couldn't move. And across the square, neither did Claudia, though tears fell down her cheeks and the color was draining from her.

Magic moved through Lemon's veins like ice. She thought she might die, freeze or wilt or whatever happened to witches too stunned to go on. But then Ruby wrapped her arms around her mother, and she thought of her, how despite everything Esther had kept moving forward.

So she forced one foot to move and then the other. She walked past Fritz, who was scanning the crowd. Lemon did not care what he was looking for. Had he known? Had he been in on the lie? Elias tried to grab her sleeve, but she shook him off. "No. Go make sure my mother is safe."

And she walked. The walk seemed to take ages, but it couldn't have been long. There was not much space between them, and the square was rapidly clearing. She did not know where her father had gone and for a brief moment that terrorized her, that he might jump out again. But she was safe, as she had always been, in Hecate's Hollow, and he was just a Hathorne in a witch town. Lavinia had come to her aid, and she had to believe soon others would have as well.

Somehow Claudia was in front of her, and all Lemon could hear was her sobs, broken only by apologies. Claudia reached out, but as her fingers skimmed Lemon's skin, she jerked away. "How could you?"

Claudia shook her head, but she had to have known, and that was what Lemon could not make sense of. Her father, the man they had evaded for two decades, brought to her town. It explained every strange apology Claudia had made, but it did not explain everything. And Lemon needed to understand.

"Why? And do not touch me." She took a step away, and Claudia made a choked sound. Only minutes ago, Lemon had been contemplating their life together. Now, she could not see past the moment, past the desire to shake her, to strike her.

"I didn't know when I came," she choked out. "And then I saw you, standing on the edge of the ravine, wet and caught in a sunbeam and I didn't know, not exactly, but you looked so much like him. And I thought about leaving then, but you were falling, and I caught you and I just... Lemon, I couldn't tell you."

Bile crept up her throat. Lies. It had all been lies from the first moment. "That's why you were drawn to me. I share his blood. You are a most accomplished liar, Claudia Auberon. It's nearly impressive, you vile, filthy blood sucker." Claudia winced as though struck, and Lemon was glad. She wanted her to hurt as badly as she was hurting.

"Lemon, please. I am so sorry. I should have told you. I know I should have." She fell to her knees, wrapping her arms around Lemon's legs. "You are the best thing that's ever happened to me, and I was horrified that you would leave me. And I just kept pushing it to the back of my mind, lying to myself, saying you wouldn't recognize each other. I thought it could be quick. That your mothers might not notice. I know it was stupid. It never could have worked, but I just wanted to be cured. I just wanted to be with

171

you." She clutched at the bare skin of Lemon's legs, fingers digging into her tattoos. *Not sweet.*

"Let me go." Lemon had never felt like this, never known the sharp sting of such a large betrayal. All of her dreams fell like grains of sand through her fingers. "You lied to me." She tried to move away, but Claudia held tight.

"Please. Please, don't give up on me."

"Let me go." She needed to get away from her, to make sure her mom was okay. To figure out what they were going to do now that her father knew where she lived.

She did not hear their approach, maybe they had been listening the whole time, but Gunter and Elias reached down, their hands on both of Claudia's arms. Gunter's wig was askew, his make-up ruined. "Come on." He pulled at Claudia and finally she let go.

Lemon almost tumbled over at the sudden release. Claudia's sobs echoed over the square and broke through the din of the crowd as Elias and Gunter led her away. She twisted her neck to look at Lemon. "I'm so sorry."

She continued to stand in the square, unsure of what to do, and it was Fritz that found her. His brown eyes were wide and his cheeks were tear stained.

"Did you know?"

He shook his head. "I still have to help her. I need to go, but your family is at home. The ingredients are still there." And the unspoken question. Would they still help?

She didn't know. All of her thoughts were cruel and vicious, clawing and tearing at the sympathy that usually filled her, making her feel like someone else. "I can't right now, Fritz. I need to see my moms. I need Ruby."

"Okay." He nodded, gravely.

And Lemon turned back towards her home, through the remains of the Founders' Festival, with everything inside of her feeling broken.

How could Claudia do that to her? The words were a constant refrain through her mind. She had to know it would fail. Once she realized Esther and Amaryllis would be there, she must have known, explaining her apologies that morning. Would Lemon have ever known if they hadn't been there? She wasn't sure. It had been so long, her father had become more of a boogeyman than something real. But he had recognized her.

And now her mothers were in danger. She bit the inside of her cheek, refusing to cry anymore, and tried to come up with a plan. But she didn't know. She didn't want to think of Claudia, but she couldn't stop. She was so mad and so hurt, and she understood rage in a way she never had before.

But was it more for Claudia or for her father? She turned towards her house and wondered what she would have done if she was Claudia, afraid and cursed. But she pushed the thoughts away. She wasn't ready for forgiveness.

Her house was quiet, and she was glad no one was crying, though Amaryllis was pale and Esther was red with fury.

"We have to this time," someone said. And she wanted answers, to be told the tale of the night they had left. But she did not turn towards the sitting room where the voice had come from. Instead, she scooped Athena into her arms and headed up the stairs.

The cat curled beside her as she got into bed, pulling the covers up to her chin, trying not to think of the potion ingredients on her dresser, the feeling of teeth on her neck, the laughter, and friendship, and desire she had found in the past few weeks.

And it worked, because none of that was what she dreamt of. Instead, it was car lights on an oak tree in Charleston, blue eyes so full of love and anger. Her mother's sobs and then driving until the sun came up.

She awoke that night in a cold sweat, and she could smell the magic, the sharp scent of charms and wards. Voices still rumbled downstairs. Lavinia and Betta. The townsfolk come to make sure their house was secure. Making up for their inaction.

Lemon wanted answers, but all she could do was sleep.

Chapter Sixteen

The house was still as she poured her cereal, staring out the window. Some of her fury had abated, replaced by the need to do something. Was Julian—Giuseppe—she didn't know what to call him, still in town?

Her heart skipped a beat. If he was gone, so was Claudia. Good. But was it? She was a piece of shit liar, but she had been fleeing the same man her mothers had once fled, and Lemon never asked them questions about the sins they might have committed to free themselves.

She dumped her cereal down the garbage disposal, no longer hungry and paced the rooms of her house. No matter what the reason, she didn't know how to move past the lying. Maybe she could understand her not telling her at first, but how could she keep it up? While they made plans for a life together, Claudia had been lying. Right to her face, without missing a beat.

But what had she expected? Only an accomplished liar would be able to smuggle illegal goods into the country. She should have asked more questions. She was a fool.

She swung for the doorframe and the old house held firm, leaving the wood untouched and her knuckles bleeding. Above her, whoever had spent the night stirred. There was too much anger inside of her to face anyone. All she wanted to do was scream until her lungs ached.

So she grabbed her jacket from the hallway closet and her car keys from where they hung by the door. Hecate's Hollow had not yet woken up. The streets were empty, the remains of the festival cleaned, reminding Lemon of another sleepy town, her back pressed against glass, teeth on her neck.

She pressed her foot to the accelerator of her car and it purred in response, leaving the town and everything in it in her rearview. Without fear for Claudia, she left the top down and the chilled air blew past her, lifting strands of her hair.

Her father. Julian. Giuseppe Diggory. He'd occupied so little of her mind for the past two decades but there he had been, older than the few memories she held of him in her mind and just as violent. Had he actually taken on the moniker Julian or had that just been another of Claudia's lies?

Valley views and the red rock sides of the mountains flew past her. She barely saw them, focused only on the yellow lines of the road zipping past. Lemon let out the scream that had been building inside of her, letting the rushing air take it away. It dulled the roaring beast inside of her but it didn't erase it. She'd never been so angry—or so hurt.

She pulled over into one of the viewing areas along the road and leaned against her pink car, dragging her fingers through her hair. She closed her eyes and turned her head towards the sky, letting the sun beat down on her, burning red beneath her eyelids. When she opened her eyes, the whole word was bathed in white and she pushed off of the car to gaze at the valley below.

Looking from the peaks had always made her feel small in the best way, putting all of her worries in perspective. But today the sense of ease did not come. Still, she stood staring; her knuckles white on the guardrail.

She could hear her phone buzzing against the dashboard of her car, and she turned back. She'd left without a word, consumed with her own rage, but there was still work to be done. Giuseppe knew where they were, and he had only grown more dangerous. He'd cursed Claudia. What was to stop him from doing the same to her mothers?

Just let me know you're okay. I love you.

She stared at Ruby's message until her phone went dark and sighed before responding. How could Claudia be so selfish? All she had to do was tell the truth. Lemon would have still helped her, but she would have never brought him to their town.

Again, unwanted understanding trickled in. Claudia was desperate, and when they'd met, she hadn't known Lemon. She had run, but unlike her mothers, there was a timer on her escape. All of those problems plus the sudden urge to drink human blood, the inability to walk in the sunlight.

And yet none of it excused the lie that put Lemon's whole family in danger. Claudia had made promises about the future to Lemon, slept with her, all the while knowing the truth. Lemon stood for a long time, listening to the sounds of the mountain, broken occasionally by a passing car.

She got back in her car as the sun rose higher in the sky, bathing everything in yellow spring light. Lemon could feel the call of the mountains, the songs of creeping vines and blooming flowers, just begging to be made into potions, but she did not stop.

When she passed a sign for Roanoke, she knew it was time to head home. If nothing else she needed to talk to Fritz. He could have the ingredients. She wasn't that cruel. However mad she might be at Claudia, she wouldn't doom her to a life of servitude to a monster. Her desperate lies would not damn her forever. Lemon owed her that if she owed her anything.

She slowed on the way back, no longer driving at speeds that would have sent her car flying over the mountain if she was not a witch. Everything with Claudia had seemed so fun at first, quite literally something out of a fantasy, her own fantasies. And like all fantasies it had crashed and burned.

But she would make sure this tale did not end in tragedy. She had the whole town behind her. If nothing else, she would make sure her father stayed away for fear of the law, and then Lemon would find a way to move on. Time would move as it always did, and she knew eventually, like everything else, this would be nothing but a memory. She would be no worse off than she had been weeks ago.

The ride had smoothed some of the jagged edges of her betrayal and anger. The town was still calm as she drove through it. No sign of trouble. Elias and his mother were outside, and they waved as she passed but Lemon didn't slow. She loved Elias, but she did not want to hear his sympathy right now.

The lights were off in the Red and White Apothecary. How long until her mothers felt safe again? How long until they actually were? He had been in her town, her sweet, friendly little witch town. She'd spent her whole life avoiding the cities, missing concerts and vacations because of the worry of her mothers. And in the end he had found them without even meaning to.

She pulled into her driveway and gave her car a pat as she got out. The engine was warm beneath her fingers. The smell of tea wafted from the open kitchen window and she found her mothers and Ruby inside. They said nothing as she pulled off her coat, and then her shoes, leaving them in a pile in the mudroom.

Her footsteps sounded against the hardwood as she walked through the kitchen, pouring herself a cup of coffee and putting bread in the toaster.

"What happened the night we left?" she asked, finally voicing the question that had been sitting in her throat for twenty years.

Her mothers stared at each other, silently communicating in the way only they could. At the table Ruby froze, mouth slightly agape. And then Amaryllis nodded to her wife.

"I tried to kill him." Esther settled into the chair beside Ruby, her hands around a steaming cup of tea. "And I failed, but there was head trauma and from what I've heard he lost his memories for a while."

"But magic doesn't work on Hathornes." Lemon chewed her lip. She had asked the question but she wasn't sure she wanted to hear any of this.

Esther shook her head, and Amaryllis moved beside her, placing a gentle hand on her shoulder. "No, and that's how he kept your mother trapped for so long. But magic is not the only way to kill a man. I poisoned him, and I beat him, and I thought he would die on the kitchen floor when I left." There was no regret in her voice.

"Mom," Ruby choked out, her emerald eyes brimming with tears.

"It was nothing he didn't deserve. Lemon was too young to remember when it started but I have heard plenty since then. I remember the first day you brought Lemon home from school. Amaryllis came to pick her up and she was bruised, hurt beyond what simple magic could quickly heal. He would have killed her, eventually."

"I'm sorry I didn't stop him myself, Lemon. You are like Esther more than you are like me. You are fearless and brave and you help whenever you can."

Lemon abandoned her coffee to hug her mother. "I wish he had died."

"I thought he had for a while. He was in the hospital for a long time, I heard later. And he didn't remember us. His memories came back slowly over the years but he had a new life by then. I do not know if he looked for us. It wasn't long before we'd cut all our ties. I had no way to check in on him."

Lemon had feared that she might have sympathy when she heard what happened to her father but none came, only deeper hatred. "Do you think he'll come back?"

A tear slipped down Amaryllis's cheek, and she brushed it away. "The way he looked at you yesterday, I think there's a good chance."

"What do we do?"

"We stick together. We are a family and he is no one. I know you are mad at Claudia, and so am I, Lemon, but he is still out there ruining girls' lives. I will speak to the sheriff today. There is a reason we moved to a witch town. There is no one to protect him here. If nothing else, what he has done is illegal."

They all jumped at a knock on the door, and Lemon stood. Whatever was out there, she had brought this to her family, and it was recognition of her that had brought Giuseppe down upon them again.

But it was only Fritz. He looked like he hadn't slept at all since she'd seen him last. His clothes were ruffled, his hair in disarray and indigo half circles laid like bruises under his eyes.

"You can have the ingredients. Whatever you need," Lemon told him, holding the door open.

But he didn't move. In fact, his eyes were vacant, and he made no acknowledgement of her words. Panic rose in Lemon, her mind cataloging everything that could have happened to him, fearing another curse. And for a second her anger dissolved like mist in the sun.

"Fritz." She placed her hand upon his arm.

He shivered at her touch and his hand disappeared inside his jacket, pulling out a folded sheet of paper from the interior pocket. "She's gone." He took Lemon's hand and put the note in it.

Her stomach dropped as she opened it. She did not know Claudia's handwriting but the delicate, loopy letters fit the woman she must have once been.

I love you. Do not come looking. Stay safe.

Lemon read the note three times and then she refolded it on the already worn lines. How many times had Fritz read it?

"I don't blame you, Lemon, truly I don't, but she's my sister." Lemon did not speak, unable to form any words. Her mouth was dry, her hands shook. His next words were barely above a whisper. "*Please*. Help."

Desperation laced his pleas and rattled inside of Lemon. Julian had gotten what he wanted. Most of the curse had been a cruel joke, but all of it had been a means to an end. A woman who could not leave him, forced to do his bidding. He wanted from Claudia what he had wanted from Amaryllis—control. And maybe it was the deep buried piece of her that still cared, maybe it was her nature, or maybe it was the injustice of it all but she found herself wanting to say yes.

But she couldn't bring herself to move. Doing this would mean seeing her father, standing against him. And it was different than standing against the shadowy figure of Julian. It was cutting into an old wound, healed and scarred, ripping it open again. Lemon had always been compassionate, but she wasn't sure she'd ever been brave.

"I'm in." Ruby's voice came from behind Lemon and Fritz fell apart. Ruby rushed forward, catching him in her arms before he fell and they both sank down on the porch. Athena slipped through Lemon's legs, curling her tiny black body beside them.

The compassion between them was nearly palpable. Lemon expected a rush of acidic jealousy but it didn't come. Instead, she pondered the future. And the question was, what could be done?

And then a new emotion did spring to life inside of her, shame, cold and sudden, filling her veins like ice water.

If her anger had not overtaken her, if fear of her father had been greater than her frustration with Claudia she could have done what Fritz had meant to do. If she had been brave instead of furious, she could have hit him, gotten the blood they needed. She shook it off. There was no good down that path.

She helped pull Fritz to his feet and led him inside. Amaryllis already had a cup of tea waiting. The smell of calming herbs and the thrum of magic vibrated off of the cup. He slipped into the wooden chair, wiping at his eyes.

Ruby stood in the doorway, sadness etched on her face, for only a moment before she composed herself. The only sign of her discomfort left was her arms wrapped around her torso.

Would Lemon really allow her sister to do this? She felt for Fritz, and despite everything she knew no one deserved what happened to Claudia, but she couldn't save her at the expense of her sister.

Esther sat beside Fritz, taking his hand in hers, and Amaryllis moved around both of them like a nervous chicken. It was all so surreal. Memories of the last twenty four hours, hell, the last month, rolled and collided in her mind. She'd gotten all the pieces of the puzzle of Claudia but she still didn't understand the picture it made.

With a deep sigh, Ruby moved towards Fritz and Lemon reached for her, though she hadn't meant to. Her fingers grasped her sister's elbow and blue eyes met green.

"It's dangerous, Rubes. And I'm frightened."

Nothing moved behind Ruby's eyes, they were nothing but shards of frozen emerald and Lemon was not sure if it was fear or anger that she held in them. "I know. And I'm furious that I'm having to do it. I'm mad that I trusted her and she betrayed us. But..." She pulled at the strands of her hair, straightening them. "I'm not doing it for her, Lemon. I'm doing it for you. For all the things he did to you and Amaryllis. She's my mother, too. And I'll never forgive him. I haven't, not for a single day."

Her sister intended to kill her father. Fear ran through Lemon's veins, chilling her to the bones.

Ruby lowered her voice, and she moved further away from the kitchen and its inhabitants. "As far as anyone will know I'm going to help a friend. The incident in the square was public. Everyone saw him attack our mother." She reached down, scooping up Athena, holding her tighter than a normal cat would allow. "I won't spend the rest of my life terrorized by that man, Lemon. I won't."

There was so much courage in her sister. Lemon knew she'd never possess as much tenacity as Ruby, but she *was* full of love. Her mothers had filled her with it from the moment they had driven away from her father. And she hoped the two might be similar enough. That in a pinch, love might substitute for bravery.

She nearly threw her arms around her sister but feared Athena's retribution. Instead, she held her by the shoulders. "I can't promise you'll always be safe but you'll never be in danger alone, Ruby. Never."

She smiled, the shards of ice in her eyes melting into tears. "Okay. But, Lemon..."

"You don't need to explain. I know what you intend." She gave Ruby's shoulders a squeeze. "I'll go get the things for scrying."

She left Ruby and headed upstairs, towards the third bedroom where they kept the things that didn't fit elsewhere—old chairs in need of mending, tables they'd picked up on the side of the road, several mid-century ceramic cats, boxes of photo albums. The treasures of the third room seemed almost endless, though they couldn't compare to what was in the attic.

She knelt in front of a chest, breathing in the smell of cedar and leather that held it together. It required no key, or it had once but it had been lost before their mothers had moved out. The chest creaked as it opened, silver chains with crystals at the end swinging from the top.

She rifled through the maps at the bottom. Her first instinct was that they must be close, but that was ridiculous. They could have hopped on a plane and flown across the Atlantic already. She wasn't sure their scrying was that good, so she grabbed two maps; one of the southeast and one of the country.

The sun shone through the crystals and she ran her fingers over them, lapis lazuli, amethyst, quartz, rhodochrosite. They were gorgeous, a rainbow of magic. She watched them until they stopped swinging and hung still in the sunlight. She pulled the rhodochrosite from its hook, running her fingers over the smooth pink rock.

She stood and nearly tumbled over the chest, startled by Fritz in the doorway. "Oh, sweet baby Dolly Parton, you scared me."

He laughed. "Sorry. I was heading for the bathroom but this room is thick with magic. I got distracted."

"Oh, yeah." Lemon motioned for him to step inside. "It was mine and Ruby's room when we were little, back when we had no idea what we were doing. You can see all the burn marks on the floor. And Ruby has this thing with buying stuff that she says she can feel magic on." She pointed to the ceramic cats. "And I don't know. It's just all our stuff."

"It's neat." He picked up an ancient book, the leather cover worn and frayed. "I love old spell books."

"Yeah, me too." Lemon admitted. She had collected them for a few years. "You can look through them sometime, if you want."

"Thanks." He put down the book and took a step closer to Lemon. "If we find her I hope you'll hear her out. She's not—"

Putting up a hand to silence him, Lemon pushed by. "I can't listen to this right now, Fritz. I just can't."

"But..."

"No. I'm going to help but that's all I'm agreeing to."

Chapter Seventeen

The map of the Smokies was spread under Ruby's hands. She traced the mountain range and then ran her thumb down to the Atlantic. Lemon knew her sister missed the rest of the world more than she did. Would she leave if the threat of her father was gone?

But it didn't sting the way it once might have. She could see her and Fritz, some condo highrise in Atlanta or New York. And Lemon could live without fear as well. She could fly out to see her. She would still be a witch, there would still be that feeling of otherness, but she would not have to constantly watch her back.

"It will work better with some of your blood," Ruby said, holding her hand out to Fritz.

He pulled out the chair beside her, sat on it backwards, and held out his hand, palm up. Ruby slid his sleeve up his arm and picked up the dagger from the table. He barely winced as she cut a shallow wound across his forearm. It dripped onto the crystal and then her thumb slid over it, and the wound stitched shut.

"Ready?" Ruby asked and Lemon nodded. They intertwined their fingers, murmuring the spell. Magic warmed Lemon as it ran through her, like soup on a chilly day, comforting and filling.

Fritz backed away, watching with Amaryllis and Esther, who had their arms wrapped around each other. Esther placed her free hand on his shoulder as the crystal swung over the paper, wide arcs from one side to the other.

The sisters continued to chant. Lemon tightened her grip on Ruby's fingers as the magic flowed through the room. It was thick and metallic, leaving the taste of old coins on her tongue. The crystal pendulum slowed as the blood ran to the bottom. It swung over Kentucky, then Virginia, and finally Pennsylvania.

They chanted louder, their voices flowing together like a song and the blood finally fell, landing near the border of Pennsylvania and New York. It was at least 400 miles away, but the blood did not advance. For the moment, at least, they were not moving.

"Okay." Ruby stared at the map, like it might have more secrets to uncover, and Fritz took the seat Lemon vacated. "Well..."

There was a knock on the door and Lemon went for it, eager to get out of the room and away from thoughts of what the next few days would hold. Her courage waned with each moment, replaced with fear of hunting the bogeyman who had haunted her for decades.

It was Elias, his dark hair sticking up at odd angles, and his glasses perched near the bottom of his nose. "Are you okay?" He looked her over. "I'm sorry I didn't come sooner. But the town is behind you. My mother is leading a citizens' force to monitor the streets."

Lemon didn't expect the tears that sprang to her eyes. She tried to blink them away, but they fell, splashing hot on her cheeks. "I love you guys so much."

"I saw Fritz's car out front. Was it really your father? That's the word going around. Everyone's real sorry they didn't stop him."

Lemon glanced behind her, headed onto the porch and sat on the swing. "Yeah, it was my dad. Julian was my dad, and she knew the whole time."

Elias sat beside her and pulled her towards him, stroking down her back. "Where is she?" There was a mixture of sympathy and revulsion in his voice.

"She went to him."

Elias stiffened under Lemon, his hand stilling on her back. Silence grew. What had happened was a horror, even Lemon could see that. Laughing, joking Claudia, tethered to a monster. Would Lemon have helped her if she had known? She wasn't sure, no matter how many times she turned it over in her mind.

A cardinal flew onto the porch railing, chirping at them. Another joined it, a sparrow and then a magnolia warbler. She did not know what it meant until Elias whispered to her. "You're practically vibrating with magic."

She laughed, and the birds scattered, flying off to land in the yard as more joined them. She missed hiking the mountains. Not in the way she had with the others; she missed being alone in her own element, feeling the magic, watching rabbits hop from the tall grasses of the valleys, hawks glide over the peaks, and minnows dart through the streams.

She missed being Lemon, free and connected to the earth. "Fritz asked for help and Ruby agreed. We scried. She's in Pennsylvania. I'm going with them."

"I'll go too," Elias said. His brown eyes locked onto Lemon's, and she knew there was no room to argue. He was part of this and they could use the help. But what would she do if something happened to Elias? Sweet Elias who watched Hallmark movies with her and had a secret collection of Star Wars figurines.

She pushed off the bench, needing to move, so full of frustration she couldn't sit still. "I'm so mad at her Elias." She paced the porch, the ancient wood creaking beneath her feet.

He didn't look at Lemon, instead he kept his eyes on the gathering of birds in the yard. "You have every right to be."

"But?"

"But she must have been terrified. She said she felt drawn to you. She thought she was coming to some savior and then... Well, you look so much like him. She must have realized before she knew you at all. Then she was deep in the lie."

"But she brought him here." She pounded her fist on the porch railing and it cracked, spider web fissures glimmering with magic spread out under her skin. Her frustration wasn't over the initial lie. She could understand why she hadn't said anything to Lemon before. But she couldn't excuse the rest of it.

Again, something like guilt crept into Lemon's chest, spreading like frost across glass, its icy tendrils plunging into her. She'd seen the fear and guilt on Claudia's face so many times, growing worse once they had solidified their plan. And she'd been so afraid to lose her she hadn't stopped to ask, not in a real way.

If she had made her feel safe, if Claudia had really trusted her, would she have told the truth? Anger flared, melting the guilt. Hadn't she done enough? Hadn't helping a stranger been enough.

The door opened and Ruby and Fritz came out. There was so much of him that reminded her of Claudia and then so many differences, his skin, tanned and golden and hers pale, his eyes brown and hers amber, his eyebrows bushy, his arms thick with muscle. But the almost crooked smile was the same, the thick brown hair. What would it be like to see Claudia without the curse?

Elias pulled Fritz into a hug, and Ruby looked across their shoulders at Lemon. They didn't need to embrace for understanding to pass between them. There would be healing later, if they made it out of this, time to find answers and understanding. Time would move as it always did and with it would come the dulling of the aches that plagued her now.

But the truth was, Lemon had never contemplated death. She'd thought of it in the same way all people did, knowing one day the world would continue to turn without her. But she hadn't dwelled on it, hadn't wondered if she'd done enough—she didn't think she had. Would her father kill her? Maybe not, but would she live if he killed someone else that came with her?

Should she put her foot down and refuse to let the others join her? Should she scream at Ruby and Elias until they stayed safe in the Hollow? She was too chicken to do it; she knew that. Without someone at her side, she'd never confront her father.

When Elias let Fritz go his eyes glittered with tears in the midday sun. He pushed himself up onto the porch railing, his legs swinging just above the floor. "You should know she wasn't always like this. When we were kids Claudia was like the sun. She was so bright, and so full of life, so funny. And life, it just wore her down. Our mom did the best she could, but when you're poor, that's working all the time. And then when I needed hormones she worked even harder to make sure I could have them. She was a good mom but the cost of living doesn't give a shit how much you want to be with your kids. And it wore us down too, until Claudia was desperate and alone at college, feeling unlike all the rich kids." He ran his hand through his hair, pulling at the roots. "I don't know where I'm going with this, but I wanted you all to know that I know what she did was wrong, but Claudia is good. Deep down, underneath all the bullshit life has piled on her, she's good and she's kind. She's just so fucking broken."

Elias clapped him on the knee. "Life's a bitch, man. We've all done things we regret, the terrible stuff you keep locked away, and only turn over in the dead of night. I'm going to help, if only for the little girl she once was, the little girl Lemon was when she showed up here, knobby-kneed with pockets full of lizards."

Fritz nodded. "I know I'm asking a lot. More than I should ask of people who barely know me, but it's my sister. And she did everything for us. She'd send money back. She helped me pay my doctor's bills."

Though her throat was dry and her palms hurt from how tightly she clenched her fists, Lemon forced herself to speak. "Witches stick together, Fritz. We'll get her out of there." She glanced towards Ruby who nodded back. "And we'll end this."

He looked up towards Ruby, her hair gilded gold in the sunlight. "He's more dangerous than you know."

"That's where you're mistaken. Everyone in this house knows exactly how dangerous that man is. And I'm done running. You know what it's like to watch your family suffer. Well, so do I. And I'm done watching the people I love hide. He came back, and he'd used his years away to terrorize more witches. I'm done. I don't know my plan yet. I don't know exactly what I'm going to do but Giuseppe cannot win this."

Lemon's heart pounded so hard and fast she worried it would break through her chest, but Ruby's words emboldened her. She thought of freedom, of days without worry, of her mothers no longer looking over their shoulders. She knew there should be something inside of her, some hole that she longed for a father to fill, but it wasn't there. It had been filled by Amaryllis and all the townsfolk who had loved her just the way she was—Dr. Mills dragging a Christmas tree up the steps their first year there, Elias's mother feeding them dinner when their mothers were too busy trying to keep the shop afloat to come home, Betta McCray lending her anything she needed from her shed whenever she started some half-assed home project, Lavinia plying her with sweets.

"Lavinia." Lemon let out a squeak. "She'll know. She has to know." So many dead husbands it had bought her a shop. "Y'all figure out a route, see if you can narrow down where they are, and I'll be back."

She ran inside, pulling on her shoes, and then she was running down the lane, bolstered by having a plan, some semblance of hope. Wind blew through her hair and the grass was springy under her feet. She may not have the sense god gave a goose, but she was going to do this, however stupid it was.

Betta McCray was outside of her house, clearly gossiping with her neighbor Emmy, who leaned over the white picket fence between them. They both turned towards Lemon, eyes going wide, but she just waved and kept walking. "I can't. Sorry! I'll be back!" Soon enough the whole town would be gossiping. Good, let them all spread the story of a strange man attacking her in the square. Hopefully, they'd harbor her if she killed him.

And really, should it be illegal to kill your own father? Obviously yes, generally, but what if he really sucked? He brought her into this world, couldn't she take him out? She was sure there was a saying about something similar.

She ran up Main Street, her dread turning into mania, her thoughts becoming a pinpoint. Save her sister. Get Ruby through this. She couldn't stop her. Ruby helped the people she cared about. She always had. But Lemon could protect her.

And while Claudia hovered at the edge of her mind, it was Ruby that occupied the bulk of her thoughts. Ruby, who would always go down swinging for her. Lemon had to be strong enough to do the same.

Lavinia wasn't at her bakery but the girl behind the counter, in the way that small town folks do, told her she was at her house. The walk up to Sycamore Lane could have been time to talk herself out of this. There were certainly those who would say it wasn't wise, but she kept walking, her mind made up beyond changing. Anything for Ruby.

Lavinia was out in her garden, her back hunched over fragrant herbs and straggling flowers. Lemon paused, taking a moment to fall in love with the mountains all over again, season after season, each one with its own kind of beauty. And, though spring was the best of all, bursting with color and life, the sounds of birds and the soft thumps of newborn hearts reaching out to her, reminding her that life marches on, fall was still beautiful. Fall was when things changed, when life slowed and she planned and prepared for winter. And this year there was so much to prepare for.

She cleared her throat, so as not to startle Lavinia, before pushing open her gate and got a beaming smile in return.

"Hey sweetness! I've been thinking of you all day and hoping you'd show up. Didn't want to be pushy." She straightened, dusting soil off her knees. "Come on in."

Her home was a Victorian like Lemon's, but her green thumb was evident in every inch. Even in October, flowers spilled from boxes outside the windows, roses crept up the sides of the porch, and vines clung to the sides, giving the house the air of something living.

Inside were more cats than Lemon could count, sprawled in spots of sunlight, batting bits of strings, and making Lemon wish she had a few more at her house. None of them darted at her entrance, a testament to the care of Lavinia, or just the fact that they'd seen Lemon enough times to decide she was no threat.

Lavinia continued to her sitting room, full of thick rugs and velvet pillows in deep jewel tones. The plants continued through the house, hanging high enough to keep them away from the cats, their vines wound around knick knacks and picture frames.

"Settle in. I'll get tea." She disappeared through an arched doorway.

Lemon took a seat in a mustard yellow chair and was immediately rewarded with an orange tabby in her lap. She rubbed under his chin until Lavinia returned with a tray of shortbread cookies and sweet tea.

"You've got the look of someone fixin' to ask a question." Lavinia sipped on her tea as cats threaded themselves between her feet.

"I am, but I'm not quite sure how to start." She fiddled with the hem of her shorts until the cat in her lap slapped at her fingers. "It's about all your... erm."

"About all my dead husbands?" Lavinia offered, and she wasn't quite grinning but she wasn't mourning either. "For you, and for your mama who arrived here still bruised and broken, I'll tell you something others have only guessed at. My first husband left, and I was too ashamed to admit it, so I reported him missing. I loved him, in the way you do when you're young and everything is new, and having him leave tore me up. The next two seemed nice, like men do when they know who they are, and know if you saw it you'd run screaming. And I've spent a lot of time asking myself how I didn't notice twice, how I didn't see the warning signs before they were flinging me around the room like a rag doll. Now I stick to cats and every time I get lonely I buy a new one. The cost of litter is high and they'll ruin your furniture, but I'm a witch, so it all evens out."

Lemon couldn't help but laugh. "And now they're dead."

"Indeed, they are. I was luckier than your mama, stuck with a Hathorne."

Lemon cringed, but she could trust Lavinia to help her. After all, she was admitting to at least two felonies. "That was my father in the square, and now he has Claudia. I'm so goddam mad at her for lying, but I have to stop him. Except he's a Hathorne."

Lavinia sipped her tea, sat it down, and wiped her mouth on a paper napkin before answering. "Well, that don't require nothing but a little extra thinking. You can't use spells on them, and potions are a gray area that trend towards no, but if you stay medicinal, you're good. Magic doesn't work *on* them, but it sure works around them. I've got some books on it." She stood up, careful of the cats at her feet, and walked over to an enormous oak bookshelf. "Go to my desk and grab a notepad. I've got so many ideas."

By the time Lemon headed home, her head felt like it may have grown a few sizes, packed full of knowledge by Lavinia, who knew herbs and potions better than any witch Lemon had ever encountered. She'd been interested in Lemon's powers, asking her to help with a few things she couldn't quite figure out. By the end of two hours, Lemon couldn't wait to return. She had so much to learn.

She'd made simple spells, creams and salves for the apothecary, but Lavinia had opened a whole new world to her, full of things she'd never imagined. Lavinia knew how to push magic to its limits.

At their house, Ruby was on the couch, a joint burning in her fingers and tarot spread out on the coffee table before her. She was frowning at whatever she saw. Elias's laughter boomed from the kitchen along with the delicious smell of butternut squash and rosemary.

Fritz peeked out, an apron around his waist, and Lemon gave him a thumbs up. "I think I know what to do. Have they moved?"

"No. They're still in Pennsylvania. We can leave tomorrow."

"The sooner the better," Lemon said, making a mental list of what she wanted to pack, the herbs she needed to grab from the apothecary, the dagger she kept tucked under her mattress. And she was frightened, as anyone would be, but she was hopeful too. If she got this right, she could free her whole family. Weeks ago she'd dreamed of pushing her magic to the limit, now she wasn't sure there was one. Without the weight of her father, what could ever hold her down?

Chapter Eighteen

Watching Fritz was giving Lemon anxiety. He'd already made three laps around the house, and the sun was not yet fully over the horizon, painting everything in hues of pink and orange. Usually, when she woke up early enough, she enjoyed the sunrise, but his constant footsteps and the mewing of Athena at his feet was setting her on edge.

She had the potions, brews, and tonics Lavinia had told her about. She'd stayed up late, grinding herbs, digging soil, boiling and mixing until her house smelled stronger than the apothecary. Speaking of, how was she going to pay her mortgage this month? Maybe she'd ask Claudia for a loan in exchange for saving her life. She'd seen her shoes, she had the cash.

She pulled a drag on the very secret cigarette she kept in her bedside drawer and tried to use her mind to bore a hole into Fritz's back as he started yet another lap around the house. They were packed. Three suitcases were piled in the back of Fritz's SUV. Now they were just waiting on Ruby to find the old atlas she was looking for and they would go.

She dropped the cigarette onto the ground and put it out with her shoe, flicked it into the garbage can, and sat down on her steps. Elias came out the front door and Athena darted back into the safety of the house. He sat beside her.

"You ready for this?" Elias asked.

Lemon forced herself to nod. "I just hope we can find her." They had the town name but that barely narrowed it down. Would the scrying work well enough to find out exactly where he had Claudia? And then when they found her would she come? She was still under the thrall of the curse, bound to Julian, as Lemon had decided to think of him. She couldn't think of him as her father, there were too many emotions wrapped up in it. He was Julian, criminal and kidnapper of Claudia.

"It's been a long time since I've been out of the mountains." Elias picked at a worn spot on his jeans.

"Just don't let anyone know you're a witch." It wasn't illegal, it shouldn't matter, but she didn't trust the world or the people in it. All it took was one bigot, and maybe a group of his idiot friends, and they would have more trouble than they needed.

The door creaked open. "Okay. I'm ready." Ruby had the old atlas tucked under her arm and a coffee in her hand.

Fritz stopped his pacing, walked across the yard, and kissed Ruby so hard she nearly dropped her coffee in her effort to return his enthusiasm. Something caught in Lemon's chest, but she refused to dwell on it. They broke apart, Ruby's face nearly as red as her hair, and got into the car.

Lemon and Elias were in the back seat, and the smell of herbs permeated the entire SUV, until Fritz rolled down the window and the grassy smell of the mountains blew through.

Highway 81 would take them most of the way to Pennsylvania. Lemon had left Hecate's Hollow before, but rarely further than a town or two over and never out of the mountains. Not that they were exactly going to flat land, but it wasn't long before she no longer recognized the surrounding peaks, until the town names on the exit signs became unfamiliar.

Was she really doing this? Was she crossing state lines to save a woman who had lied to her time and time again? But she'd also fallen on her knees, begging Lemon for forgiveness. Lemon thought of all the times she'd screwed up in her life. What if she'd never met Ruby? What if her mother had stayed, or worse been killed by her father? Where would Lemon have ended up?

When she was a teenager and she'd been mad at a girl at school—she could barely remember why now—Amaryllis had told her you don't have to forget to forgive. And Esther always told her holding hate in your heart only poisoned yourself. She wasn't ready for forgiveness, but she wasn't used to hate, and truth be told, that wasn't what she felt now. Once the dust had settled, and she wasn't fuming with anger, she knew that what she really felt was hurt and betrayal and while those felt a lot like hate, while it was easy enough to let them fester into it, she couldn't. Not if she was going to save Claudia and end a lifetime of terror.

But there was a pocket of her heart, her very soul even, carved out to hold hate, and all of it was for Julian, as it had always been, since she had been old enough to understand the world. Even when her father had been smiling and laughing, she'd never opened up to him like other children did, knowing one wrong word would set him off again.

That he had become a smuggler, or whatever the word for it was—she wasn't exactly up on the terminology of criminal enterprises—didn't surprise her at all. To others he was charming, handsome and jovial. And he was smart. He'd seen the way it went for other Hathornes, either full of hate, going into law enforcement or just posting diatribes online about witches, or the other way, ignoring their magic, pretending it wasn't part of them. He chose the middle ground of manipulation. His magic let him find a witch in any crowd, and he used his charms to manipulate them. So why stop at witches? And he apparently hadn't.

"You alright?" Elias turned from staring out the window of the back seat. Under his glasses his eyes had heavy bags. She knew he'd argued with Gunter about coming, but he was human and they wouldn't risk it.

Lemon shrugged, glancing towards Fritz, who'd been chatting with Ruby for most of the trip. He had the decency to pretend not to hear her when she replied, "I really thought she and I could have something."

"I won't tell you what you have to put up with, Lemonade, but if we do this, you've got the rest of your life. You aren't even thirty. You might find things look different without all of this over us."

"And I might find they don't."

He turned back to the window, watching the interstate signs zip past them, and she thought he wasn't going to answer. When he did, she could barely hear him. "No one will blame you either way."

Ruby twisted in her seat, the seat belt cutting into her shoulder. "I love you, Lem."

"I love you too." There wasn't much more to say. She could talk over what had happened with Claudia until her throat hurt, but she didn't want to. It was all too messy. She was mad and hurt and sad and worried. So she just let her emotions flow as they came, not fighting them.

The most prominent was frustration. She was tired of talking about it. Why did she need to have a relationship with Claudia? Why did they care? She was helping her, wasn't she? "Okay, so what do we think? They're probably at a hotel, right? Something nice?"

"I hope not. It's only going to be harder if we have to get past desk security." Fritz passed a slow moving Volvo, his hands tight on the steering wheel. "I should have dealt with him years ago. I knew he was bad the moment he showed up."

"Don't blame yourself," Elias said, echoing what Lemon was thinking. "Pieces of shit are always insidious."

As they left North Carolina, they pulled into a rest stop diner. The whole thing smelled like grease and syrup and the lights were too bright, but the waitress was pleasant enough and called everyone hun or sugar.

Lemon ordered a club sandwich and a plate of pancakes with bacon for Ruby. It was several more minutes before she made her way in from the car where she'd been scrying again. "Same town, but I got a closer read. It's not in the town proper though." She pulled out her phone, zooming in on a map.

"A house, hopefully," Fritz said, practically finishing his glass of sweet tea in one gulp. "It would be easier that way."

Everything was moving too fast, and Lemon wished she could slow down time. Claudia had turned up and upended her entire life in a matter of weeks. Now she was traveling to Pennsylvania of all places. Her sister seemed half in love with the man sitting across from her, and she couldn't blame her. Fritz was everything she would have chosen for Ruby.

Lemon dipped a fry deep into a ramekin of ranch and watched it drip off the end. She had explosive potions, potions to create thick smoke, she had her own magic to use on Orlo. But she wished her mother was there to help them track, though she'd never seen her do it on a human. They hadn't even asked Amaryllis, knowing it would be too much.

"If it's still sunny, we'll need cloud coverage to get her out," she told Ruby, glancing around at the other patrons, but no one was paying them attention. She stretched her arms over her head and caught a glimpse of Elias. "You okay?"

"Hmm?" He glanced up from his plate. "Yeah, just wondering how exactly I went from working at the Shop 'N Go to chasing down an international thief and his vampire companion. You know, I'm barely a witch."

His magic had never been strong, but it hadn't mattered to Lemon. "We all deserve a vacation after this."

He laughed, loud enough to draw the attention of the waitress, who came over to refill Fritz's cup. "The most I want to do after this is go camping. I'm not leaving the Hollow again for years to come."

"I was thinking..." Fritz stirred the ice in his drink, looking anywhere but at Ruby. "I know my mom isn't a witch, but I might try to get her to move to the Hollow. She'll resist at first but it'd be good to know she was somewhere that people would look out for her."

"They're hiring at the Shop 'N Go, and we're probably the only place in America you make enough at the grocery store to pay your rent."

Lemon took a bite of previously frozen burger and listened to the conversation develop. Did Fritz really want to set down roots here? She looked at Ruby, laughing around her mouthful of pancakes. But maybe it wasn't her, or at least not entirely. How many hours had he spent at their house in the last month? Maybe he was just a man who wanted to see his own mother thrive the way Amaryllis had.

They ate and paid and piled back into the car. Thirty minutes in, Lemon's ass was completely asleep. She closed her eyes, leaning her head back against the foam headrest. The hum of the road nearly covered the pop music coming from the front of the car. She went over spells in her head, making sure she had them memorized.

Less than four hours until they made it to the spot Ruby had circled on the map. They'd need to stop again, try to find a local map, scry again. Lemon's thoughts strayed, wondering what her mothers were doing, thinking of all the flowers she'd failed to pick and dry this year. And then, when she was half asleep, lulled by the movement of the car, she thought of Claudia, the way she had looked in the passenger seat of Lemon's Thunderbird, the curve of her smile and the way her hair curled at the ends.

And the bright, hot, alive feeling Lemon had felt whenever she was with her reared its head. Lemon had spent most of her life just this side of afraid, only feeling alive when she wandered the mountains, always putting the excitement of life on hold. But not with Claudia, whatever else she was, whatever the curse or her own choices had made her into, she had filled Lemon with life. She didn't know what each moment would hold, and it excited her, made her yearn for things she hadn't ever dared to want before.

Her thoughts became more disjointed as she drifted off to sleep, dreaming of vampires, of falling from mountains, and soaring with birds. She dreamed of her mother and the night they had fled, her father's hand reaching for her, always reaching. She dreamt of garnet lips and soft fingers, pale skin turned golden by the flow of blood, of steam from mountain springs and rivers flowing endlessly. And she dreamed of fear, the frigid hand of it around her heart.

When she awoke, it was to Elias prodding her gently, his glasses slightly askew as though he'd been sleeping as well. It was still light out, the autumn sun only beginning to give away its domain to the moon, but they were no longer on Highway 81. Wherever they were was smaller, the road surrounded by trees, red maple and white ash.

Ruby was out of the car, leaning against a wide tree trunk and staring at something on her phone. Fritz paced, doing the same.

"We lost signal and must have taken a wrong turn. Fritz isn't sure where we are," Elias explained. "We were trying to find somewhere that might have a map of the Poconos."

Lemon nodded, still pulling herself out of sleep, and opened the car door. It was quiet, no sounds of highway or human life anywhere nearby. "Any luck?"

Ruby shook her head, red curls bobbing. "I'm trying to look at the downloaded map and see where we are, but we might have to just start driving until we get a phone signal because I'm shit at this."

Her sister looked steady, much steadier than Lemon felt, which was impressive considering she knew she intended to kill Julian. "Are you nervous?" she asked, coming over to peer across her shoulder, but she'd been asleep for an hour and could offer no help.

Wind whipped through the trees as Ruby shoved her phone into her pocket, and it was strong and sudden enough that Lemon suspected it wasn't natural but her sister's magic, giving away just how nervous she really was. "Yeah. I mean, I'm not second guessing myself, I could write an entire novel on the reasons I want to kill that man, but I'm frightened. I can't take it back once it's done. And, I'm not him. I don't know what I'm doing and I'm scared I'll hesitate."

What was there to say? This was all uncharted territory. Lemon did not know where to begin or any words to say to comfort Ruby. They had lived like wood nymphs, traipsing through the forest, reading cards, mixing potions. They had never used their magic like a weapon. Murder had to change a person. Who would they be when they returned? Would the Hollow still feel like home? She had no answers to any of those questions, and part of her wanted to turn and run back to the comfort of their mothers' arms, to hide under the covers like a child, to let this become someone else's problem.

Instead, she knelt on the ground with Ruby's phone, pulling sticks and leaves towards her. She cleared a patch of soil and traced a rudimentary map in the earth. She thought of Claudia, pulling her picture into her mind, all the beautiful things she had helped Lemon to feel.

Her mind and her magic spread out, reaching towards Claudia, and Lemon murmured a spell. The leaves fluttered, dancing across the forest floor. The map she had created twisted through the soil, inching further away from Lemon before coming to an abrupt stop.

A leaf at the end of the winding street crumbled to dust and in its place was a green sprout, its leaves turned towards the sun.

"Shit, Lemon." Ruby knelt down, comparing Lemon's map to the one on her phone, her eyes narrowed in concentration. "I think we found her."

Terror moved down Lemon's spine, making her shiver. There were so many things to fear at the end of this journey. Not just Julian, that fear was slippery and dull, though she knew it shouldn't be. She had feared him for so long that even now it lacked urgency. The fear of Claudia was hot and raw, mixed with feelings she could not name and did not wish to explore. Julian had long ago lost his hold on her heart, but Claudia had held it so recently, and she had crushed it in her fingers with deceit. Yet it still beat, traitorously, in Lemon's chest, buzzing with anticipation.

Fritz made his way over to them, casting dark shadows across the ground. "She's my sister," he said in response to a question no one asked.

"And Julian is my father. Fate is cruel, isn't she." Lemon stood, brushing the leaves off her legs. "My mother always said it's the one thing we cannot escape."

He put out his hand, helping Ruby to her feet. Elias was leaning against the car, his expression far away. Looking at him, Lemon regretted letting him come. But they would need the help.

They crowded back into the SUV. Lemon wasn't sure she'd ever spent as much time in cars as she had the last few months. She walked around town and most of her driving was for pleasure, just to feel the wind through her hair and the beauty of being alone.

A few miles down the road, the trees gave way to open fields. Minutes later Ruby was able to get a phone signal. She found a spot on the map that matched the one Lemon had made. Less than half an hour away.

There was a collective intake of breath as the automated voice directed them to take a left. What had they gotten themselves into? Lemon's heart beat faster in her chest and she wiped her clammy palms on her pants.

This was both the stupidest and bravest thing she'd ever done. The world's bravest idiot. She stared out the windshield, wondering what it would be like to be born normal, to not have magic running through her veins, for witches and Hathornes to be talking points she could rant about for clout on social media, if none of it was her life.

But it was her life, and the road continued to disappear into the rearview while danger drew ever closer.

Chapter Nineteen

They almost missed the turn as they drove downhill. The entrance was tucked away behind rows of trees and lush bushes, dense with leaves. The driveway was barely more than a dirt trail, most of it grown over with weeds. As they headed down the path, the air in the car grew thick with anticipation and the metallic tang of magic.

There was not yet an adversary to fight, but their fear sparked through the SUV. Overhead the clear sky gave way to clouds and the rumble of thunder. Lemon looked towards her sister. Ruby's fingers were digging into the armrest.

Gravel crunched under the tires, and Lemon was sure that if this was the right place, they would hear them coming. She closed her eyes, falling into the magic that swirled at her core, finding that link that had drawn Claudia to her. She could feel her, in truth she had felt her for weeks. Not exactly tangible, but in the way she could feel the birds that flew above her, or the moles under the ground. Unexplainable, magical, but there.

As they continued to drive up the long, straight driveway, Lemon wondered if that connection had always been there. The idea seemed silly, unreasonable, and yet she wondered. Was it what had pulled Claudia to Julian, what had made a beautiful college student attach herself to a criminal? Or was it desperation running through Lemon's body, trying to make sense of why she was doing something so undeniably stupid?

There was a bend in the driveway, and a large house came into view. Fritz pulled the car over to the side of the driveway, and they were all silent as they got out.

Lemon looked around at her companions as she opened the trunk. They each caught her eyes, one by one, in silent understanding. There was nothing more to stay. They'd made their choices. In actuality, this had been inevitable from the moment they had agreed to help Claudia. They knew of curses, they knew of the world and Hathornes, and they knew that blood would not come easily. They had all decided long before they had left to find her.

Lemon strapped one of the utility belts in the trunk around her hips and began loading it with potions and vials until it was heavy.

If this was not the right place, they were going to scare the shit out of whoever lived there. But it was, she knew it, the same as she knew which ingredients to pull from a shelf, the same way she knew which trails to take and when to water plants. The universe had always held Lemon in its gentle grasp, and now it was asking for something in return. The stars and planets had led her to this point, and it was her father at the other end. Maybe she had been moving towards this moment, this confrontation, her whole life. This, by blood and design, was her battle to fight.

She looked up at the sky, brimming with angry gray clouds, and sent a silent plea to the universe, to Mother Nature, to whatever was out there—Let it be them. So many times Hathornes won, let them lose this once. The jails were full of witches, just as the stocks and pyres had once been. Let Lemon win.

"Oh, we're fucking idiots," Elias said, grabbing for the last vial in the trunk.

"Complete morons for sure," Fritz agreed, clapping Elias on the shoulder. "And you'll have my eternal gratitude."

"Just gotta survive." Elias forced a smile onto his face.

"Ready?" Ruby asked, and the four of them started towards the house. It was wooden and run-down, on a massive piece of property. The house looked as though it might have once been a farm, with dilapidated fences stretching out behind it, the wood rotting and falling at irregular intervals.

Ruby's fingers found Lemon's wrist. There was a small static burst as thunder rumbled overhead, and the wind picked up, rustling through the leaves and covering their footsteps. But the path towards the house was wide open, and anyone looking out would be able to see them.

Lemon started to run, and the others followed, her eyes darting from window to door, waiting for someone to burst out of it, but they never came. And then she was at the porch, her feet moving up the steps and her thoughts hardened, reducing to a pinpoint. Live. Get Claudia.

That was her mission. She and Elias would get Claudia out, Fritz and Ruby would handle Julian. There might have been a certain symmetry to Lemon ending her father, to being the one to snuff out his life, but she did not argue with Ruby when she had handed out roles, scared she would hesitate and that it would cost them everything.

But she hesitated at the door, her fingers hovering over the knob. She reached into a pocket of the utility belt, pulling out a potion Lavinia had taught her to make. Smoke in a bottle.

She turned the handle and to her surprise it moved. Not locked. The door creaked open, and the voices in the house went silent. Lemon's heart stuttered, but Fritz pushed past her as Orlo appeared in the long hallway.

"You." Fritz did not reach for potions but for the knife at his hip, unsheathing it, and advancing on Orlo.

Lemon froze, transfixed at the scene unfolding in front of her, but Elias pushed her shoulder and she broke from her trance. There was no use in stealth. The two men tumbled, bottles breaking, and the hallway filled with smoke.

Lemon ran through it, trying to peer into the rooms as she passed. She screamed Claudia's name, and the response came from above her head. She looked up, trying to see through the smoke, and found Claudia at the top of the staircase, Julian at her side.

There was a bruise blooming across her milk white cheek. Her eyes were sallow, no longer amber, they had turned a dull yellow, but they grew wide at the sight of Lemon, and she lurched forward, but Julian grabbed her around the waist.

At the front of the house Orlo screamed, and something thudded. Lemon had to use all her self-control not to turn and look. Beside her Elias vibrated with contained magic.

"Lemon, this does not have to end poorly." Julian tightened his grip on Claudia.

"You're right." She fingered the vials through the fabric of the utility belt. "You can let her go. Leave."

"Aren't you curious to hear my side of the story, Lemon? I've been looking for you."

His confession stirred nothing in her. There was no comfort this man could offer to soothe the past. She did not wish to pour his poison into healed wounds. "I haven't wondered about you at all."

"And yet you've followed me across the country."

Another thunk. This time it was Fritz who yelled. Claudia struggled harder to get away, clawing at Julian. Dark anti-magic swirled around both of them, and Claudia clawed at her neck, making a terrible gurgling sound. Lemon's heart skipped a beat at the same moment recognition left Claudia's eyes and she collapsed.

Lemon was running up the stairs before Claudia hit the ground, all rational thoughts gone from her mind. She threw the vial in her hand and the room filled with thick smoke. She could hear Elias behind her, but she couldn't see him, could not even see the steps beneath her.

Julian was moving, and she grabbed for him but tripped over Claudia's prostrate form, and went down, falling away from the stairs, her nails digging into his arms. She pushed herself to her elbows and came face to face with Claudia. Her eyes were blank and unblinking and Lemon scrambled to pull her close. A sob broke from her lungs as she felt her chest rise and fall. Not dead.

Elias was locked in battle with Julian, but her father had six inches on him. She dragged Claudia's lifeless body further from the fight, doing her best to ignore the sounds of fighting breaking out in the house. Let her wake up. It was a constant refrain through her head.

Elias screamed her name, and it cleared her mind. The belt was hanging off of her, bottles smashed, the potions hissing and eating away at the fabric. She felt for what she could, not sure what potion it was, and stood. The smoke was clearing and she could see bodies moving. Where was her sister?

There was no time to look for her. She leapt, landing on Julian's back, and digging her free hand into the skin of his face. She smashed the potion into his mouth, hoping it was poison. There had been hemlock among the others.

He shrieked through the shards of glass in his mouth and threw himself backwards, away from Elias's swinging fists. Lemon was slammed into the wall, her head colliding with the edge of a doorframe and her vision went black.

She fell to the floor, holding her head, blinking away the darkness at the edges of her sight. Elias swung, connecting with Julian's bleeding mouth and her father reached for him. Elias screamed at the contact, his veins turning black.

Lemon swallowed the fear that swelled inside of her and pushed herself up from the ground. Her fingernails were broken and bloody, and she thought she felt blood trickling down the back of her head, but she stood firm.

This was how the Hathornes won. But not today. She looked at Claudia on the floor and thought of her mother. If he won, how many more lives would he destroy? She glanced around, looking for something to help her. Elias's screams tore through her chest and her body trembled. She should have brought a weapon.

The utility belt lay on the floor. She reached down, picking it up and smearing it with blood. Her eyes locked on Elias's as the black magic running through his body made its way up his arms, paralyzing him.

Drawing on the magic inside of her for strength, she threw the belt over Julian's head, wrapping it around his throat. With all of her remaining strength she pulled, and the darkness flowing from his hands stopped and Elias broke away, panting. For a moment Elias stood, then like Claudia his eyes went hazy and he fell.

Lemon screamed, trying not to think of her sister and Fritz. The sounds below had stopped. She squeezed the belt tighter, her arms bulging.

Julian kicked out, knocking her legs from underneath her. She fell to the ground and he stood over her, his face bleeding, his neck red and raw. He kicked again, his foot driving into Lemon's side and pain bloomed through her.

A drop of blood fell on Lemon as he leaned down, crouching over her. He clicked his tongue. "It was such a disappointment when you started showing magic. I'd hoped and prayed you'd be better than your mother. But what do they say about lying down with dogs? I guess it's on me."

Lemon smiled. He was bleeding so much. She reached up, running her hand down the side of his face, feeling the hot liquid between her fingers. "I prayed Esther had killed you."

He punched her, and her head bounced against the wooden floor behind her, her ears ringing. "You stupid little—"

He cut off at the sound of Ruby calling for Lemon. She laughed through her pain. Her sister was alive. And the house was big, but it would only be moments before Ruby found her.

"You're going to die." She smiled at the monster above her. "And no one will miss you."

A terrible smile curved his lips, and he stood suddenly. Lemon rolled, every inch of her body aching, towards Claudia, scared he meant to take her with him. She wrapped her arms around Claudia's body, holding her tight to her chest. But Julian was not moving towards her, instead he was bounding down the stairs.

She buried her face in Claudia's shoulder, and breathed a sigh of relief as she heard Fritz yell out, then another thud. She could not stop the tears that flowed, great sobs that shook both her and Claudia.

Arms wrapped around her and she tried to resist but Elias shushed her. "It's okay," he murmured, pulling both of them into his lap.

"Lemon!" Ruby had never looked worse, her hair was a tangled mess, there was a deep cut, freely bleeding under her eye and most of her body was bruised, but she had the strength to pull Lemon to her feet and wrap her arms around her in a nearly bone-crushing hug. "He got away. I'm so sorry. He got away."

"Orlo?"

"He's dead." Fritz looked as bad as Ruby, but they were both alive, and for that moment it was enough for Lemon.

"I've got blood." She held up her hand. Some of it had been wiped away, but there was enough, coated between her fingers and underneath her nails.

Ruby just nodded and started to turn, but Fritz touched her elbow and a look of understanding passed between them. With a final glance at his sister, he went down the stairs.

Claudia was starting to stir, and Elias had already recovered. He wiped the hair back from Claudia's face and gazed down at her as though he could will life into her through his eyes alone. "I've got you. It's Elias. You're safe."

Lemon lowered herself back to the debris covered floor, taking Claudia's hand in her own. She rubbed her thumb over the back of it, feeling the tendons underneath her skin. "Claudia, please, open your eyes."

She obeyed, blinking slowly and then she gasped, pulling her hand from Lemon and clutching at her chest. They all watched her with apprehension as she coughed and sputtered. She grimaced as she pushed herself to sitting. "I'm sorry I didn't do more...the curse."

"It's okay. You don't have to explain."

Fritz reappeared and life came back to her eyes. He smiled sadly and passed a backpack to Ruby. Lemon knew what was in it, she had packed it herself. Everything they would need for the potion. Her sister glanced at her hand, and Lemon held it out to her.

Her fingers were warm and soft, and she muttered spells over Lemon. At first nothing happened, and Lemon worried it was not enough blood. She willed her own magic towards Ruby, hoping she had the strength for it. Her sister placed her free hand on her arm and the air between them grew thick. The blood on her hand swelled into droplets that disappeared and reappeared in the vial.

Claudia sobbed, her whole body shaking, and Lemon wanted to hold her, but she was so tired and couldn't force herself to move.

Instead, Fritz wrapped her in his arms. "There's a kitchen downstairs." He led her slowly down the stairs. Most of the bottom of the house remained untouched but there were signs of their struggle, frames fallen and broken, glass shattered across the floor.

Orlo's body, the hilt of a dagger protruding from his chest, bled out to stain the rug beneath him. Lemon stopped, looking down into his unseeing eyes. "We should clean up as much as we can, hide the things we brought with us. We'll have to call the police."

Claudia moaned but there was no other choice. Their crimes would be found eventually, and it would be worse for them. Their fingerprints were everywhere, along with their blood. And now they had proof of Claudia's curse, though the man who had done it was gone. Whatever Claudia had agreed to, this was a kidnapping.

"I'll call," Elias said, looking around the room. "We were rescuing a friend. We knew he was dangerous, but we thought with our numbers he wouldn't put up a fight."

"They'll want to know why we didn't call them," Lemon said, looking around. She bent down and scooped up one of the utility belts. "I can handle that. I'm his daughter. I thought he would listen, and he attacked us." Fear dissolved under the need to make a plan. "I'll be back. Ruby, get started on the cure." Maybe she should make it herself, but she worried her feelings, good and bad, for Claudia would seep in. Let Ruby, who loved her brother, do it. Lemon no longer cared about strengthening her magic. She just wanted to go home.

She didn't wait for a response but headed back up the stairs, gathering up the belts and what she could of the vials. There wasn't much but glass, so she knocked over other pictures and vases, covering the floor with more, making the vials unidentifiable.

Without Ruby's interference, the sun had returned. Lemon headed into the woods, reaching out to the animals that were nearby. She did not know them as she knew the creatures that roamed her mountains, but they still came to her.

"Take them," she pleaded with the small eyes looking up at her. "Please." And to her relief they did, gathering them in beaks and mouths and tiny fingers. "Thank you." She reached down, digging her fingers into the cool soil, blessing it with the last reserves of her magic. She prayed for it to grow fertile, for the animals of the forest to have a season rich with berries and pollen and fruit. She did not know if she had enough magic left to help, it was nothing she had tried before. Her own forests grew abundant with all the magic nearby, but she'd read of the spell, and she owed them her gratitude.

When she returned, the house was full of the smell of magic. Claudia leaned against the kitchen counter. There was so much for Lemon to say to her, but she did not know where to begin. How could she tell her of the fear she had felt when she fell to the ground, or the relief when she had stirred, without mentioning her anger, without screaming at the danger she had put everyone Lemon loved in? She was selfish and cruel, and yet Lemon wanted to take her in her arms, to kiss her, to twist her fingers into her hair.

She walked to her as the sound of sirens met her ears, and reached out, tracing a filthy finger down her cheek.

"Lemon." She captured her hand in her own. "I am so sorry. Please forgive me."

Part of her wanted to say yes, but it was not so simple. What had broken between them was not something an apology could fix. "I'm glad you're okay."

Ruby cleared her throat. Despite the bruises her skin was shining, her eyes glowing with the magic she had done. "I think this is it."

Claudia shuddered under Lemon's hand. "The cure?"

Boots sounded on the porch. "Hello?" And then a string of expletives as the cop made his way inside.

Ruby glanced towards the doorway but she continued to move, ladling the chartreuse liquid into a cup. "It should work."

Claudia's hands trembled as they took the cup.

"Stop!" the cop's voice boomed.

And Claudia lifted the cup to her lips and drank.

Chapter Twenty

The effect was immediate. Magic filled the room, thick and metallic, all of it coming from Claudia. Another police officer appeared behind the first, but he stood just as transfixed as the first, though he moved his hand to the gun on his hip.

In front of Lemon, Claudia changed, her eyes no longer yellow but the brown of the soil Lemon had dug her fingers into. The color of her skin deepened, golden and full of life. The incisors visible in her smile shrunk, and as they receded, so did the magic.

"I'm me." She felt her face and ran her tongue over her teeth. With a shout of joy she spun and pulled Lemon to her, kissing her hard. "I don't want to bite you! Thank you Ruby, thank you!"

"Okay," one of the officers said, his voice full of trepidation, clearly unsure of what he should do.

Fritz stood on the other side of him, shoulder to shoulder with Elias, and grinning nearly as wide as Claudia.

"I think we can agree, she was the victim of a crime." Elias looked over the two uniformed men, standing slack-jawed.

"And we are supposed to believe that is why there is a dead man in the dining room?" asked the second officer. He was taller and stockier than the first, with black hair graying at his temples. His name tag read Pennell.

Claudia moved forward and Lemon could not take her eyes off of her. She had always been beautiful, but unlike the shows and movies she loved, it had not been increased by vampirism. It was as though a veil had been lifted from her, like varnish over a painting, revealing all the incredible details. "I was kidnapped by Julian Pluth, or Giuseppe Diggory, however you may know him, but I assume you have heard of him." She paused, and it was clear from their faces that they did indeed know him by his name. "That is his associate Orlo Bostic."

"And he cursed you during this kidnapping?"

"No, he cursed me before, when I refused to work for him or sleep with him. He kidnapped me when I went to his daughter for help. He attacked her and her mother then, just as he attacked her mother years ago. They came to save me, but I unfortunately cannot tell you the details, as I was quickly rendered unconscious when I tried to flee."

Pennell looked between Claudia and Lemon, and then slowly at the others. "How did the man end up dead?"

"I stabbed him," Fritz said, holding out his arm and pushing back his sleeve. There was a deep cut, red around the edges. It had clearly been worse before his magic had kicked in but it was still gruesome. "After he stabbed me, while he was trying to stab my girlfriend." He nodded towards Ruby, who still had blood smeared across her cheek.

They should get a lawyer. Lemon knew that. She'd seen enough episodes of Law and Order but a lawyer would mean sitting in custody, it would mean money she didn't have, and it would mean not stopping her father who was still out there. What she really needed was for these cops to not hate witches, and to not arrest them.

She looked at the badge on the other. Tarver. And then Ruby started to cry, fat tears that fell from her big blue eyes and down her rosy cheeks. "I know we should have called you. I know this wasn't the right way, but we had to find out where she was. He's a monster.

He tried to kill Lemon when we were children. She would come to school bruised, and I went to the cops then and they didn't help. They weren't like you." She blinked and blinked and more tears fell.

"They didn't listen. And we had to run from him. My mother helped. We've grown up together, hiding from him, and look at what he did to her!" She gestured wildly towards Claudia. "We got here, and we parked back there. We wanted to call the police, but we heard her screaming and we just ran. I thought maybe because Lemon was his daughter, he wouldn't hurt us but he wouldn't stop and neither would Orlo. There was no time."

Jesus. She had no idea Ruby had such a talent. She'd seen her fake tears a few times to get out of trouble in childhood but this was something else.

She wiped her hand across her face, smearing blood and tears, but somehow not looking grotesque. Her long eyelashes were wet with tears and she kept moving closer to the officers. Every bit a damsel in distress. "I've never hurt anyone before. It's all my fault. I should have stopped him, but I was so afraid. And then Lemon was screaming and screaming. She's my sister, ever since we were little. I hadn't been able to protect her then, and I couldn't protect her tonight. Please, I know we did this all wrong. That's why I had to make the potion, I wasn't trying to disobey you, but I needed you to see what he did to her. He tried to make her a slave to him. It's the only reason she found Lemon, because she shares blood with him. Blood with a monster." She whimpered, lurching forward and Tarver caught her in his arms, steadying her.

"Okay. And where is Julian Pluth now?"

Ruby let out another sob, and Lemon was surprised to find her own eyes full of tears, though she wasn't sure the officers would be quite as moved by her plight. "He got away. I don't know where he'll go or what he'll do, but he's dangerous and he can't be far yet."

The two cops exchanged looks. She knew what was going through their heads. If Lemon and her friends were telling the truth, they had a wanted criminal in their jurisdiction. The dead man had a criminal past as well. Pennell nodded to the other and walked away, already speaking into his radio. God bless Ruby.

"We're going to need to take some more statements. Where do you live?"

"In North Carolina. I want to go home."

"I'm sure you do, but you won't tonight. However, we've been tracking him. There's been an influx of illegal ingredients. Look, it's clear there was a struggle, and I've arrested the man in the hallway enough times to know he's dangerous. I'm not arresting any of you, right now."

Lemon bit her tongue to keep from saying anything. He'd seen the curse reverse itself. But there was a dead man, she reminded herself, and Claudia was a criminal as well. God, why had she done this? But she had. She'd cured Claudia's curse. "Thank you. He was my dad, you know. Even though I remember him bouncing my mother off the walls, I still thought..." She didn't want to mention the curse, to remind this man she was a witch. But she was also a human, and maybe there was something in him that could sympathize. At the very least, he had to know any half assed lawyer would win this case. And maybe that was another point in her favor. "If you catch him, I'll testify to whatever you want. I haven't seen him in twenty years before this, but I can ID him. I'll cooperate with anything you need."

"So will I," Elias said. "If you can't catch him on anything else, you saw the curse reverse. Ruby still has the vial of blood, you can test it against him."

Travers nodded. "Look, I don't condone anything that happened here, but I know self defense when I see it. And you called it in. How about I give you all the name of a hotel near the station?

You check in, clean yourselves up." He looked towards Ruby. "And we'll talk tomorrow. Now, we've got your vehicle tags, and I'm going to take a copy of your IDs. The man on the floor, do you know if he was..."

"He was a witch. He was the one who did the curse for Julian." The excitement of the curse lifting was fading from Claudia's eyes, and she looked tired. She leaned on the back of a chair for support. "I can show you where he's hidden stuff, he's got wolfsbane and elephant tusks here. It's under the floorboards."

Pennell reappeared. "And I found this on the porch." He held up a bag, and while Lemon wasn't exactly worldly, she knew drugs when she saw them.

"Come on." Claudia moved forward, nodding to the cops, who followed her.

Lemon deflated when they left, glancing towards Ruby, who was wiping at her eyes. She didn't dare say anything and could barely believe her luck until she remembered Julian was gone. And he was a criminal, that was all they had on their side. If he had just been a man, she doubted they'd be walking free. But just being a man had never been enough for him, and finally it might catch up with him.

The hotel was decent enough, and they got half price as police guests, which wasn't Lemon's favorite thing to be, but she got it. They had killed a man. She needed to go talk to Ruby, make sure she was okay, but first she needed to be okay herself.

The shower was as hot as she could stand it. The water flowed over her while she tried to figure out exactly how she had ended up at this place. She wasn't made for this life. She wanted to go home, to curl into her mother's arms and sleep for days. But she didn't think she was going to jail. Which was fair. Her only crime was breaking and entering, and she hadn't broken anything, and he had kidnapped her—her whatever Claudia was.

When the water ran clear, no longer cloudy and pink, she grabbed the shampoo and scrubbed her hair. Was Fritz okay? He'd been the only one to strike a killing blow. Were any of them? She wasn't sure she'd ever be okay again. God, she missed Hecate's Hollow. She finished her hair and started on her body, running the tiny, lavender scented bar of hotel soap all over her skin.

She wanted a drink, a smoke, to blast herself high into the sky, anything but standing here, in this blue tiled tub. And they hadn't gotten Julian. He would still live, out there, ready to torment them if he wished.

She turned off the knob and got out, looking at herself in the mirror. Her head hurt. When more cops had showed up, they'd insisted she see the paramedics they had brought with them. They'd been kind, and she hadn't needed stitches. They'd rarely seen witches before and were intrigued by how she healed, but assured her she didn't have a concussion, which she supposed, was good.

And it hadn't hurt her case. She'd clearly had the shit beat out of her, they all had. She could see it on so many faces though, the desire to blame them—witches, others—but coming up short. The dead man was a criminal, the house was full of illegal ingredients and worse, all cleverly hidden. So in the end she'd gotten hard earned sympathy.

She wished Claudia hadn't kissed her. She knew being queer wasn't doing her any favors with the crowd she needed on her side. That felt dirty too. When she had watched Ruby pretend to cry with her half-truth story, she'd wanted to scream. She'd saved Claudia.

She was a goddamn hero. But, instead of praise, she was worried they'd knock the door down and arrest her.

Someone *was* knocking at the door and she wasn't sure who she was going to find. The jolt of emotions that flew through her when it was Claudia, beautiful, human, Claudia, was too much to analyze in her weary brain.

"Can we talk?"

Days ago she would have slammed the door in her face, and part of her was tempted to now—to yell that she had saved her, but she would never forgive her. But she'd seen her with Julian, and all she felt was sorrow. She held the door open and stepped back, letting Claudia in.

She was wearing Ruby's clothes, but Ruby was shorter and curvier than Claudia, and they hung on her oddly. She looked lost, like a child wandering the streets alone, searching for their mother.

"You lied to me. You knew who he was, and you never said anything."

Claudia looked down, pulling at the hem of her dress. "I'm so sorry. I wish I had a reason to give you, that I could explain it. I can tell you how I didn't realize at first, and how afraid I was. I can tell you how my mind hasn't been right for weeks; how part of me spent every single moment of the day desperate to run away and find him. I can tell you how scared that made me, and how I thought you were my only hope. I can tell you more than that; how the part of me that was still me only wanted to make you laugh, to keep you around, to never let you go, and how fucking afraid I was that everything would fall apart the moment I told you. But I know that's not enough. I thought..." She sighed and looked towards the ceiling.

When she looked back at Lemon her eyes were clear. "I thought if I could keep your mothers away then he might not recognize you, that you wouldn't recognize him. And I know that's no better, that it would have just been more lies. So I just want to apologize, Lemon, and tell you I've never been more sorry for anything I've done in my life. I've spent every minute since I was with Julian lying, it's all there was. I hated it at first, I guess I hated it always, but it got easier, and my mom wasn't starving and Fritz could go to school. So I told myself it was fine. And then lying just became what I did. And I swore I'd be better when I left him, and I meant to, I still do. I want you to know that even if you never forgive me, though god I hope you will, I'm going to be better. I'm not going to waste this."

The emotional turmoil Lemon had felt since she had seen Claudia at the top of the stairs only grew worse with each second. She wanted to kiss her, wanted to throw her onto the bed and rip Ruby's stupid dress off of her. She wanted to scream in her face and tell her to leave, that she'd never trust her again. So, she stood still. "Will you stay in the Hollow?"

"Not if you don't want me to. I won't impose on you, Lemon. You've done more for me than I deserved."

"Fritz wants to bring your mother."

Claudia laughed, wiping away a tear that fell. "She'd love it there. I hope he does."

Lemon took a step closer, pushing away the still wet hair that was plastered to her face. "When I realized who he was, something inside of me broke, and it was because I'd trusted you. I'd looked at you, and I'd known you were lying, but like a fool, I'd still trusted you."

She nodded, eyes wide and unblinking, full of tears. "I'm going to see somebody. Talk to a therapist—if I'm not arrested. I'm so sorry. I wish we'd met some other way, that I'd gotten away and just stumbled into your town and seen you behind the counter. And I hope you find someone you can trust one day. And if they're not good to you, you tell Fritz and he'll tell me, and I'll kick their ass."

Lemon took another step closer, and perhaps she truly was stupid, but her heart pounded in her chest. "I want you to stay in town."

Claudia's shoulders sagged with relief. "Please..."

Lemon waited for her to finish her sentence but nothing came. Timidly, she lifted her hand, touching Claudia's face, running her fingers over her lips. "Your eyes are brown."

"They usually are." Claudia laughed. "I missed it. You know I spent my whole life looking at the mirror and thinking about the things I wanted to change, but once I changed I just wanted to look like me again."

Lemon pressed her forehead to Claudia's. She smelled like cheap lavender soap, the same as Lemon. "I can't forgive you right now, Claudia, and I can't say I trust you. But... god help me, I'm not ready to give up either."

"I'll earn it back." Claudia kissed her, gently and slowly, one hand on Lemon's face, the other at her waist.

"I'd try to seduce you but every inch of my body hurts."

"Then can I hold you? Please?"

Nodding, Lemon took her by the hand and led her to the bed. They crawled under the scratchy sheets, but it was Lemon who held Claudia. She rested her head on Lemon's chest and she stroked her hair, imagining Claudia's life, all the things she'd been through. No, she hadn't found forgiveness yet, but she had found understanding. She understood her fear; how it could drive someone to extremes. She understood how desperate and isolated she must have felt, how she would have wanted to hold on to her one chance at escape and not risk it.

She reached across Claudia, taking her phone from the side table and sent a text to Amaryllis: *We're alive. We all made it. We broke the curse. I love you and I'll see you soon.* And then she sent another to

Esther: *Everyone is okay. The curse is broken but Julian got away. Be careful. I love you.*

"I think I'd like to get a cat," Claudia said, her voice sleepy. "I always wanted one, but I was gone too much."

"You should name it Lestat."

"Too soon." Claudia giggled, a sound Lemon had never heard from her before. Her body shook with it. "Maybe I'll get two or three. That way they'll never be lonely."

"Neither will you. We'll get through this, and you'll be happy. We'll find somewhere for you to work and we'll go apple picking and carve pumpkins. You'll see your brother whenever you want, and you'll know your mom is safe. And one day, you'll wake up and this won't even haunt you. It will be the past, and you'll just be you, whoever you've decided to become." She wasn't sure who she was trying to convince, herself or Claudia, but she could see it in her mind, see them laughing under the sun, having a future.

Eventually, Claudia's breathing slowed and Lemon kept holding her, glad to have her in her arms, warm and safe. Her eyes grew heavy, her thoughts became strange, and Lemon fell asleep too.

Chapter Twenty One

Sometime before Lemon woke up Ruby had found a lawyer. She certainly wasn't the best, and didn't look long out of law school, but she seemed competent enough. She assured them that if it went to trial the case would be a slam dunk. Claudia had clearly been cursed and kidnapped, half the town of Hecate's Hollow had seen Julian attack them in the square. And she didn't think the police in a small town would want to risk the ire of the witches rights movement.

Lemon started to argue, but Ruby's hand had tightened on her knee, so she shut her mouth. The police had seen Claudia transform before their eyes, they would have the blood match if they needed it. Witches had been screaming and protesting about it for years. Why would the cops bring protesters down upon themselves instead of pursuing a case against Julian? He was a Hathorne, but he traded in black magic. Maybe the lawyer was right. She would believe it when she saw it.

When they walked out of the police station, Lemon pulled her sister aside. She looked her over, mostly healed, but there were still yellowed spots running up her arms, remnants of bruises. "Ruby..."

Her sister pulled her into a tight embrace, burying her face in Lemon's shoulder. "I'm so glad we're all alive."

"You helped kill a man, Ruby. Are you okay? Really?" Lemon searched her sister's face, all the curves and freckles she knew so well.

Ruby shrugged. "I've been better, but I think I'm going to be okay. I don't feel guilty. I'm glad he's dead, but I wish none of this had ever happened."

"I'm sorry." Lemon had dragged her sister into all of this. Julian wasn't her father, none of this needed to be her problem. Ruby had just been an empathetic child, and it had disrupted her entire life.

"None of this is your fault, Lemon. I helped you because I love you. I'll always help you. Like you said, we'll never be in danger alone." She let her go as the others exited the station. "You've gone along with every plan I've ever come up with since we were little girls. You've always had my back, and I'll always have your."

"But this is bigger than skipping school or hiking in the snow." She looked at her feet, shame creeping in. She'd never wanted Ruby to be in danger, to have a man's blood on her hands.

"It doesn't matter, Lemon. I'd go to hell for you. Wouldn't you do the same for me?"

Lemon looked up, into earnest blue eyes. She would. There was nothing she wouldn't do to keep her sister safe. "I would."

"Then you understand. So please, stop feeling guilty." Ruby kissed her forehead, and they headed towards the others, waiting in the shade of a group of trees. "Have you heard from the moms?"

"Yeah, I messaged them last night to update them. Got the usual back." She stopped in front of Claudia. They'd woken in each other's arms, but had not said much as they got ready. Lemon wasn't sure what to say, but they had an eight hour drive ahead of them.

"Hey." Claudia smiled, revealing straight teeth. No points to be seen. Seeing her was still jarring, so different than she had been in the weeks Lemon had known her. Somehow it made it easier to work out her feelings, the cursed woman she was before, and the one she was now. Lemon only hoped she wasn't being foolish. She tried to believe people when they showed her who they were, but did that count for people who were drowning? Could you judge anyone on the worst moments in their lives? She wouldn't want to be judged for hers.

"Ready to go home?"

As they walked back towards Fritz's car, their fingers brushed, just the barest of touches, but it sent a thrill down Lemon's spine. She wanted Claudia, wanted to learn all the secrets she kept, wanted to know the way she looked when she was dreaming, the things that made her laugh, her favorite foods and biggest fears. She wanted to know the person who had been hiding for all those years.

And if she found something she didn't like, she wouldn't regret it. Life was full of lessons, of people who blew past and didn't stay, but it was also full of beauty and love.

She could not know what the future held, but she looked forward to finding out, and she suspected she would find something beautiful. Some flowers just needed a bit of tending, nothing flourished in the wrong soil, but with time and a gentle hand they would bloom.

Their knees bumped together as they traveled down the highway, pressed together in space too small for three adults.

"We should still try to find him," Fritz said, after a long stretch of silence filled with nothing but trees and other cars whizzing by.

"I've been thinking that the whole time. He knows where we live." Elias glanced towards Lemon.

Claudia put her hand on Lemon's leg, running her thumb over the fabric of her jeans. "I wouldn't be surprised if he's already out of the country. I worry about him less now, and more in half a year when he's had time to regroup."

It was odd how he was Lemon's father, but also wasn't. A new name, an older face she barely recognized, and Claudia knew him better than she ever would or would ever want to. "We should come up with some kind of plan. When we get in, we can visit the sheriff, though I'm sure they already know. And we should get a security system at the house."

"I vote for electronic *and* magical. I've been texting my mom this morning. She's going to get word out around town." Elias was doing his best to make himself small on the other side of Claudia, but he was still man sized, leaving him smashed against the door.

Lemon squashed the urge to apologize again and just nodded. She tuned out the conversation that followed, letting her mind wander until they pulled off to get lunch at a McDonalds that had seen better days. But there was a stand boasting 'best jams in the state' across the street that she wanted to check out.

She dashed across the pavement with Claudia on her heels, chasing the smells of strawberry and fig. She paid for a cup of boiled peanuts from a truck outside and turned around to find Claudia standing with her face turned towards the sun, arms thrown wide at her sides.

Instead of interrupting, Lemon stood and watched as a smile spread over her face and her cheeks heated until they were pink and rosy. They grew even redder when she caught Lemon staring at her. "It's just nice to be in the sun and not worry."

Lemon offered her the styrofoam cup and looped her arm through Claudia's, leading her into the interior of the country store. It smelled like sugar and was full of little jars of jam sitting on antique furniture. The gray-haired woman behind the counter stood up at their arrival, smiling brightly. "Let me know if y'all need any help."

They browsed for a while, picking up the jars and looking them over, examining pots of honey and little knickknacks. Lemon grabbed a few magnets. "To remember the weekend by," she teased.

"I know you're joking, but I won't ever forget this. This is the day my life starts over. I get a second chance. I never thought I would." She picked up a baseball cap with *Virginia is for Lovers* written across it and put it on her head. "I'm excited, Lemon. I really am."

Lemon kissed her, hoping she wasn't drawing the eye of the shop owner. She let her hands linger on Claudia's arms as she pulled away, looking her over. "I can't take you seriously in that thing."

"Too bad. I'm becoming one with the Smokies, just like you always wanted. I'm going to get one of those belts with the big buckles too."

Pulling Claudia behind a display of printed t-shirts, Lemon kissed her again. She made slow work of it, running her tongue along her teeth, tasting her, until Claudia pulled away, bright eyed.

"I'm going to prove it to you, Lemon. You're my knight in shining armor. I'm going to make you so happy." Claudia leaned in, kissing Lemon's cheek, then moving along her jawbone until she nipped at her ear.

"I'd like to revisit that knight and princess thing sometime but I think the owner of this establishment might chase us out with a broom soon. Not to mention everyone is waiting for us."

But Lemon was reluctant to leave, tucked away behind the tackiest t-shirts she'd ever seen. This was a perfect moment. She could picture the life spread before her, full of Claudia, but also family and her town. All the festivals and parades with someone she could grow to love by her side. Her sister happy with someone who looked at her like she hung the moon. Julian on the run, her mothers no longer looking over their shoulder. There would be picnics in the square, hikes through the mountains where she could show Claudia all the places she loved. Life, a real life. Lavinia could teach her everything she knew, all the spells and potions the Appalachian magic made possible.

They checked out, buying more than they needed, and distributed jam and honey and candied nuts amongst the SUV as they crawled back inside. Ruby took over the music, and Sylvan Esso crooned at them through the speakers.

Lemon extracted her phone from her pocket, a true feat in the cramped space, and checked her messages. Neither of her mothers had responded to her last text letting them know her ETA, something Amaryllis and Esther had drilled into her head since she was little. *"How can we know you're missing if we don't know when you're supposed to be home?"*

Ruby turned around, offering her the last of her chicken nuggets and Lemon took one, shoving it into her mouth and watching an argument start between Elias and Fritz over the best show Netflix had produced. Ruby chimed in with The Witcher, making Fritz groan and Claudia offered Stranger Things which they all agreed was good but possibly not the best.

Then Elias brought up The OA and outrage over the cancellation of the show lasted them well into North Carolina. Lemon finally ended the discussion by saying she thought Year in the Life had some of the best episodes of Gilmore Girls, purposefully setting off his sister, and finally forcing Fritz to pull off at a rest area, desperate to get away from an argument over Team Logan and Team Jess between Claudia and Ruby that did not seem likely to end in anything less than bloodshed.

Lemon leaned on the car, watching Claudia head towards the vending machines for a soda, and pulled out her phone again. She had social media notifications and about twenty emails of varying levels of unimportance, but still no reply from either of her moms.

She dialed Amaryllis first, letting the phone ring and ring until her mother's cheery voicemail asked her to leave a message. When Esther didn't answer either, she dialed the apothecary. It was the middle of the afternoon, someone had to be there. But it rang and rang and Lemon's heart beat harder in her chest.

She searched through her contact list and rang Betta McCray. Her fingers tightened around her phone and she walked away from her car, pacing the sidewalk and weaving between families heading towards the bathroom.

"Hey, honey! What's going on? You need me to feed the cat again?" Betta's voice was upbeat and loud enough to cover the baby crying in the background.

"No, it's..." She didn't want to scare the shit out of her neighbor when her mothers might just be busy with customers. "So, you know how crazy things have been with me, and I can't get either of my mothers to answer the phone. I know you've got a lot going on with those kids but—"

Betta hissed a warning at one of her kids. "Is this about that man? Yeah, of course, Lemon. I'll call Lavinia and get her to look in at the shop and my husband can swing by their house. Did you... did you not beat him?"

Nothing traveled faster than news in a small town. "I cured Claudia, but he got away. I'm sure I'm overreacting but I'm worried. I'm only about an hour away. I know I should have probably waited but—"

"Nonsense, honey. Now, you hurry home. See you soon." The line went dead.

Lemon tried to convince herself she was overreacting. There was no reason to worry until she had something to worry about. Until her sister found her, her eyebrows knitted together and her phone in her hands.

"No one's answering my calls."

"I asked Betta to go check on them." Lemon felt as though the temperature had dropped. They looked at each other, understanding without words, and ran to grab the others.

Fritz sped between cars, and Claudia clutched Lemon's hand in the backseat, her thumb stroking slow circles, and no one spoke except occasional murmurs of reassurance. They all jumped when Lemon's phone rang. Betta's name flashed across the screen and Lemon swiped to accept it.

"Hey!"

"Hey sweetheart. They didn't come in today, but it sounds like they had the day off. SaraLee was making out with that god awful boyfriend of hers in the back. You need to find someone better to work the shop, she couldn't pour piss out of a boot if the instructions were on the bottom. Anyway, she's back at the counter and her boyfriend's who knows where, but he's not in the shop. I stopped by your mamas' place and everything looked fine. I'm betting they're out in the hills somewhere, one of their walks, you know how the reception is up there."

"I'm sorry I made you do all that Betta." Lemon let out a long breath, relief washing through her.

"Oh, no worries. I got Emmy to watch the kids and I'm at the bakery right now so you improved my afternoon. Plus, I got to yell at SaraLee, and that's always heartwarmin'."

"Thank you. Seriously. I owe you a night of babysitting."

"Of course. And be careful what you promise when you're thankful, or I might take you up on it."

Lemon laughed. "I'm not worried. Bye Betta." She hung up and nodded to Ruby. "No sign of foul play and they had already planned to take the afternoon off."

Ruby pulled her hair off of her neck, fanning herself with her free hand. "They never tell us a damn thing. I'll still feel better when I see them."

"Me too." But Lemon wasn't surprised that her nerves had gotten the better of her. For all her hopes and dreams of a new life, she doubted she would rest until someone found Julian. But she could work on that when she got home, sit down with the sheriff, do some scrying, check the tea leaves. He couldn't hide forever, and if he did she hoped he'd have the sense to stay far away from Hecate's Hollow.

The road was already familiar to Lemon, and it wasn't long before they pulled into town. Gunter was waiting outside of Elias's house and he threw his arms around him as soon as he got out of the car and kissed him so thoroughly Fritz drove away before they finished.

"Where are you going to stay?" Lemon asked as they turned onto main street. She couldn't believe she hadn't brought it up sooner.

Claudia shrugged. "I have absolutely no idea. I don't even have any of my stuff. So I guess I'll check into the motel, and maybe you'll take me shopping tomorrow. I've got a bit of money left over but I'll need a job."

Out of the corner of her eye, Lemon saw Ruby nod. "Stay with us. The house has five bedrooms. I'm not saying move in forever but there's room for you both, and if you really intend to stay, you can save up to get somewhere decent."

"Are you sure?" Claudia asked, glancing towards her brother, but from the lack of shock or interest on his face, Lemon suspected Ruby had already discussed this with him. She'd yell at her later for not asking Lemon first, though to be fair, their life had been eventful lately. Fritz staying with them was barely newsworthy. Still, he was a man, and there'd been a distinct lack of them in the Victorian since... well, since Lemon had known it.

"Honestly, I'd prefer it. It'll be two less people to constantly worry about."

Fritz pulled into the yard, parking under the oak that Claudia had once stood under, bathed in moonlight.

"Okay." Claudia nodded excitedly. "Yeah, that would be nice."

But as she dragged her luggage into the living room, Lemon couldn't shake the feeling that something was off. It rose goosebumps on her arm and she rubbed her hands across her biceps. "I know this is terribly inhospitable, but I want to go over to my moms' house. I'll be back in like half an hour tops."

"I'll come with you." Ruby scratched the cat under the chin and then stood.

The walk to their mothers' house wasn't long, but the sun was still fully overhead, beating down on their necks. But Lemon's chill continued, making her hands clammy and her throat dry.

"Something feels wrong, Rubes."

"I know," she whispered. As her breath met the autumn air, the wind kicked up, blowing through the grass in the surrounding lawns. Ruby's hands were clenched at her sides. Their mothers' house came into view.

There was nothing to see. The same brick house; their car in the driveway. They must have come back since Betta's call. Lemon tried not to let her mind race. She'd been known to get ahead of herself before, but the chill would not subside.

Lemon was the first up the steps to their porch, and she put her hand on the door. Unlocked and unlatched, it pushed open when she touched it. She called out for her mothers as Ruby rushed ahead, but before Lemon stepped inside, she sent off a single text. And then she followed.

Chapter Twenty Two

From the moment she stepped inside Lemon knew something was wrong. Not in the worried way she had had for hours, but from the sharp taste of magic that lingered in the air. She walked shoulder to shoulder with Ruby, peering into rooms as they passed.

There was a broken picture frame on the floor in the hallway and drops of blood on the credenza where it had stood.

"Mom!" Lemon yelled, feeling magic rush through her veins.

The answer came in a muffled yell, and they rushed to the end of the hall. Ruby pushed open their bedroom door and stumbled, catching herself on the doorframe.

"Don't move," Julian said, walking away from the window, his hands clasped behind his back.

He looked worse than he had the last time she'd seen him, a man clearly on a bender, with deep circles under his eyes and unwashed hair. She recognized nothing in him, no feeling of familiarity between them. This man may share her DNA but there was nothing of a father in him. And she'd beat him before, far away from her home. He'd made a mistake. She knew it as sure as she knew she was a witch.

She looked to her mothers and recognized the effects of anti-magic on them. Her eyes locked on Amaryllis and then Esther, and she tried to convey that they would get out of this. The terror this man had brought upon so many would end here. It would end in their little brick house, in a witch town he should have never entered.

"Julian." Lemon took a step into the room, blocking Ruby, willing her to stay back. "Or Giuseppe. I'm not sure."

"I left that name behind when that witch attacked me." He moved suddenly, grabbing Esther by the shoulder and she cried out.

"Stop!" Lemon commanded. Her phone vibrated in her pocket, but she didn't dare reach for it, only praying her message had gone through. "Why are you doing this?"

He walked away from the bed, where her mother lay and towards Lemon. She moved closer to the dresser, eyeing all the things on it. Julian's voice was hoarse. "She took everything from me, and now she comes back and she takes more."

"No one took anything from you. We *left* you. It was a choice." She moved again, this time closer to the window beside Amaryllis, hoping he didn't notice her glancing outside. "People will always leave you eventually. Don't you understand? There is nothing in you anyone wants."

"Watch your mouth." But Lemon wasn't worried about his words. She was worried about the noises escaping from her sister, worried she would try to attack him and get hurt.

Her phone vibrated again, and she spoke to cover the sound. "Why? You know, Claudia is falling in love with me. It must be awful, the daughter that got away and the woman you couldn't have. She is beautiful, and far too good for you. The same as my mother was. So much money, but you can't buy love, can you?" She glanced at Amaryllis and then at the window.

Something moved in her peripheral vision, but she couldn't chance looking out the window again. She moved as much as she dared and continued to taunt him as anger grew on his face. "Did you know the police barely cared about Orlo? Called him a criminal. And your prints are all over everything. They even saw Claudia cured, and we've got your blood in a vial. It was stupid to come here. They'll catch you. That Hathorne blood in your veins won't do you any favors when you're on trial for black magic dealings." She spat in his face.

It worked. He finally lunged for her and she jumped aside. He fell towards the window and Esther brushed her fingers against the glass. The window cracked, giving way, and he fell through it. Before he stood, it had knitted itself back together, under the magic of her mother.

Stupid man. To come to a witch town. There were so many people in Hecate's Hollow who could have told him you should never strike a witch.

Betta McCray and her husband, Jimmy, were outside. Lemon took off running as Jimmy swung, and by the time she had made it out of the house Julian was on the ground. Jimmy was huge, even compared to her father. He was the tallest man Lemon knew and with the muscles of someone who did manual labor all day. And he had one knee on Julian's chest.

"Get your fucking hands off of me. That Hathorne magic shit don't work on me. Betta, baby, where's the sheriff?"

As though in answer to his words, the blue lights showed up, and Betta waved her arms as Lavinia came running into the yard, her dark curls flying behind her.

"Motherfucker." She crouched beside him and Lemon watched in horror and fascination as she pulled something out of her pocket and shoved it into Julian's mouth. Just like she had taught Lemon to do.

He gagged and was still gagging, as Lemon made her way over to him. He screamed, twisting his body and tried to throw Jimmy off him. "What did you do?" He looked at his hands.

"Shut up. Your magic will come back. Eventually. Over here, sheriff."

"Lavinia, my moms and Ruby are inside. He did something to them with his magic."

"Motherfucker," she said again, looking Julian up and down. "I'll help 'em out."

Jimmy and Betta stood on either side of Julian. Betta clutched her purse like a weapon, and Lemon had no doubt she'd use it like one.

"So," Sheriff Wilson said, looking over Julian. "You really were as stupid as the Pennsylvania police thought you might be, and they're no geniuses themselves. I should have had more watches on this place, but I thought, no the man isn't stupid enough to come to a witch town and attack witches." Julian tried to run, and the sheriff moved quicker than Lemon would have thought the old man could, grabbing him by one arm and smashing him into the side of the house. It was only seconds before handcuffs were on him. "You know you'll be tried here, right? At least for the hostage taking and breaking and entering."

Betta moved towards Lemon as Ruby emerged from the house. "I'm sorry. I thought they were okay. I swear their car wasn't here when I checked." She pulled Lemon into a perfumed hug as Jimmy helped Sheriff Wilson drag Julian to the car.

There was so much more Lemon wanted to say. She wanted to scream and rage and beat her hands upon his chest until they were both bruised, but what would that do? Instead, she would get to watch from the gallery as he was tried at the courthouse. She'd watch as he was found guilty and then as he was taken to jail miles away. Because her mothers had picked the right place years ago.

"It's okay," she told Betta, breaking away to grab Ruby as she fell. "It's okay," she repeated, because it was going to be. That had been nothing but the death knell of a man who knew he had been caught.

"You girls okay?" Jimmy asked, massaging his knuckles. He was a man of few words and Lemon had been the recipient of even fewer of them, but she threw her arms around his neck. "Thank you for coming."

"Of course. Knew I'd make it faster than the police when you messaged Betta. That was smart with the window. I thought you'd seen us through it but she wasn't sure." He nodded towards his wife. "I had to convince her not to shoot."

In response, Betta jangled the handbag she was clutching. "Didn't want to hit one of you."

"Jesus, Betta." Ruby laughed as more police cars pulled up. She groaned. "Not more cops." And it was a little annoying that they'd be the ones to get justice for them, but Lemon figured it was better than a murder charge. And at least it would be the police here, in her town, not the shitheads in some big city who wouldn't give a damn about all the crimes he'd committed against witches.

"Don't say shit." Jimmy advised. "Call Rudy Macintosh. You need a lawyer no matter what they say. Don't trust Sheriff Wilson just because he's old and watched you grow. Cop's a cop. Oh, is that your girl?" He glanced across the street, to where Claudia was running for her, brown hair streaming behind her back.

"Shit, Lemon! I knew I should have come with you." Her eyes caught on the car with Julian inside, then towards the corner of the house where Esther and Amaryllis were coming around. Her face fell. "Oh, God." She walked over to them slowly. "I am... I'm so terribly sorry."

Amaryllis put a hand on her shoulder. "Stop. I forgive you. I kept my daughter in his home. I know fear. And I won't begrudge you for trying to get help."

Claudia began to weep and Amaryllis pulled her into her arms while Esther watched on. Lemon wasn't sure she was as forgiving as her wife, but they would have time for those discussions later.

Now wasn't the time, as the lawn filled with townsfolk and Betta told the story far too loudly.

Hecate's Hollow would never let her down. It was one of the truths of Lemon's life. One she often forgot. But it wasn't just the Hollow and everyone there who loved her so much that had saved her. She'd been strong. She'd come up with a plan. She'd sent a text, and though she'd only meant for Betta to call the police, she'd gotten the help she needed.

There had been a time, not so long ago, when Lemon would have frozen. She would have stood as stock-still as Ruby had and watched. But she'd held her ground, and she'd gotten him outside. She barely felt like the hero. Jimmy had been the one to bloody his nose and Lavinia had taken his magic, but maybe that's how things should be, not one big hero but people who cared about each other coming together.

So Lemon sat in the cool grass outside of her mothers' house and wept. And it wasn't long until familiar faces surrounded her, until tissues were thrust upon her, and someone was dragging her up. She shook them off, worried they were going to lift her on their shoulders and carry her home.

She busied herself with hugging her sister. "We did it, Ruby. We won. It's over."

Ruby looked up at her, her emerald eyes wet with tears that spilled over and ran down her cheeks. "We won."

And there was so much more to say to her sister, but she had a lifetime to say it, so she let Fritz pull her away. She watched them for a moment, the way his big brown eyes watched her sister's every move, full of love. She watched her mothers, the way they held hands, their fingers intertwined. She thought of the way their love had gotten her through all the struggles in her life. And she would later learn they *had* been off all day, wandering the hills, hand in hand like they were now. It wasn't until they got home that they found Julian waiting, swearing he would make them pay. The way it was only minutes until Lemon showed up.

There were so many things she would learn later—the way her father had abused so many other women through the years. Women who came forward, braver than Lemon could imagine, to help put him away. The way he'd never looked for Lemon like they'd always worried. She also learned where Claudia kept her jewels though the police never did. She learned from Lavinia the ways to mix potions to steal the anti-magic from someone's veins, how to do spells she needed to know but hoped she'd never use.

She got to watch as Claudia fell in love with the town, taking over SaraLee's job at the shop, and learning all the magic she'd never known growing up with a human mother. And Lemon helped them pick out wallpaper for that same mother's house, helped install the new sink and made sure the air conditioner worked.

It was days after the police had driven away. Ruby and Fritz were laughing from the kitchen and Lemon was tending the garden, when she felt Claudia behind her. She pulled off her gloves and stood up, wrapping her arms around Claudia's waist.

Her eyes were the deepest brown, warm and inviting, and Lemon often found herself lost in them. Now, they were crinkled at the edges, holding back a giggle as she kissed Lemon in the sun. She smelled of rosemary and magic and all Lemon could think of was taking her upstairs. But as Lemon intertwined their fingers, the giggle finally escaped her lips, and she whispered, "I'm going to fall in love with you so fast."

Tallie Rose

CHECK OUT THESE OTHER BOOKS BY TALLIE ROSE

Vampire Fairytale Retellings

Calla Falling

Briar Constance Series

As Played By Gods

An Echo of Gods (Coming Soon)

Sea and Flame Series

Sea and Flame

Scale and Smoke

Coming Soon

Romancing the Gorgon

If you enjoyed this book please leave a review and consider signing

up for my newsletter at www.tallierose.com.

Printed in Great Britain
by Amazon

24906794R00142